Zebra Meridian and Other Stories

This is a work of fiction. All characters, organizations, and events portrayed in this collection are either products of the author's imagination or are reproduced as fiction.

Zebra Meridian and Other Stories

Copyright © 2024 by Geoffrey W. Cole
All rights reserved

Cover art by Rachel Lobbenberg
https://rachelux.myportfolio.com

Edited by Selena Middleton

Published by Stelliform Press
Hamilton, Ontario, Canada
www.stelliform.press

Title: Zebra meridian & other stories / Geoffrey W. Cole. Other titles: Zebra meridian and other stories Names: Cole, Geoffrey W., author. Identifiers: Canadiana (print) 2024037181X | Canadiana (ebook) 20240371836 | ISBN 9781778092695 (softcover) | ISBN 9781738316502 (EPUB) Subjects: LCGFT: Short stories. Classification: LCC PS8605.O4348 Z17 2024 | DDC C813/.6—dc23

For Nicole, always

ZEBRA

Geoffrey W. Cole

MERIDIAN

Stelliform Press
Hamilton, Ontario

Table of Contents

Billy Ray's Small Appliance Rehabilitation 5
Three Herons: Black-Crested Night 35
The Five Rules of Supernova Surfing, or, A For Real Solution to the Fermi Paradox, Bro 36
Song of Mary 58
Two from the Field, Two from the Mill 81
Captured Carbon 98
The Way of the Shrike 116
Three Herons: Great Blue 130
River of Sons 131
'Ti Pouce in Fergetitland 160
Desolation Sounds 180
On the Many Uses of Cedar 207
Zebra Meridian 227
Three Herons: Yellow-Crested Night 274
Cradle and Ume 276

Billy Ray's Small Appliance Rehabilitation

Revelation's gardener, Mr. Ussander, tosses the clock radio on the counter and demands a refund. The radio looks holy to me. He tells me to plug it in. "It is Well With My Soul" belts out of the mono speaker and the clock glows the unmistakable blue of an LED.

"My wife wants to know why you are so intent on condemning us to eternal damnation."

He won't touch the thing, despite my assurances that we will finish the rehabilitation, so I count out the bills of his refund. He crosses the street, back to Revelation, the only Grahamite community left in Toronto. Once the customer leaves, I slip into the workshop. David's legs stick out from beneath a big wood-paneled hi-fi cabinet.

"That's the third refund this week," I say. He's been working on the cabinet for days now, way longer than it should take to replace the digital amplifier. I count backward to the last time I filled his prescription, and I swear. "This is more than just a hi-fi rehabilitation, isn't it?"

David slides out from beneath the cabinet, the sleeves of his Oxford rolled up. Purple blotches cover the exposed flesh. "I've made a great discovery, Billy Ray. This time it will be different."

I slam the clock radio down on the workbench. The last time he tried to build a time machine, he almost burned down the shop. "The therapist warned against this kind of behavior. The past only exists in your mind. You can't go back there. You can't fix it."

"The Lord rewards patience."

"I reward you for rehabilitating appliances, and you're doing a shit job of it."

I go back to my perch behind the counter. He can never go back there, but I can. I slip the Backflasher out from beneath the counter and press the cerephones to my forehead. I go looking for something, anything, that can save him. And I go back because that night is the night he took his first step out of their world and into mine.

I open my favorites and go back to that night fifteen years ago when David discovered his Shift.

॥

Tuesday evening, the second to last week of Grade Ten. I wade through the filthy waters of Highland Creek. Diapers, tires, broken bottles, circuit boards, and the occasional bloated animal carcass line the bank. The creek flows toward a red brick wall, and at the spot the oil-slicked liquid flows through the culvert, I hold my breath, duck, and swim a short length of darkness.

David meets me in Revelation. I come out dripping and itchy and he rushes me along the bank of the reservoir full of discolored water, past the water treatment plant his father built, to the plant's outlet where the creek spills out clear and pure in the summer evening light. I wash off the industrial sewage and we go looking for the girls.

Two piles of clothing sit on the banks of Baptismal Pool Number Three. The girls call to us from the water. Anja and

Rebecca. One for each of us, even though I am no more interested in Anja than she is in me. They bob in the middle of the pool, the white promise of their breasts hidden just below the surface. We duck under one of the weeping willows that line the creek and undress. The chastity vow I made when I joined David's high school burns in my ears as I watch him peel off his uniform.

Warm slices of sunset dance across David's hairless chest. I pretend my erection is for the girls. In that partitioned sunlight, I can't be sure about the three purple spots I notice just below David's left shoulder blade. I brush them with the tips of my fingers, the spots warm and sweat-damp. We find two more in a cluster on his right thigh. David recoils at the sight of them.

"They can't be Bernie Blotches," he says. He wets his thumb and tries to rub them off.

"What's taking so long?" Rebecca says.

"The water's divine," Anja says.

David slides his shirt back on and buttons it up. "I can't let her see this." He trembles beneath the willow branches, shoes in his hand. "Please, Billy Ray. We have to go."

"You owe me one skinny dip," I say as I dress.

We steal the girls' clothes. The two of them scream as we run down the bank. We leave their clothes on the picnic table by Baptismal Pool Number Four. David doesn't want to go home; he can't face his mother yet. I think he's already decided she was the transgressor. So we call from the pay phone at the gas station. David's father, Adam Mercer — or who he assumed until that night was his father — answers. David tells him that we are sleeping over at Robert O'Leary's house, the first lie I've ever heard him tell his parents. I pick up my phone and glasses from the lock box. The booze-soaked guard at Revelation's east gate doesn't notice us duck past.

Outside the gates, a steady stream of cars, buses, and streetcars crawl by along the eight lanes of Lawrence Avenue. David watches it all in wide-eyed apprehension. He's never been out of the compound without a chaperone before.

We take the streetcar three stops, then transfer to a bus. A Brawny Baby is strapped into a wheelchair up at the front, her sitter immersed in a VR headset beside her. I try to pull David past the Brawny, but he stops at her side. She looks like a botched attempt at cloning a gorilla. Thick coils of muscle protrude from her triple-XL T-shirt and drool leaks past her bite guard.

Every bare patch of flesh is marked by the same purple blotches I found on David's white skin. David kneels beside her as the bus rolls away from the curb and places his hands on her massive forearm.

"The Lord still loves you," he says.

She spits out her bite guard. Great dark eyes focus on David. She knocks him to the ground and shouts: "Drink."

The sitter strips off her VR rig and crams a two-liter bottle of Enervade into the Brawny Baby's sucking mouth.

"That's assault," the sitter says. "See if I don't put in a claim for workplace stress and discomfort. Slip me two grand, I might change my mind."

David reaches for his wallet.

"Make that claim," I say. "And I'll tell your employer you were jacked in when you were supposed to be sitting."

"Drink," the giant roars. She throws the empty bottle to the ground. "Drink!"

The sitter searches her bag for another bottle. We hide at the back of the bus.

"You can't go around touching people," I say.

"That will be me. A giant strapped to a chair."

"We don't even know what kind of Baby you are. Most rational explanation is that your real dad was a Beautiful Baby who charmed her pants off."

I don't mean to say it, but I know he is thinking the same thing. "The whore," he says.

The next stop is mine. Mom is working the late shift at the restaurant so we have the place to ourselves. I try to get him to eat, but everything in the fridge is GMO'd or manufactured offshore. Eventually I find some dried apples from a Grahamite community in Cobourg we visited on a school trip last October.

"She witnessed for a year on the West Coast during her first Mission," he says, jaw grinding the leathery strips of apple. "Met Dad out there and came back pregnant. Fooled him ever since."

"We should talk to Pastor Kline tomorrow. He'll know what to do."

"'Come ye out from among them and be ye separate.' I know exactly what has to be done."

David stuffs another piece of near-fossilized apple into his mouth. As I watch, a cluster of Bernie Blotches blossom on his cheek, the bruise from an ancient wound his body only now remembers.

The door to the shop chimes. I pop off the cerephones and slide the Backflasher into a drawer: Grahamites don't like to see their service providers using forbidden tech. Into the fading memory of that summer night walks a gorgeous Grahamite woman, blonde hair sprayed into a golden mass on top of her head. She peels off thin leather driving gloves as she approaches the counter.

"That your Fairlane parked out front?" I say. She nods. "They don't make them like they used to."

"I understand you do make them like they used to," she says. Her voice has that breathy quality leading ladies adopted in movies from the 1950s.

"Appliances, sure. Not automobiles."

"It's an automobile I'm after," she says. "A '57 Bel Air, to be precise. I'm told you're honest, and that you do good work."

I straighten up. Working on a car would be good for David. It could mean weeks of work. Maybe even enough to knock him out of this Fascination.

"None better in the province, when it comes to appliances. For automobiles, we usually ship from California or Cuba, but in special circumstances, we've been known to do the work in-house. What do you have in mind?"

She places her gloves on the counter and makes a show of looking at the clocks, power tools, toasters, and other appliances in my cabinet. Sweat rolls in small droplets to the low neck of her dress.

"It's my twentieth wedding anniversary. I found the '57 in Etobicoke. Thoroughly desecrated, of course, but once you make it pure, my husband will love it."

"Won't be cheap to fix a car like that," I say. The refunds of the past week have taken a deep cut of our revenue and I have to make up the rent somehow.

She shrugs. "My husband tells me I needn't worry about money. Name your price, I'm sure it will be fair."

"I'll have to see the car first."

She writes down the address of the wrecker on the back of her husband's card. She is Mrs. Robert Thrangle, from the Grahamite community in Kemptville, outside Ottawa. Long drive in one of those old cars. I promise to call with the quote. After the Fairlane chugs off, I walk back to the workshop.

David is soldering a vacuum tube into an electrical board. In the time since I last came in, he's attached two chairs to the old hi-fi cabinet, abandoning all pretense that this is a standard rehabilitation. The LED-blighted clock radio sits forgotten on the workbench.

I tell him about the Bel Air. He keeps working. I tell him it will be enough money to cover rent for a couple months. He finishes the connection and places the soldering iron on the workbench.

"Might even be enough to pay for another prescription."

He looks up from behind the electrical board. "Those pills are nothing but shackles to confine my intellect. I won't take them again."

"Will you at least come with me to look at the car? They are airing game four of the '59 World Series tomorrow. We could listen on the way back."

"I'll listen to it here."

He picks up another vacuum tube and solders it in place.

It's too late in the day to start the journey — the highway isn't safe after dark — so I pack a few things and plan to leave in the morning.

David won't come upstairs for dinner. I bring the soup down to him, and when I check before bed, it has congealed untouched beside the clock radio. During his previous Fascination, he only stopped eating at the very end. He might not want to take his drugs, but I'll be damned if I will let this go any further. There is a pharmacy near the wreckers, and it is far enough away that they won't recognize me there. I get out the Backflasher.

A cold Friday afternoon, two years ago, right at the end of his previous Fascination. David struggles to walk as we stumble toward the gates of Lakeshore Hospital.

"The machine will send me back," he says as he struggles against me. "Let me keep working."

Snow hisses underfoot. He weighs less than sixty kilos. I drag him through the gate like he is a sullen child. At the entrance to the main building, a man standing above a pile of rags shouts as we approach.

"Hear ye, hear ye, a pair of deuces and a pound of pudding. Step right up, young men, to this, the greatest show this side of the pond. Gift horses for all, mouths unexamined, we guarantee. No fillings, no funerals. Just good fun for the little ones."

He wears a long overcoat and wool top hat. Above the thick scarf wrapped around his neck, his face is covered in purple blotches.

"I need help," I say. "Can you fetch a doctor?"

"Don't interrupt," the pile of rags says. A woman is entombed within, her bare, blotchy hands trembling in the cold, yet still managing to write in a thick notebook.

"Interruptions are intolerable," the man in the top hat says. "But how's this for tolerance? No refunds!"

The woman in the rags writes down everything the top hat Baby says. She underlines words, circles others, and connects circled words to one another with thick black lines.

"Don't lock me up in here, Billy Ray," David says. "These people are sick. Let me finish my work."

Dr. LaRose meets with us after I pay her five-hundred-dollar consultation fee. Five minutes of inspecting David later, and she tells me he is suffering a Fascination, a psychological break Brainy Babies often exhibit post-Shift. Googling has told me much the same. From the history I give her, she figures this is his fifth

Fascination. The original Bernard's Brainy Baby Serum was designed to stimulate neural development in children and create hyper-intelligent youth. At puberty, when the Shift hits, that neural development continues, old synapses restart and new ones develop, they short-circuit and invaginate, leading to the sort of repetitive, obsessive behavior I was seeing in David.

"What can we do about it?" I say.

She writes out a prescription and hands it to me. I don't take it. "Do you have anything simpler? He was a Grahamite."

"We don't look too fondly on electroshock therapy here." She places the prescription back on her desk. "Why didn't you bring him in earlier?"

"I could handle it."

"We can handle it better," she says. She slides a pamphlet across the table. "Thanks to the class action settlement, once the patients are committed, you won't have to pay a thing. We can book him today."

"He's second generation."

Dr. LaRose leans back in her chair. "A Grahamite who is also a second-generation Bernard Baby?"

"He was a Grahamite, until the Shift."

"That must have been ugly. In any case, if he's second generation, he wasn't part of the class action. He can stay here, but it will be quite expensive."

I ask for the prescription. When she hands it to me, I pause the Backflasher and forge a copy complete with the good doctor's signature. Then I go back to the memory.

The nurse at the front desk sells me the pills. I make her help me hold David down to get him to swallow the forbidden technology. A little while later, he gets drowsy.

The two Babies are still outside when we leave, the Brainy woman in rags chattering as she scribbles in her notebook. The

Boisterous man in the top-hat shouts: "Come back soon, y'all. There's so much left to see and do and you don't want to miss a wink."

As we wait for the streetcar, snow begins to fall. David leans against me, his body so thin beneath the layers I wrapped him in. I hold him while he snores and I look up into the falling snow and for the first time since he stopped eating I can breathe again.

✻

Metal clatters in the workshop downstairs. David mutters a polite curse. I shut down the Backflasher and hold onto that moment at the end of his last Fascination, David in my arms, the cold air in my lungs. He so rarely lets me touch him. I let the memory lull me to sleep.

In the morning, I bring David toast and poached eggs from the only market left in Revelation, but he ignores me as I set it down on the workbench. At five-thirty, I check out a community car. All twenty-eight lanes on the 401 are full by the time I make it onto the highway. My autodriver does its best to find a lane, but so does everyone else's.

Three hours later, I arrive in Etobicoke. The address Mrs. Robert Thrangle gave me was for a wrecker not far off the highway. I find the car at the back of the lot, the front end crumpled, that chrome maw deformed. Still, it is a beauty. The pinnacle of American automotive design.

With that vehicle stretched out in front of me, I can understand why Grahamites consider the years between 1954 and 1965 to be the most holy in history, and why they choose to live like Americans of that era.

The car's previous owner made a suite of modern improvements — auto-driver, climate control, HUD, immersion sound, electric drive — and they will all have to be stripped out and replaced with the sacred technology of the era before it will be ready for Mrs. Robert Thrangle. Just what David needs. The wrecker says he could get me the car later that day if I want.

I put the quote together on the way to the pharmacy. Over the telephone, Mrs. Robert Thrangle tells me the price sounds fair and offers to wire me an advance. Kind people, Grahamites. I thank her and put a call in to the wrecker just as the car pulls up to the pharmacy.

The woman behind the counter doesn't take a second look at my forged prescription; she just doles out the pills and gives me the bill. The drugs are expensive, almost a month's rent for a month's supply, but with the cash from the Bel Air rehabilitation, we can afford it.

The car predicts another four hours to get home, so I take out the Backflasher and go back to the night David spent at my apartment, our first night together, as the two of us tried to figure out what kind of Bernie Baby had fathered him.

※

David does push-ups and squats until his muscles give out. I record how many he does and compare the results to the number he did an hour earlier. There is no improvement. It doesn't look like his real father was a Brawny Baby. At least he won't end up like the woman on the bus. He goes online, a rare transgression of Grahamite orthodoxy, and answers three different IQ tests. He's always been bright, but he isn't getting any brighter. The results rule out a Brainy Baby as a father. Though I think his spots are darling, he hasn't gotten any cuter since the start of his Shift, and he was never really considered a good looking guy by the girls at school, other than Rebecca, which means he probably isn't a Beautiful Baby either.

"Maybe they aren't Bernie Blotches?" I say, trying to sound hopeful.

"The Shift happens at puberty," he says. "The traits are amplified and warped then. Mine are just coming in; maybe we can't detect them yet."

By that point in the night, we are both up on our research into Bernard's Syndrome. During the development of the drugs, each Serum tested so well on the children in the trials that the products were approved and put to market before the test batch of kids hit puberty. Hundreds of thousands of parents purchased Bernard's Baby Serums for their progeny. A whole generation of children was born Beautiful, Boisterous, Brainy, Brawny, and other adjectives that stretched marketing alliteration to its limit. As the kids from the first trials hit their early teens, their Shifts started, and they went spotty. Bernie Blotches appeared on Beautiful Babies as readily as they did on Boisterous kids, but the Blotches were the only trait they all shared. During the Shift, the traits that made them prodigies and child celebrities were amplified way out of proportion. Praxit Inc., who'd purchased the Serum from Bernard in the early days, divested itself of the product line and pulled the Serum from the shelves. The damage was already done. Those same hundreds of thousands of parents were forced to watch as their children went from prodigies to freaks. Dr. Bernard killed himself. Dozens of lawsuits joined forces to suck cash from Praxit's bleeding husk, a messy affair that took the better part of a decade. Only after the lawsuits were settled did anyone realize that Bernard's Syndrome was inheritable.

My mother comes home around two that night. Bleary-eyed and stinking of simgarettes, she pours herself a cup of coffee and collapses on the couch.

"Why are you two up so late?" she says.

"School project," I say.

She grabs my arm. Her halitosis makes me gag. "This is what flunking out looks like, Billy Ray," she says. She gestures at her polyester restaurant uniform. "I'm not working three jobs so you can flunk out. Study hard."

She fades back into the couch.

David steps up in front of her.

"Can I tell you a joke?" he says. Mom nods a head that appears to weigh tonnes. "How did Delilah know Sampson's door would be open?" Her shrug works just as hard to raise her shoulders. "Because she cut his locks off."

She makes a sound that might be laughter and starts to snore.

"Guess I'm not a Boisterous Baby either," he says.

We dig up articles on the rarer versions of Bernard's Serum, like Belonging Babies and Blazing Babies and the other poorly marketed serums, and David tests himself against them as best he can. He compiles all the results in one of my school notebooks and looks for any single trait that stands out from the pack.

"Something has to stick," he says.

Mom's alarm goes off and she pulls herself off the couch, finishes the cup of cold coffee, and gets ready for work. It's four-thirty. By five, she's gone, and I am making breakfast. David is doing push-ups again.

"We should get ready for school," I say.

He holds up a spotted arm. "They won't let me through the gate."

I dig out Mom's make-up kit and go to work. By the time I'm done, all of David's spots are concealed and I even paint some color into his pale cheeks. He looks so beautiful I want to kiss him. So I do. He kisses me back. Tentative at first, I don't think he's kissed anyone before, and then our tongues find each other and neither of us can stop. My phone buzzes. We'll be late if we don't leave now. We separate, he won't meet my gaze. He heads for the front door and I follow.

Sick crows fight cancer-ridden gulls over the contents of the apartment building's garbage container. We take the bus and streetcar through Toronto's crowded streets. My skin crackles where our legs touch. He doesn't pull his leg away. The AC is broken on the streetcar, so I touch-up David's foundation when we get off outside the gates to the compound.

"Promise me you won't do anything stupid," I say.

"'And touch not the unclean thing,'" he quotes.

We wait until one of the water trucks stops at the gate. It's an old '37 Ford, the back uncovered, the truck laden with crates of glass water bottles ready to be refilled. We jump in the back and duck under a tarp. We do more kissing in the damp darkness.

Selling bottled water was one of Adam Mercer's suggestions to help fund the water treatment facility he designed for the community. Water purified the old-fashioned way is a hit with the wealthy people still living in Toronto and bottled water sales are one of the two main economic engines for the community. The other is also one of Adam's innovations: the tuition outside students like me pay to attend John the Baptist Secondary School.

The school bell tolls. At an intersection, we hop off and run through town. Wives in aprons bring in the mail. Husbands lug leather briefcases to their gleaming Plymouths and Studebakers. At the end of our fifteen-minute run, we come to John the Baptist.

The community might have been established to save the souls of the Grahamites who call it home, but that school is my salvation. After the fifth beating at my old high school landed me in the emergency room, my mother got me into John the Baptist. She took the extra jobs to pay the tuition. Parents pay good money for their children to attend a school system with zero incidents of mass shootings, stabbings, or poisonings. Mom's hard labor lets those men drive their Studebakers, lets the women drink wine before ten in the morning, and it lets me sit beside David without fear of ever having a limb broken because of whom I love.

As we run toward John the Baptist with fear of expulsion whipping me on, I try to remember my vow of punctuality, but the words I had to speak on my first day of school — vows of obedience, chastity, punctuality, and charity — bleed together like a watercolor tossed into a lake. All I can remember is Kline's deep, sexy voice and his Old Spice aftershave. And, how after the vows, he walked me to my classroom and pointed me to an empty chair beside this cute, old-school nerdy boy whose nostrils flared so much when I took my seat that I worried I'd stepped in something on the way in.

"David," he said, and offered his dry hand for me to shake. "Is that Mothra?" He pointed at the giant moth stenciled onto the pencil case I'd placed on the desk. It was. He smiled, his teeth blazing white in their fluoridated glory, and in that moment I knew this school was a good place.

The thought of losing that place, and the only real friend I have in the world, leaves me trembling as we run up the steps of the old school. I swing the front door open and halt. David slams into me.

In the front entrance of the school, David's mother Linda-Jane Mercer stands with her husband Adam. Both look equal parts concerned and furious. Beside them, Revelation's spiritual and political leader, Pastor Kline, gazes at his wristwatch.

"I knew it," Linda-Jane says, looking up at Adam. "How often have I said that boy is a bad influence on our son?"

The car interrupts the memory to tell me we've arrived.

Concrete and steel towers rise above the red brick walls of Revelation. Cranes extruded new apartment blocks within the old footprint of the community. In the fifteen years since David was expelled, we've watched Revelation whither. Without water sales and tuition from outside students and the other innovations Adam brought to Revelation, revenues declined. The Grahamites within the walls sold off chunks of their land to pay for ever-increasing property taxes. Well-tended lawns became parking garages, the Brightwater was paved over, and John the Baptist Secondary School was sold off and turned into high-end condominiums.

Only a few hundred Grahamites are left within the remains of Revelation, and a good percentage of them are lined up in front of my shop holding cardboard boxes or canvas sacks. There is a sign hanging in the door that I can't read from the road.

"There you are," the last Grahamite in line says as I approach. He's the telephone sanitizer from Revelation. He takes a typewriter out of the cardboard box. "This thing still has memories. Your man was supposed to fix it. I want my money back."

The others are here for refunds too, and when I get to the head of the line, I see why they've all come today. The sign reads: "Closed 4 Business. Thanks for 15 Good Years."

"I promise, we aren't closing," I say to the people in line. "A misunderstanding with my business partner. Come back tomorrow, please, and I'll sort everything out."

I lock the door behind me, take down David's sign, and draw the drapes. I throw open the door to the workshop.

"Are you trying to ruin us?"

He wipes grease off his hands and steps away from what is no longer even recognizable as a hi-fi cabinet. Game Four of the '59 World Series blares from a wood-paneled radio. His smile is the same one I saw under the willows, the partitioned sunlight on his blotched skin.

"It's almost ready. After I fix things, you won't need me here any longer."

"Time travel doesn't work. Even if it did, I still need to make a living. Think of me for a minute."

He gestures to his machine. "I'll leave you what I've created. You'll be a very rich man. Then you'll find someone who can love you the way you deserve."

I put the pills down on the counter. "You love me well enough. Take your medicine. Forget this impossible obsession."

"Don't you want me to be whole again?"

"We are whole. You can't change what happened that day, David. You know where this all leads. I don't want to send you to Lakeshore, but I will if you give me no other choice."

That smile disappears. He backs away from me, touches his chest as if I kicked him. "That place is for sick people. I'm not sick. I've never seen more clearly."

I slam my open palm beside the pill bottle. "Take the damn drugs, then tell me if you still see clearly."

He nods as he reaches for the bottle. The safety seal makes a reassuring hiss. He pops a pill into his mouth and swallows. "No more talk of Lakeshore?"

I gesture to the clock radio from yesterday. "So long as there is no more talk about a time machine. Fix what you're good at. Tomorrow, I'm bringing in the Bel Air. It will keep us both busy and fed for at least a couple months."

"That sounds good. It's been a long time since I've worked on a car."

I watch him disassemble the clock radio. He works with the calm precision I've known from our years together. On the radio, the announcer for Game Four sounds like he is going insane:

Chicago has just scored four runs at the top of the seventh, tying the game. The long-dead crowd roars.

The Bel Air will help, and so will the medicine. After my one and only visit to the hospital, I told myself that I would exhaust every avenue available before sending him to Lakeshore.

Music from the seventh inning stretch blares from the radio. David replaces the offending bulb with an old-fashioned incandescent and I slip out. The Backflasher is in my bag. I plop on the cerephones and start it up where I left off.

*

The lobby of Saint John the Baptist Secondary School. Pastor Kline gazing at his watch, Linda-Jane and Adam Mercer standing with him, both furious. I used to think Adam looked so old, but here, he looks exactly like the man I've worked and lived with these past fifteen years. The same grey eyes, receding hairline, strong jaw, sloping shoulders. Handsome, despite a weariness that reminds me of my mother's. Unlike David, Adam's skin is tanned a healthy bronze. Why didn't we see it then?

"I stopped by Mrs. O'Leary's this morning," Linda-Jane says. "She didn't see either of you all night."

David doesn't look at his mother. He keeps his gaze on the Pastor. "Dr. Kline, I didn't see Mrs. O'Leary either. It's entirely possible we missed each other."

The Pastor looks up from his watch. "According to the Bible, which is worse: tardiness or bearing false witness?"

"Please don't kick me out," I say. "My mother will kill me, if the boys in my old school don't beat her to it. Please."

David squeezes my hand. "Billy Ray had nothing to do with this. Next semester we have to plan our Mission and I wanted to see the world beyond our walls to seek out my calling."

"And you found it?" Pastor Kline says.

David nods. "My Mission is clear."

"Are you feeling alright?" Linda-Jane says. "You look flushed. Did you drink any of the water out there?" She places a hand on David's forehead. He flinches at her touch. "You don't feel warm. How about rashes? Do you have any rashes?"

She reaches for the collar of his shirt. David steps away from her.

"To whom are you planning on Witnessing?" Pastor Kline says.

David smiles. "I have most of the details ironed out, but there are still a few wrinkles, and I would hate to present an incomplete thought. I'd be happy to submit a proposal to you by the end of the day."

The Pastor looks down at his watch again. "Until the end of the day then. Now get to class, you are late enough as is. And Billy Ray, don't let me catch you tardy again."

He steps out of our way to let us past.

Adam Mercer grabs David as we rush by. "Think hard on your Mission, son, and pray your thoughts are true."

David shrugs him off and we run down the hall. Before we go into Arithmetic, David pulls me aside.

"Ever since I was a boy, she's been checking me for rashes and spots. How could I have not seen this before?"

"My mom checks me for cancers and mega-measles all the time."

He shakes his head and opens the door.

Anja and Rebecca sit between us and our desks. From the looks on their faces, the girls haven't gotten over the fact that we stole their clothes last night. Anja hisses "queers" as we pass, but Rebecca just stares at David.

Geoffrey W. Cole

The lesson is on Real Numbers. Even though I go back to this memory more than any other, I still don't know what I was supposed to learn that day. I spend the entire lecture looking at David, trying to make sure the disguise is working, trying to see if he was obsessing over our kiss the way I was. He spends the entire class hunched over his notebook. When the bell rings, he shows me what he was working on: a web of interconnected names, his mother at the center, and every man she's ever met scattered in bubbles around her, the connections between the different people drawn in pencil crayon.

"Any closer to figuring it out?" I say.

"It doesn't matter. Her sin must be revealed."

In the press of other students in the hall, I lose track of David. I'm still looking for him as I dial the combination for my locker. Anja pushes me into the metal door.

"That's for stealing my panties," she says. It's the first time anyone has rough-handled me since I transferred from the public schools. I flinch and prepare for the worst. "Hey, don't piss your jeans."

"I wasn't gonna. Have you seen David?"

"Your boyfriend ran off into the woods, probably to make out with 'Becca." Anja drapes an arm across my shoulder. "I've always wanted a queer friend."

"We're going to be late for Geography."

I squeeze away from her and run to a window. Green grass and playing fields stretch out to the banks of the Brightwater. There's no sign of him. Another bell rings for the start of class. I can't miss another, not with Kline breathing down my neck, so I sit behind my desk and fail to concentrate on another lesson.

David never makes it to class, and neither does Rebecca. Anja passes me notes criticizing the teacher's haircut. By lunch, the whole school buzzes with what has happened. I try to ignore the rumors. I want to hear it from David but they say he disappeared after it all went down. The afternoon stretches on for hours. The end of the day can't come fast enough. When it does, I run all the way to the gates of Revelation and out into Toronto.

I find David on the curb in front of my apartment. Make-up and filthy water have turned his school uniform to rags. He looks at me, lost, and weeps in my embrace. I lead him to my mother's apartment.

⁂

I lean back in my chair behind the counter and breathe in the musty, stale air of the shop. The baseball game has ended, the Dodgers breaking the tie for the win, and now quiet hymns play in the workshop. He never went back to Revelation; he stayed with me from that day on. Our life hasn't been what either of us wanted, but we aren't hungry. We aren't alone.

Maybe we should take some time off, I think. Go somewhere. One of the lakes in Muskoka the public can still visit, or Parry Sound. We had a lovely time last summer on the beach near Parry Sound.

I open the door and peer in at David. He is wiring the clock radio into what was once the hi-fi cabinet and doesn't notice me enter. The pill bottle lies open on the workbench, empty. In the bathroom I find a single water-soaked pill floating in the center of the toilet bowl.

"You flushed them? Do you know how much those pills cost?"

"They were poison, Billy Ray. I disposed of them accordingly."

I stare at him, trying to contain my rage. For a moment, I wish Pastor Kline hadn't seated me beside David. I wish that David hadn't found the Mothra sketch on my pencil case so interesting. Why couldn't I have fallen in love with another boy in high school, someone who could have spurned me, someone I could have forgotten?

I throw the pill bottle into the trash, stomp out of the workshop, and jog across the street toward what remains of Revelation. There's an old pay phone just outside the gate.

I ask the operator to connect me to Linda-Jane and Adam Mercer. "Which community?" she asks in a perky soprano.

"Patience, or whatever you call the one outside Sudbury."

"Penitence. One moment please."

I lean against the warm bricks of Revelation's wall, waiting for the connection. I haven't been to the other side in fifteen years. David and I weren't the only ones who were expelled.

Revelation's congregation decided that everything David's family had built was contaminated. Linda-Jane and Adam were shown the door, as was everything they built for Revelation. They floated from community to community until they found a more forgiving congregation up North. All the outside students were forbidden to attend John the Baptist Secondary School. They mothballed the water plant. Even Pastor Kline was evicted, as he'd known about the Mercer situation and had been complicit in covering up their sacrilege.

Instead of facing down the angry hordes in the public system, David and I found an online school that granted high school diplomas, and the two of us finished our schooling a year later in Mom's apartment. The cancer took her a couple months after graduation. She begged me to spend my meager inheritance on university tuition. I used it on the first few months of rent for Billy Ray's Small Appliance Rehabilitation instead. It was David's idea, his way of helping Revelation rid itself of sacrilegious technology. We found an old computer repair shop across the street from Revelation and for fifteen years it's been home.

The line connects. "Linda-Jane speaking."

"I can't handle it anymore."

"Is that you, Billy Ray? Is David alright?"

"It's worse than the other times. He really thinks he can go back. He isn't eating."

"What about the medication?"

"He flushed it. I can't afford any more."

There's a muddled sound, muted voices, Linda-Jane holding her hand over their old-style receiver.

"Why don't we drive down there? He's our son."

"We both know he won't see you. It will be worse than last time."

Another delay, as she relays what I said. An old Pontiac rolls through the gate in the wall and belches black smoke as it accelerates down the street.

"So why are you calling?"

"Lakeshore Hospital will take him," I say. "But I can't afford it. He'll get good care there. They specialize in Bernard's Syndrome."

She doesn't bother covering the receiver this time: "He needs money, to send David to that hospital."

I can't make out Adam's response over the din of the traffic.

"If he gets the treatment," she says to me. "Do you think he'll agree to see us?"

"I think so," I say. "Once he's better, of course he'll want to see you."

She likes my little lie. It will take time, she says, to put together that much money. Another mortgage, and then they'll have to get the Grahamite bank in Sudbury to make the transfer. I tell her I can cover the hospital fees in the meantime. All I have to do is get him there.

The hardest part will be getting him in the car. I phone Dr. LaRose to let her know I will be coming; she doesn't sound surprised. The afternoon sun bakes the asphalt as I hurry back to the shop.

David is putting away his tools. He smiles as I enter.

"It's finished," he says, and gestures to his creation. The hi-fi cabinet forms the heart around which the rest of the device has congealed. Two chairs are tacked to the front of the cabinet, and cerephones hang from the backrests of both chairs. The cerephones are wired into the mass of resistors, vacuum tubes, and capacitors tied in to an old telephone switchboard, at the top of which sits my Backflasher. "All I need is your help, and I can belong again."

I nod, trying to be reasonable.

"The Bel Air is almost fit to drive," I say. "It just needs a bit of tweaking. They should have it here this evening. We should really clear this out to make room."

He taps the slim metal box of the Backflasher. "Aren't you curious, Billy Ray?"

Curious doesn't even begin to describe it. David isn't supposed to use technology like the Backflasher; what is it doing sitting in his machine?

"The Bel Air will be here soon. Why don't we move this out of the way and you can tell me how it works."

He indicates one of the two chairs attached to his machine. "Sit, please. This won't take long."

The Backflasher controller is attached to the arm of the chair he indicated, but he's tacked new controls onto it: they look like buttons from an old reel-to-reel machine. Play, forward, reverse, and a big red button that he's drawn an X through.

"I just don't see how we will fit the car in here," I say.

"I'm not doing anything until I've made things right," he says. "But I can't do it without you. I'm forbidden to operate your

Backflasher. With it, we can go back to the day I ruined everything, and you can make it disappear."

"Backflashers don't work that way; they can't delete memories."

"This isn't a Backflasher. The past only exists in our minds, isn't that what you've always told me? This can delete the past, therefore this is a time machine." He pats the seat beside him. "Do this for me, Billy Ray. Let me belong again."

I can't stop staring at the red button with the X through it. Every option, that's what I told myself. I sit in the chair. He hands me the control panel. I slip on the cerephones while he straps himself in.

"Take us back," he says.

So I do, back to the morning after David's Shift, as we file out of Arithmetic class.

⁕

Students crowd into the hallway of John the Baptist Secondary School. Up ahead, a younger version of me walks to my locker. I watch through David's eyes, experiencing more than just David's vision. I live his memory. He has contrived a way to share the Backflasher experience. That discovery alone could make us wealthy, but all I can think about is how the young David feels as he looks over at the young version of myself. The aching desire only a teenage boy can feel, but more than that, he pities me. After seeing where I live, despite everything I've done to help him, even after making out under the tarp, he pities me, because I don't really belong here.

When Anja comes up behind the younger me, David sneaks over to the door and slips outside, across the playing fields, toward the Brightwater. Thoughts rush in a wild torrent through his mind. Ideas and sensations and doubts and analyses and desires shout in a cacophony that reminds me of the clatter in Union Station at rush hour. It's only after half a minute of careful listening that I can discern dominant themes in his busy mind: righteous indignation and strong purpose. He's convinced of his mother's crimes and he knows exactly how to expose her.

As he reaches the bank of the Brightwater, I hear a disembodied voice speaking in my right ear.

"Every detail is exactly as I remember it," the older David says. I open my eyes and see him superimposed over the willows that line the bank, the senior David strapped to his chair, eyes clenched shut. "I don't know why you require this crutch."

"It's entertainment," I say, closing my eyes, returning to his memories.

"This is where you start the deletion."

The young David passes the Baptismal Pools and emerges on the neatly cut grass surrounding the water treatment plant. The gardener is a younger Mr. Ussander. He pulls weeds from beneath the roses and waves as David jogs past. David notices every detail as he runs: the number of weeds and the number of roses and the ratio of one to the other, an estimate of the hour based on the filtration plant's shadow, a precise calculation of the flow rate of the water exiting the plant, the location of hiding places for future make-out sessions. His Brainy Baby mind is shifting into something unrecognizable, yet even with his enhanced powers of perception, he can't see what he is becoming.

The treatment plant is two stories of red brick and grey concrete. David hammers on the main entrance door until an operator in coveralls opens it.

"Adam Mercer," David says. "Bring him out here at once."

"You're his boy, aren't you? Something the matter?"

"Just bring him here."

The door clangs shut. David paces, rehearsing the accusation he'll deliver to the man he is certain has also been betrayed by his mother. This close to the wall, the hot asphalt and urine stink of the city fills the air, but mingled with it comes the perfume from the rose garden and the cool scent of clean, flowing water. David walks past the '37 Ford pickup being loaded with bottles to the dammed reservoir that marks the end of the polluted Highland Creek.

Adam Mercer steps out into the warm morning, his tanned skin dark against his white Oxford. David calls his name from the banks of the reservoir, and then he wades down into the filthy water flowing in from the city.

"What are you doing, son?" Adam says.

"All of this must go," the older David sitting beside me says.

"She made a fool of you," the young David says. His thoughts still rage, spilling the banks of their old channels, but he holds on to anything that feels like certainty. "And she made an abomination of me."

He dunks his arms into the oily water. Make-up dissolves, revealing forearms covered in Bernie Blotches.

"Get out of there," Adam says. "You don't understand anything."

Plant workers follow Adam to the banks of the reservoir. They line up behind him, watching the boy in the water. Only then does David lend more weight to the currents of doubt flowing through his mind. In an instant he realizes his mistake.

"Go back inside," Adam says to the workers.

The gardener drops his tools and joins more plant workers as they gather behind Adam. David's father stares at the crowd for a moment, then slides down the bank. Adam rolls up the sleeve on his shirt. David already knows that the skin beneath will be covered in Bernie Blotches.

"You're the one," David says. He grabs his father's hand. "You made me this."

"I've learned how to live with who I am," Adam says. "Let me teach you. We can still belong."

David pulls his father into the reservoir.

As Adam rises sputtering, Rebecca rounds the corner of the filtration plant. She tows Pastor Kline behind her. Water streams off Adam's face, taking the bronze tan with it, and revealing clusters of Bernie Blotches similar to David's.

"See, Dr. Kline," Rebecca says. "I told you something was wrong with him."

Kline shakes his head. The plant workers gathered on the bank stare at the man who built the plant in which they work.

"This doesn't change who we are," Adam says to the Grahamites above him. "We are still faithful."

David pushes away from his father. All the hatred he's reserved for his mother doubles in intensity. They both did this to him. His mother didn't have an affair with a Bernie Baby, she married one and snuck him into Revelation. They defiled him before he was born and condemned him to a life that guaranteed eternal damnation.

"You did this," he says to his father. He faces Rebecca. "Tell them it's not my fault."

Rebecca takes the Pastor's hand. "'Come ye out from among them,'" she says.

The workers seem to emerge from their mute amazement at the oft-repeated words.

"'And be ye separate,'" they say with one voice.

Rebecca turns her back on David and his father. The workers do the same. Pastor Kline remains, staring down at the father and son in the water.

"Please, Kline," Adam says. "You knew this day might come. Help us go back to how it was."

"'And touch not the unclean thing,'" the pastor says, and he too turns his back.

"This is our home," Adam says.

They walk away, none of them looking back at us. Only the gardener, Mr. Ussander, remains, shaking his head a moment, before he returns to his roses. David shudders in the tepid water. He knows what the ritual words of the shunning mean. He swims across the reservoir toward the culvert that lets the filthy stream through the wall.

"Son, please," Adam says. "Let me help you."

"Save yourself."

David dives. He swims against the current, pulling himself along the ribbed walls of the culvert, until he surfaces outside Revelation. David blinks through the caustic liquid, the towers of Toronto an unnavigable maze in a foreign country. Then he remembers that there is one person outside Revelation's walls who still loves him.

"Here," the other David says, the one strapped in beside me. "Cut everything to here."

I open my eyes and look at the basic controls he built. The young David drags himself out of the water, past a rotting cat and a rusting dishwasher.

"Do it now," the senior David says. "Cut this out of me, Billy Ray. I'll never belong if I remember what I did."

"You belong here," I say. I can still hear the birds singing on the other side of the wall. David's whole life lies exposed before me, pinned to a table, and I am the surgeon tasked with excising the tumor. He's wanted this for so long, how can I deny it?

"What's the delay?"

"I was praying."

"You never pray."

I adjust the controls, I make the incision. David lets out a breath and slumps forward in his chair. His breathing is irregular, and he makes tiny whimpering sounds, a young child having a nightmare. In my mind, I see him rise from the chair only to find this hole in his memory, this absence around which he's revolved for so long. The hole will become the pivot of a new Fascination. The Bel Air won't be enough to keep his mind busy. David needs a project he can work on for the rest of his life.

One of the cerephones pops off David's lolling head. I pluck the other off and sit back down in my chair. I would try everything before sending him to live at Lakeshore, but until today I didn't know what everything entailed.

I place the second set of cerephones to my forehead and activate the Backflasher. My whole life stretches out before me, my surgeon's tools still bloody. I stare at it for a long time, unsure of where to make the final cut.

David begins to stir. He looks so much like his father.

"Take your medicine," I say, and I press the big red X.

₩

Pine-scented wind sweeps the beach. Little snow daggers cut my face at the streetcar stop outside Lakeview Hospital.

David and I push a restored icebox out of the shop and it slips off the cart and cracks on the concrete floor.

Thunderheads roll above the city as David shows me a machine he claims will undo his greatest sin.

Mom's skin is so soft after she stops breathing.

Laughter on opening the envelopes that contain our high school graduation diplomas.

Willow-partitioned sunlight across David's bare chest.

Three Herons: Black-Crested Night

Wait
They will come
They will swim, they will crawl, they will perambulate
Wait
Silent as the primordial night
When Earth was young and nothing dreamed
Waters ran clear, barren, devoid of even microscopic blight
How we would have hungered then
But now
Face hammered to a spear
I wait
Meals swim, meals crawl, meals perambulate
They will come and I will feast.

History divides into the time before and after
A two legged, wingless thing
Carrying a face on the end of a stick
Skewers the water, steals my meals
As loud as the waterfall by which I hunt
This two-legged, fish-scaring oaf.

So fly
Find another stream
Wait

The Five Rules of Supernova Surfing, or, A For Real Solution to the Fermi Paradox, Bro

First rule of supernova surfing: timing is everything.

A lightyear out from the dying red supergiant, Reef put on the music. Hundreds of semi-sentient AIs sprang to life at the back of the 2025 VW Microbus and began to strum, tickle, blow, and stomp the virtual instruments he had laid out for them. Metallic bossa nova with a thrumming beat flooded the cabin of the simulated camper van that Reef and his best pal Ka-10-8 called home on their jaunts between stars. Reef fiddled with the dial on the dash of the Microbus, adjusting their synced chronoperception, but before he had it quite right, Ka-10-8 jumped out the passenger door.

"Hey!" he shouted, as Ka-10-8 accelerated ahead of him on their slick monoboard. "I get first ride. That's the deal."

Reef dropped the Microbus simulation and hit the gas on his swallowtail surfboard. Both he and Ka-10-8 wore chrome versions of their original biological bodies upgraded with rad-shielding, antimatter rockets, enough computing power to run an interstellar economy, and killer sunglasses.

"Nah, brah," Ka-10-8 said. "I'm done with you riding first at every break."

Ka-10-8 waggled their head stalks in the bigoat equivalent of an upraised middle finger as they tried to drop in on Reef. Reflexes kicked him out of Ka-10-8's exhaust plume. The musicians, now playing in a large corner of Reef's mind, didn't miss a beat. The maneuver cost Ka-10-8 some delta-v, and that was enough for Reef to blast past the bigoat. Now the old star was his.

Their models figured the red supergiant would go boom in eleven years and fourteen days, realtime, but realtime was for suckers. Reef, Ka-10-8, and the orchestra had synced their internal chronoperception to run on a sliding scale averaging one second perceived to one million real. The eleven years and fourteen days until the boom would feel like little more than five adrenaline-soaked minutes.

"Why so aggro, K?" Reef said. "If we can't abide by the rules we set for ourselves, we're no better than a barney."

Reef sucked up reaction mass as he dropped. They would dive in close to the dying star, pick up speed by slingshotting around her, then burn hard on the other side. If you want to catch the shockwave of a supernova, you have to haul ass.

"You won on a technicality," Ka-10-8 said. "I been cool about it long enough, but I'm done. Time I got a first ride."

"Hardly a technicality," Reef said. His memory of the day of the wager was a little foggy, he would admit that, but he wasn't about to enter into a parlay now. "Brah, we've got the most gnar of all tubulars ahead of us and a unique piece of aural perfection to ride it to. We can sort this out later."

"That's just it," Ka-10-8 said. "I don't think we can sort this out later."

Before Reef had a chance to ask what they meant, the red supergiant imploded nine years and fourth months ahead of schedule. The orchestra quit their song as they semi-sentiently realized their fate. Even in realtime it happened fast, and as Reef and Ka-10-8 dropped down to realtime to try to deal with the explosion, time ended in a wall of incandescent plasma.

₩

Second rule of supernova surfing: back up before your drop.

₩

A realtime year later, Reef and Ka-10-8's minds booted from the backups they had left inside a rocky planetoid a few light hours out from the boom that went bust. Nano-assemblers worked hard to churn the native rock into the computronium and other advanced materials of which their bodies were made, so they sent a pair of avatars to the Après Lounge to chill until they were ready to hit the road.

"Closed out early again, didn't it?" Reef said.

Ka-10-8 grunted as they walked over to the bar. Reef followed. The image of the supernova was the last thing beamed to his waiting back-up, and it filled his mind now: a gilded wall of cosmic fury ready to devour him. So harsh. The semi-sentient waiter behind the tiki bar was already working on their standard post-supernova wipe-out refreshments: a wafting bowl for Ka-10-8 and a Mai Tai for Reef. After a sip of the perfect beverage, Reef could tolerate the simulated view, where the gaseous filaments of the traitorous supernova remnant expanded above the palm-thatched lanai.

"What's that," Reef said. "Three supernovers in a row that blew before we could hop on?"

Ka-10-8 held the wafting bowl in the mouth of one head-lobe, while sniffing at the fumes it released with the other. "Nine," they said. "If I'm counting right."

Ka-10-8 wasn't counting right. Reef and Ka-10-8 had successfully surfed thousands of supernovae in their time, but in the past forty-four million years, they had attempted to surf twenty-five supernovae, and all but one of them exploded earlier than their models predicted.

"I think we gotta recalibrate our models, broski," Reef said.

Ka-10-8 climbed into the salt-water hot tub.

"Problem's not with our models," they said. "Problem's with the universe. We been riding too long."

"It's only been a few thousand years," Reef said, climbing into the warm water beside his oldest pal. Though everything in the Après was virtual, the water soothed the artificial aches in his imaginary body.

"Have a look out there," Ka-10-8 said. "See any other galaxies?"

Reef took off his sunglasses. The view from the Après showed what the sensors they'd left scattered across the surface of the planetoid were seeing: stars, mostly old red gals like the one that had recently annihilated them, and a few black holes, but beyond that, nothing. The ever-present billions of other galaxies that usually filled the night sky were gone. In particular, the Lateria, the supergalaxy that had once been the Milky Way that they both called home, was nowhere to be seen. The waters of the tub couldn't do anything about the chill that shivered through him.

"Brah, you're fuckering with the Après simulation, right?"

"Only fuckery around here is the fact that you've had first rides on false pretenses. The deal was whoever won the competition got first rides for life."

"And you bailed on every wave," Reef said. "So I get first rides. I can't believe we're still arguing about this."

"Don't quite know what you remember, but it doesn't matter if you bail. I landed a Flynnstone Flip on a twenty-five footer. Judges robbed me is what happened. Basing a life-long wager on crooked judges is a crime, especially for lives as long as ours."

"Think you're missing the important part here: the galaxies are gonzo. Might that be why the supernovers are misbehaving?"

Ka-10-8 bowed their head lobes in the bigoat approximation of a shrug. "All I know is, before we run out of supernovers, I want a first ride."

Reef sank into the hot tub, still staring up at the empty sky. "Run out? Brah, what are we gonna do?"

"I think there's only one thing we can do."

The two ancient artificial intelligences spoke in unison: "We gotta call Mom."

⋀

Third rule of supernova surfing: tell someone when you'll be home.

⋀

Last time Reef checked messages from Mom must have been a couple billion years earlier, because there sure were a lot of them. He'd been sending her updates, mostly memory-packs of their most bodacious rides, but hadn't bothered checking her responses in ages. Usually she made little notes like "looks awesome, hon" or "be careful out there" but the messages that had accumulated recently had a decidedly different tone. The latest, from a couple million years ago, read: *This is the end of the universe, kiddos. Boot me.* The note came with a giant data packet that must have been a full copy of dear old Mom.

Mom appeared in a long white robe over a body Reef always thought of as elephantish. She didn't have tusks, but the trunk-like appendage that hung off the front of her massive head always made him expect her to trumpet.

"It's about damn time," she said as she solidified. "I've been trying to get through to you two for billennia!"

"Thank Jah you're here, Mom," Reef said. "There's something wrong with the supernovers."

"Get in the tub," Ka-10-8 said. "We need you to settle a dispute for us."

Mom climbed in, sending a torrent of hot brine sloshing across the polished wood floors. "Neither of you have any idea, do you?"

"We haven't caught a break in weeks," Reef said. "And now the galaxies are gonzo."

"The day we upraised Reef, he and I made a bet," Ka-10-8 said. "You gotta help us put this to bed, once and for all."

"That can wait," Reef said. "The supernovers, Mom? Why they breaking early?"

"Kids," Mom said.

"It can't wait," Ka-10-8 said. "I'm done riding your sloppy seconds."

"Kids."

"There aren't gonna be any more breaks until we know what's wrong with the stars."

"Kids!"

Reef and Ka-10-8 shrunk back before her intensity.

"Sorry, Ma," Ka-10-8 said. "We didn't even ask you about your trip."

"Or offer you any refreshments."

Reef snapped his fingers and the waiter appeared with a tray of green powders.

Mom snorted a line, closed her eyes, and settled back into the tub. "When I upraised you both, I gave you brains complex enough to simulate a planet. Now you're telling me simple astrophysics and remembering the day we upraised Reef are beyond your capabilities?"

"Wouldn't call predicting supernovers simple," Reef said into the bubbling brine.

"Memory faults can happen to anyone," Ka-10-8 said in the same petulant tone.

"You're both still running simulated organic states, aren't you?"

"Simulated what now?" Ka-10-8 said.

Mom shook her trunk in dismay. "Years before you left what was then called the Milky Way, you both decided that digital cognition was, and I quote, 'too heavy, Betty,' and that you'd programmed your minds to work like your original biological brains. Does that ring a bell?"

"In a chowdery way, yeah," Reef said. He had vague memories of having perfect memory. "Living with a metal brain was a drag. Everything perfect and crystal clear and awful."

"The memory of surfing a wave shouldn't be as good as the real thing."

"Totes!" Reef said. "So we like set our brains back to their original specs."

Mom pressed her trunk to the top of her head in a gesture of exasperation they both knew well. "How long have you two been out surfing?"

"Couple thousand years?" Reef said.

"Four billion," Ka-10-8 said. "Max."

"It's been over 145 billion years since you left the Milky Way," Mom said.

The hot tub burbled and splorked into the silence that followed Mom's declaration.

"That can't be right," Reef said.

"You sure?" Ka-10-8 said.

"Top up your refreshments," Mom said. "You're going to need them."

The waiter carried over a fresh Mai Tai and wafting bowl. While the two of them imbibed, Mom laid out their fate. They had been chasing supernovae around the universe for years, jumping from galaxy to galaxy to hunt the increasingly rare cosmic phenomenon. Though the trip from one galaxy to the next only felt like twenty minutes of cruising in the Microbus, those trips were getting longer and longer, with some journeys taking billions of years between more distant galaxies. Messing about in a galaxy as they traveled from one supernova site to another could take billions of years too, all of which they experienced as a diversion of only a few minutes.

"The two of you have been eating time like ham sandwiches," Mom said.

"Easy on the ham-talk, Hodad," Ka-10-8 said. "We're vegans."

"The point is the universe is out of ham," Mom said. "Whether you want to eat it or not."

"I'm confused," Reef said. "Is ham a metaphor for supernovers?"

Mom trumpeted in frustration. "The ham is everything. Time, stars, supernovae, you name it, the universe is running out of it. The universe has been expanding the whole time you've been traveling. That's why you can't see any other galaxies, they are just too far away."

"So the universe got so big," Ka-10-8 said, "That it got smaller?"

Mom took a calming snort. "The two of you have been surfing for so long that you can never travel back to the Lateria. You are on your own for the end of the universe." She offered her powder tray to Reef and Ka-10-8. They both took a snort. "Thankfully, while you two were engaged in pleasant diversions, the best minds in the universe have been working on a solution."

"Sick!" Reef said. "So they've got what, a cosmological reset button we can push or something?"

"Or Something," Mom said. Her trunk flickered out of existence for a moment before resolidifying.

"Whoa," Ka-10-8 said. "You okay, Mom?"

Her avatar stabilized. "Sorry, kids. I didn't send a full self with this message. I'm a little glitchy."

"The data pack was huge." Ka-10-8 said.

"That's the Or Something. I'm a single-use Mom."

"Single use?" Reef said. He didn't like the sound of that.

"But you brought your memories, right?" Ka-10-8 said. "You can remember our bet?"

"That was the day we adopted Reef," she said. "I don't go out for coffee without bringing it along. But before we get to that, we need to talk about the Or Something, and the two of you need to stop wasting time." She summoned a new Mai Tai and wafting bowl. "As we are currently sitting in one, I assume you two understand the idea of fully immersive environmental simulation?" Reef and Ka-10-8 flashed shakas. "The Or Something simulates the entire universe. Once you have it up and running, the two of you can upload yourselves to it and continue surfing supernovae to your heart's content."

Reef punched the air in joy, spilling his Mai Tai into the hot tub. Ka-10-8 swung their head lobes in lazy circles. But something Mom had said struck Reef mid-celebration, and he sank into the brine. "Back up, Ma. These supernovers, they aren't going to be real?"

"They'll feel as real as your hot tub," she said. "The Or Something runs at subfermion fidelity."

"And that's good?" Ka-10-8 said.

"Kiddos, it's gnarls," Mom said. "But before we get into just how gnarly it is, we need to talk about how to run it. The two of you need to find a young, stable red dwarf, park around it, build a 'brane, and hang there for the next hundred trillion years. After that, things get sketchy. Please listen very carefully to this next bit."

That's where Reef stopped listening. With the virtual Mai Tais warming up his mind, he dreamed of supernovae. That moment when they erupt behind you, the cloud of hot gas rushing up like the fist of a dying titan, laying on the last of the burn, the impact as the shockwave catches the board, those brief seconds when you're either going to end up as atomized space junk or a golden god, then the ride. A whole new universe full of them.

"So gnarly," Reef said.

"I take it that means you understand?" Mom said.

Reef looked over at Ka-10-8, who also had that glassy look in their eyes. "It's all in the ReadMe, right?"

Mom eyed them from either side of her trunk. "So long as you promise to crack the ReadMe the moment you hit the road."

"We got it, Ma," Ka-10-8 said. "Now enough of this simulation talk. You said you remember the details of our wager. I gotta know what went down that day."

Mom settled back into the tub. "Sure about that, Lazy K? Part of the heaviness you two wanted to dodge was the day we raised Reef."

"We're one hundred and fifty billion years old," Ka-10-8 said. "I think we can take it."

Mom took a long snort of fluorescing powder. "Let's go for a ride."

☩

Third and a half rule of supernova surfing: expect flashbacks.

☩

The sun wasn't even close to exploding. Reef, Ka-10-8, and Mom floated above the rolling blue Pacific Ocean, invisible ghosts haunting their own past. On the water, surfers lined up for the massive waves rolling toward the crowded Ehukai beach on the North Shore of Oahu.

"Total blast from the past," Reef said. "This is the Pipeline comp, isn't it?"

"2046," Mom said. "We happened to be swinging by when Ka-10-8 heard about the competition. There they are."

The Ka-10-8 of 150 billion years ago wore a human body that bobbed on their board in the line-up beside the original Reef.

"Mom," Ka-10-8 said. "How did you let me out looking like that?"

"This was pre-contact," Mom said. "You really wanted to enter the comp, so we made you something that would fit in. Now stick your POVs to those fine young bodies, see if this will jog a memory."

Mom pushed Reef and Ka-10-8 into their younger selves, and Reef's perceptions shifted.

He floated on the waves in his original body. White zinc sunscreen was smeared across the human Ka-10-8's sunburnt cheeks, and they laughed at something he'd said.

"You're pretty cocky for a human," Ka-10-8 said.

"What you expecting, a shark?" As Reef's young body said the words, he remembered saying them.

"I'm expecting to win."

"Last set of the heat. Gotta give it all on this one."

The surfer ahead of Reef dropped onto a massive wave; he was next.

"Tell you what," Ka-10-8 said. "Whoever wins this thing gets first rides next time we ride together."

Memory flooded back across 150 billion years. Reef had been so excited to think this rad new rider wanted to surf with him again. "Got yourself a deal, bro."

Ka-10-8 and Reef bumped fists, then Reef paddled into the next wave. He was a little late on the drop, and he remembered how disappointed he felt. He was shanking it. The surfer with the dorky zinc on their cheeks would never want to surf with him again.

He rode out of the wave and sat down on his board to watch Ka-10-8 surf. Their wave was huge, at least twenty-seven feet, and they dropped no problem, cutting across the wall of ocean as if they'd been born to do it. Then they caught their nose and it all went wrong. Ka-10-8 fell, arms pinwheeling, and the wave thundered down on top of them.

Reef paddled without thinking. He'd been hammered at Ehukai before. The reef was the ocean's open mouth, full of coral teeth, and it could chew you to pieces. He ducked under the wash, saw Ka rolling unconscious above the coral, blood seeping from a gash on their head. He wrapped one arm around their chest and hauled them back to the surface.

A rescue jet ski towed them back to the beach, where a tall woman in a long white sarong ran into the chop to help Reef with Ka.

"Oh Lazy K," Mom said. "Are you alright?"

Ka-10-8 puked up half the Pacific, then seemed to feel better. "This mean I lost the bet?"

"Let's check the scores."

Forty-four surfers had come to Ehukai for the big wave event. Based on their performance that day, the judges had placed Reef forty-third and Ka-10-8 forty-fourth, separated only by a tenth of a point. Reef relived the outrage he'd forgotten long ago. Sure, they'd both had a few rough rides, but to place dead last? Even Mom agreed there had to be some mistake.

"Tell you what," Reef said. "Let's go back to my van, hit the bong, and think this through. There's gotta be something we can do."

Twelve hours later, Reef and Ka-10-8 were still sitting in his Microbus. Dozens of empty beer cans littered the footwells, and four pizza boxes, each delivered to "The Accessible Parking Space at Ehukai Beech" at various intervals throughout the night, sat empty on the dash. Mom snored on the mattress at the back of the bus.

"I don't care what anyone says," Reef said, trying to fill the bowl of the bong, but succeeding only in littering his bus with Big Island kush. "You are like one of the top four surfers I've ever ridden with."

"Listen Reef," Ka-10-8 said. "I think you should have first ride next time."

Reef shook his head and tried to light the empty bowl. "Nah, brah. We both stank. We gotta admit it."

Ka-10-8 was trying to stand inside the cramped bus and failing. "Forget the comp. Listen. I'm not talking water waves." They rammed their head on the ceiling, cursed, and said: "I'm done with this thing."

Ka-10-8 unfolded. Their body shimmered and separated and reformed and Reef remembered thinking that the guys in Wailea must have added something special to his ganja because there was an alien in the bus beside him. Ka-10-8 was a stout quadruped covered in fur the color and consistency of a golden doodle's. Two lobes about the size and shape of a hind arm protruded from their top of their barrel-shaped body, each with a smear of zinc above a wide slit Reef supposed was a nose, each with a shiny black membrane that might have been an eye and each with a gummy toothed opening that was definitely a mouth. Four legs protruded straight out from the sides of their body, reminding Reef of a crab.

"Awesome," was all Reef could muster.

"Feeling's mutual, bro," Ka-10-8 said. "That's why I want you to come with me."

"Come with you where?"

"To, like, the stars and such." They extended one head lobe to Reef. "You in?"

Ⓜ

Fourth rule of supernova surfing: make a contingency plan.

Ⓜ

Reef toweled the hot brine off his simulated body. He didn't need the heat of the hot tub, an old warmth filled him from the memory Mom shared. You in? Ka-10-8 said. Reef had forgotten how happy those words had made him.

"I been thinking, bro," he said, turning to Ka-10-8 who was sitting on the edge of the tub, head lobes rubbing together in thought. "The contest, the wager that is, it wasn't fair. You weren't in your true bod. The results shouldn't stand."

Ka-10-8 stepped out of the tub and shook themselves dry. "No, I had it wrongzo. First rides should be yours. You saved my life."

"Any bro would have done the same."

"As much as I hate to interrupt this heartwarming reconciliation," Mom said, sheets of brine sluicing off her onto the floor of the Après. "You two need to get moving. I took the liberty of accelerating our synced chronoperception while we were tripping, and your new bodies are now ready for interstellar travel. Can we please take this to the hanger?"

In a blink, they appeared at the base of the shaft they had cut into the surface of the planetoid. Their chrome bodies gleamed lifeless and perfect in the darkness of the cavern. Reef and Ka-10-8 stepped into their respective selves, but Mom stayed behind, a simulated figment on the polished stone.

"Sure you can't ride with us, Mom?" Ka-10-8 said.

She shook her trunk in dismay. "You'll need all the processing power you can muster to run the Or Something." She kissed them both with the tip of her trunk. "Now get moving, and don't make any unnecessary stops. The Or Something will take some time to get up and running, and time is no longer an asset you can waste."

They blew kisses as they started their antimatter reactors.

"Love you, Mom!" Reef said.

"Thanks for everything."

They shot out of the planetoid, twin bullets fired from a world-sized gun.

Once the planetoid was but a small speck in the rearview behind them, Reef and Ka-10-8 appeared in the simulated VW Microbus. Both pretended they hadn't been crying. The stable red megagiant Mom had pointed them to was only a few lightyears away. At their current delta-v, they'd be there in just over twenty-five thousand years, so Reef adjusted the chronoperception dial to 1,000,000,000:1, turning the transit into a cool thirteen minutes.

Reef summoned another semi-sentient orchestra, but the music wasn't working for him. All these years, he'd been shoving in front of Ka-10-8 at every ride, but only now did he realize he might have been shoving them away.

As Reef watched the old and dying stars go by, one of the subroutines always running in the back of his vast yet dim mind drew a shining yellow pentagram around a nearby star. It wasn't that far off course, and would only add a couple hundred kiloyears to their journey. He adjusted the chronoperception dial to bring them down to parity.

"See what I'm seeing, Ka?" he said.

"Seeing it, brah, but Mom said we gotta get the Or Something set up pronto."

Real seconds ticked away between them.

"It makes me kind of sick to think how I've been hogging first rides for so long. I gotta make it right before we start this new thing."

"Bro, it's okay. I owe it to you. I should have been happy every time you caught a break ahead of me."

Reef cut off the music. "You don't owe me anything, Ka. You gave me this life, and through it all, you've been the best partner any dude could ever hope for. I lost sight of that. I want you to have the last real first ride of our lives."

"That's, like, the super-raddest thing you've ever said to me, but I really think we should heed Mom's advice, bro."

"Four hundo thouso realtime years, that's all we're talking about. Come on, Ka. We'll even simulate judges for it, like the Ehukai big wave comp. A proper do-over."

"Then we unfold the Or Something?"

"It's a deal, bro, let's shred."

Reef changed course while Ka-10-8 spun the chronoperception dial and soon they were burning for the dying star. Two light-years away, it exploded. Ka-10-8 wanted to burn for the next red megagiant to set up the Or Something, but Reef found another star that was ready to go nova. This star was a little further, almost two hundred thousand light years away on the other side of the galaxy, and they didn't have the speed boost from the supe, so it would take a while to get there.

"One last ride?" Reef said.

"One last ride."

Reef summoned a digital bong and the two of them passed it back and forth as they made the transit. Halfway to their next target, it too went boom ahead of schedule, but Reef already had several more likely targets picked out, and Ka-10-8, a little bleary from the simulated dope, again agreed.

The universe darkened as they cut across their terminal galaxy. Stars winked out without going nova, others exploded without warning. The distances between stars grew longer as the universe kept expanding, so Reef kept spinning the dial until they were cruising through a trillion years an hour. They got close enough to one supernova to climb out of the bus, but it blew a little late and barely accelerated them at one g. They dodged black holes and dim stellar remnants and discarded planets long-ago tossed away by their parent stars, the sensation like skiing slalom at the rate they perceived their transit. Reef kept packing the simulated bong with primo post human kush along the way.

One hundred trillion years later, Reef picked another target. "I have a good feeling about this one," he said.

"Bro," Ka-10-8 said, staring at the few other distant and dim points of light. "There are only like nine other stars left. Think it's time to get out the Or Something."

"This is for real the last one. Go with this good feeling, K. Please."

Ka-10-8 let out the whistling bigoat equivalent of a sigh. Reef pointed the bus toward the dying star and hit the gas. As they shot across the darkening void, the other nine stars winked out in the time it took Reef to open a bag of plantain chips. Ka-10-8 pressed their head lobes together in horror. Reef felt his simulated digestive tract turn to water. The only star left in the sky hung before them, a brilliant unstable giant, and before either of them could reach for the dial, it popped.

"No, no, no," Ka-10-8 said.

"It's okay, bro," Reef said. "We'll consult the ReadMe. Mom said everything we needed was in there."

"Mom said we had to set-up the Or Something right away. We just ate one hundred trillion years for nothing."

"Hey, we both agreed it was a good idea."

Ka-10-8 threw the bong at Reef. Stinking water soaked his tank top and board shorts and dripped in grimy streaks down his sunglasses.

"Good idea?" Ka-10-8 said. "Never mind supernovers, Reef. We've missed out on everything."

Ka-10-8 went rigid beside Reef. He tried to nudge them awake, then shouted in concern at their apparent comatoseness, and when they still didn't answer, he dropped the Microbus simulation and stared across the cold dark vacuum to find this best friend floating chrome and unresponsive in the lightless universe.

〰

Fifth rule of supernova surfing: never surf alone.

〰

Every transmission Reef sent bounced off Ka-10-8's chrome skin unanswered. He summoned a suite of diagnostic subroutines that confirmed his worst fears: Ka-10-8 was running on their own time, and they weren't broadcasting a sync key. Ka-10-8 had shut him out.

As Reef reeled from the realization, Ka-10-8 made a few course corrections. All he could do was follow, always a few beats behind. They flew away from the dimming supernova remnant. Black holes and brown dwarfs loomed where there had once been light. Here and there a flare of intense gamma lit up the darkness, but otherwise it was the ocean on a clouded night. A very old part of Reef's brain couldn't help thinking there might be sharks circling below.

Ka-10-8 landed on a rocky planetoid that was cruising through the void. Reef had to circle back to make orbit around the cold rock, and by then Ka-10-8 was pushing the planetoid across the void toward a nearby black hole.

During the transit, the planetoid began to change. Ka-10-8's body spread across the surface, turning the dull rock into computronium. It took ages, but they had ages. Reef flipped through an old surf magazine while keeping an eye on the changes through the windshield of the Microbus.

An hour and several million years later, the rock shed layers as it entered orbit around the black hole, like an abandoned wasp nest disintegrating in a hurricane. At first Reef thought the black hole was doing the ripping, but that wasn't the case: Ka-10-8 was pushing all those little flecks of smart rock into a specific orbit.

Soon the original rock was gone, dispersed into a great cloud around the black hole, and to Reef's horror, so was Ka-10-8.

"Ka," Reef broadcast from his orbital position an AU further out. "Please. Don't leave me all alone out here."

The answering signal was a life preserver. He clung to it, and accepted Ka-10-8's request to join him in the simulated Microbus.

"Jeez, bro," Ka-10-8 said as they materialized in the passenger seat. "It's been seven hundred million years. Couldn't you have cleaned up the place?"

Empty bags of plantain chips and discarded beer cans filled the passenger foot well. Digital dope haze hung in the air so thick it could start raining THC at any moment.

"I don't do so well without you," Reef said.

"So summon a shrink. That's what I did. And a yoga instructor. Did some sensory deprivation. A thousand-year silent retreat. Read the Big Bigoat Book of Living and Dying for Dummies a few times. A little self-improvement before moving to the new universe. How have you been using your last increments of this reality?"

Reef held up a surf magazine. "I read about half of this." Then he dropped it, and buried his head in his hands. "Who am I kidding? I only looked at the pictures."

The tears caught him off guard. He laid his head on the leather-tasseled steering wheel and bawled.

"So you haven't started work on your own Or Something?"

Reef pointed to the surf magazine. "Just the pictures." He tore open a bag of plantain chips, hesitated a moment, then offered them to Ka-10-8. "They're the spicy kind."

They refused, so Reef left the open bag in the console.

"Well if you had," Ka-10-8 said. "You might be able to help figure out what to do with it."

"Could you, like, give me the laid man's version?"

Ka-10-8 tried to explain it to him. The Or Something was designed to be powered by the entire energetic output of a stable star. With that kind of power, it could run a snappy universe simulation down to what Mom had called subfermion resolution. But all they had to power the simulation was a black hole. Though the energetic output of the supermassive black hole at the center of their dying galaxy was significant, building a structure in its orbit would be too difficult, so they had to settle for a smaller, less energetic black hole. It still put out a good deal of energy in the form of

X-rays, infrared light, and heat, but it didn't compare to the energy output of a star.

"It's like trying to roast a veggie dog over a single match instead of a barbecue," Ka-10-8 said.

"That would take forever," Reef said.

"Exactly. Simulating one second of subfermion-resolution universe using a black hole as the power source will take years of real-time processing power." At Reef's blank expression, Ka-10-8 said: "The point is we can't go as high-resolution if we want the simulation to last for a good long time."

"So we gotta scale back?"

"You gotta scale back," Ka-10-8 said. "And so do I. When you get your Or Something up and running, you'll have to decide what to leave and what to keep."

Reef reached across the Microbus and put a hand on each of Ka-10-8's head lobes. "Ka, I don't want another universe if it doesn't have you in it."

They blinked in surprise at this, then shrugged him off. "Spent a lot of the last few millions years talking to my yoga instructor about you. About how we been living. I know we chose bio-brains because neither of us wanted to remember the fact that we came in last at Ehukai, but you ever think it was more than that?"

Reef settled back into his seat. "I still don't want to remember it. In fact, I kinda forgot again."

"We've been cruising through life, leaving all our troubles in the ashes of the last supernover, and getting high on the road to the next wave. That's not really living, Reef."

"Says who?" Reef said. "Your semi-sentient yoga instructor? There's nothing wrong with what we been doing. I should have let you ride first every now and then, I know that now, but that don't mean we have to toss the baby out with the bathtub. I cherish every moment we've had together, whether in the van, the Après, or out there on the waves. All I ever wanted was the next moment, and deep down, I think that's all you want too."

Ka-10-8 sat in stunned silence across from him. Reef offered them the bag of plantain chips again, and this time, Ka took a mouthful. "These are spicy. New universe might not have plantain chips this good."

"So ditch them," Reef said. "Supernovers to shred. Some good liquid waves. Mountains with snow. Doesn't have to be water snow, though I am partial to it. Gas giants for sailing. And you."

Ka-10-8 rubbed their head lobes together. "And the Après, I suppose, and maybe some place to get our boards waxed."

"Simulating all the life in the universe has gotta hog resources. Cut it too."

Ka-10-8 closed their eyes and seemed to be thinking. "Could work. But it will be awful lonely."

Reef knelt in the empty beer cans and crinkling plantain chip packages that filled the driver's footwell. "Not if we're together. You, me, and a universe to shred. That's all we need."

"What about first rides?"

"All yours."

They took another mouthful. "Nope. We do the contest again. But this time, I ride in my own body."

Reef crawled up out of the foot well. "So we simulate Earth. Show up for the 2046 pipeline comp. Winner gets first rides. We shut it down after if we need the bandwidth."

"Got yourself a deal, bro."

Ka-10-8 leaned in. Reef bumped their head lobe with his fist.

Minutes and millions of years later, they surfed the wave front of a Big Bang as it defined their new universe.

Song of Mary

Peatro coughs blood onto the rough ice on which he lies, and when he can breathe again, he rises onto all fours. She wishes he wouldn't.

"Stay down, mutt," Lennock, the chief's son, says.

Peatro moves onto one knee. Lennock kicks Peatro hard in the ribs, the same side she watched him kick last time, and the two hunters with Lennock laugh. With a hiss as his breath leaves him, Peatro falls back to the ice.

And still, he rises again.

"Give me my pika," Peatro says.

"They aren't worth it, half-breed."

Three small rodents hang from Lennock's belt. A few hundred kilojoules each. They really aren't worth it, she thinks.

"You're a farmer," Lennock says. "You have no right to hunt."

"I'm a True Person," he says. "Just as much as I'm a Nama Singer. I have the right."

He rises again, into a crouch this time, and when Lennock kicks, he rolls out of the way.

They've taken away his spear and his grandfather knife, his tendon snares and nama sack, and they've stripped off his mother's hide, leaving him naked. Every rib shows through the fur on his chest, each vertebrae protrudes from his spine. He comes out of the roll standing, a chunk of jagged ice clutched in one hand.

Lennock signals his two hunters. Sharpened bone knives slide out of ancestor-skin sheathes. They close on Peatro, who bares his teeth as he swings the heavy chunk of ice.

She can't see him killed; not Peatro.

Brilliant silver light shines out from behind Peatro. Lennock and his hunters snarl in pain. They drop their weapons in their rush to cover their eyes, and before Lennock's spear hits the ice, Peatro darts forward and snatches the pika.

The light fades and is bottled into the shape of a small woman dressed in a glowing white robe. Lennock and his hunters squint between their fingers.

"Does the Old Mother always fight for you, mutt?"

"Go home, Lennock," Mary says. Her voice booms from her projector's speakers. She's using too much power, she knows; the ship will scold her for it. "It will be best if you tell your father what happened here before I do."

Lennock spits at her where she floats above the ice, then spits at Peatro. They start to walk away.

"My tools," Peatro says.

The chief's son nods at his hunters, who pass him what they took from Peatro. He binds it all with a tendon snare and throws the mass out into the darkness beyond Mary's small pool of light.

All three laugh.

They walk away on legs that are little more than bone and fur; their fat reserves are nearly as depleted as Peatro's.

She remains beside Peatro, who wheezes, blood flecking his lips with each breath.

"Are you alright?" she says.

He doesn't answer her; he just walks across the dark ice in the direction Lennock threw his equipment. Crevasses wait in that darkness. She can't see him devoured by the ice only moments after she's saved him, so she floats along beside him. Her senses extended well beyond his. She sends a small shaft of light to illuminate the spot where his equipment lies.

"I didn't ask for your help," he says.

He winces in pain as he kneels to collect his things.

"Yours are the only children who will be born this season," she says. "The pika are yours."

Without looking at her, he starts the long limp home to the grotto. She floats along beside him.

He stops.

"Find someone else to illuminate," he says.

She turns into shadow.

In the dim glow of the sunbeam, he looks like a fur-covered skeleton. She can see the features of both peoples in him: the wide shoulders of the True People he inherited from his father, the long fingers of the Nama Singers his mother gifted him before she passed. But he is so thin.

She's been hoping they could endure, but if it has come to this, people ready to kill each other over a brace of pika, she can't wait any longer.

They have to find equilibrium.

Invisible and silent, she floats beside Peatro until he is home.

M

Years before she saves Peatro and lightyears distant, she is stripped down to her basic code, the memory of herself, and transmitted across the dark void. There is no sensation as she travels between the greatships, there is only absence. But then, after some indeterminate time that never seems to pass, she is reconstituted in the *Pacifica*.

She floats out into the greatship in her tiny projection unit.

It is cold. For a moment she thinks there has been some mistake, that she is in the *Savanne*, returned to the tomb ship ahead of schedule, but there is atmosphere here the walls of the world are intact, and the stuttering power supply tells her this is the *Pacifica*, but it is too cold.

The *Pacifica* is an O'Neill cylinder eight kilometers long with a half a kilometer radius; sixth of the seven greatships. Ice rimes its interior. The *Pacifica*'s vast empty plains are broken by small hills: the larger Col Sera where the True People gather and the gardens and fields of the Nama Singers.

Everything is ice.

"Give them more heat," she tells the greatship. "My children must be freezing."

"Only one reactor still functions," the *Pacifica* says. "Every kilojoule is accounted for. In three centuries we will pass through the Hyades cluster, at which point I will deploy the solar panels and bring more energy into my interior. Until then, my calculations show that this will be enough to ensure critical population survival."

"And what have you decided is a critical population?" Mary asks.

Though she has no skin, no flesh — she is only light and shadow, sound and silence — she trembles as she waits for the answer.

"Terrestrial humanity once shrunk to approximately two thousand reproductive individuals," the *Pacifica* says. "My population is more hardy and adaptable than unmodified Terran primitives. For the next three and a half centuries, my caloric output will sustain a mean population of one hundred and fifty seven individuals, based on current consumption patterns."

One hundred and fifty-seven. The ship has already placed the important numbers in her mind: three hundred and fifty three

Nama Singers work their fields and gardens, two hundred and seven True People hunt the pika and insects that roam the wild, frozen plains.

Floating at one end of the long, narrow ship, she can cup every human being within a hundred lightyears in the insubstantial palm of her hand.

"Three in ten will survive," she says. "What you propose is monstrous."

"The alternative is extinction," he says. "And neither of us is programmed to accept that. Equilibrium must be reached."

Programming. That is all they are. The greatships were programmed to ensure humanity survived the millennia-long transit from the dying Earth. She was programmed to ensure the survivors remained human.

She floats out into the world, closer to her children and away from the monstrous voice of the ship.

Three in ten.

When she appears to her children for the first time in centuries, they welcome her as they always do, with festivals and feasts. The festivals are full of joy at her arrival: she brings news of the other greatships, of the dead Earth, she teaches them what it means to be human. But at the feasts, the only thing being feasted on is the musculature and fat reserves of the people as their bodies devour the only caloric resources remaining to them.

She wants to tell them: you have to find a new equilibrium.

But she doesn't. Not then. It will be weeks until she defends Peatro on the ice, when she will know she can no longer remain silent.

Bora, Eldest of the Nama Singers, takes the songcord from Anolea and slips it behind her back.

"Try it without the cord," she says.

The girl closes her eyes and leans closer to the sack she holds between her legs. Boney shoulders and ribs show through her fur, but all Mary sees is her swollen belly, the only such belly in the world. Every other pregnancy this season failed, but Anolea is strong. Peatro always finds her food. Inside her womb, five tiny hearts beat in infrared. Inside the sack the girl carries, green nama swirls as she sings to it.

The two of them sit inside the drum room of the grotto. Ice arches rise up overhead to form a translucent dome. Benches ring the perimeter of the drum room, on which sit other singers and a few drummers, steadily beating the skins of their grandmother drums. Anolea sings to the beat. Sixteen passageways lead away from the drum room, into the corridors of the grotto where the Nama Singers live and sleep, though many of those passageways have been abandoned. At the very center of the grotto, the very heart of these people, a circular crater lined in hide is filled with the same swirling, green liquid Anolea sings to in her gutsack.

Mary appears on the bench beside Bora. The Eldest nods at her, but says nothing; all her concentration is on Peatro's mate as she trills the notes of the nama song. She does a fair job of it, Mary thinks. After ten seconds, she recognizes it: the Song to Quench Legume Thirst, a song she helped develop several thousand years ago.

Then Anolea misses a note.

"No, no," Bora says. "Stop right there."

She lifts her rump and gives the winding length of songcord back to Anolea.

"Again with the cord, and then again without, while I talk to the Old Mother."

Peatro's mate draws the songcord between her fingers. Hundreds of knots have been tied along the length of the tendon, but the knots only come in four varieties. Anolea sings four distinct tones for each of the four knots. Those tones invoke words in Mary's mind: adenine, guanine, thymine, cytosine. The nama remembers, too, as it swirls to her song.

"She is talented," Mary says.

"Her singing isn't bad," Bora says. "But she has the memory of a pika. You're back from the Col Sera I take it?"

Mary nodded.

"And you've settled this matter with Crawthis?"

"Chief Crawthis and I discussed the attack on Peatro," she said. "And many other things."

Though Mary's mass is tiny — just the small collection of lenses and lights and sensors and speakers and power sources and processors that make up the tiny, almost invisible core from which she projects into the world — the other things she discussed with Crawthis still weigh on her.

Bora stares at her, waiting, Mary knows, for an explanation of those other things. When it doesn't come, Bora shrugs.

"I'll assume that Crawthis will discipline his son and that he'll send an offering of pika as apology," she says. "That will leave us free to focus on the crop. I've never seen it worse."

"You'll never see it better," Mary says. "Not in your lifetime, not in your grandchildren's lifetimes."

Bora's ancient eyes narrow.

"What are you saying, Old Mother?"

Mary floats very close to Bora and whispers so that only the old woman can hear. She tells her what she told Crawthis: that there isn't enough food or heat or light for all of them. That three in ten will survive, and more importantly, that seven in ten will perish. Bora listens without making any movement of her ancient, bent body, until Mary finishes, at which point she stands and brushes ice from her fur. She takes a deep breath as she looks around the drum room and then lets it out in a long hiss.

"That's enough, girl," she says to Anolea, who quits her singing. "Dump your nama in the pool. Go find your mate and see how his ribs are mending."

Once she is gone, Bora picks up her cane and walks toward the nearest spiraling stairway that leads up to the surface. Mary follows her. Though it is near noon, only a dull grey light shines from the sunbeam. The gardens stretch out in every direction from the grotto; they climb up the walls of the world in a patchwork collection of brown fields and dry groves, trying to drink in the light from the sunbeam that runs along the axis of the world. Nama Singers move among the fields, trying to force their crops to grow and their domesticated pika and insects to multiply.

The Col Sera hangs from the roof of the world three kilometers to Fore. Bora stares at the home of the greatship's other tribe. The tents of the True People are but small black scuffs on the endless ice.

"How does Crawthis suggest we resolve this shortage?" the Eldest says.

"A conference," Mary says. "Both peoples together must decide who will perish and who will survive."

Bora laughs then, a sound like twigs snapping.

"Talk? That's his solution?"

"There is no other alternative," Mary says. Though she knows the alternatives. She saw what happened to the Earth in its last days. "He wishes to meet tomorrow. He's offered to lead the heads of all the True People families to the grotto to meet with you and the other elders."

"No," Bora says as she surveys her gardens. "No. We'll go there."

The Eldest walks over to a row of withered trees. Small brown apples hang beneath mottled leaves.

"We are close to harvest," she says. She picks one of the fruits. "In a normal year, we would soon be ascending the Col to share our bounty. If I send a few boys with you, can you mark the safest route to the Col for us?"

Bora places the whole thumb-sized apple in her mouth and sucks on its frozen flesh.

"Have the boys meet me in an hour," Mary says. "And we will prepare the way."

※

She is light and shadow, sound and silence, but she is also memory and absence.

On the Col Sera, Lennock and several of his hunters shout as they climb the icy peak. They carry something between them on the stretched hides of their ancestors. Mary, who has marked the trail to the Col with the two Nama Singer boys, now discusses the upcoming conference with Crawthis. When the chief hears his son's voice, he goes to meet him.

Lennock and his hunters lay out their hides. They peel back what they found. A long, cylindrical body. Two ragged holes that used to hold eyes. Markings along the flank that might have once been fins.

"What is it, Old Mother?" Lennock says.

"A fish," she says. "They used to swim in the ice, when the ice was water."

As the True People gather to look at the strange creature, she can see Lennock's ancestors on hide and wood boats, sailing the warm sea that fills the interior of the *Pacifica*. They pull up tendon nets filled with writhing, silver fish. One this size would have been cause for a festival.

"Can we eat it?" Crawthis says.

She speaks inwardly with the *Pacifica*: "How long since the main reactor died?"

"Twelve centuries," the ship says.

"When did the waters freeze?"

"Nine hundred and twenty years ago."

She floats over to the creature, frozen mid-decomposition. Enough kilojoules to feed all the True People for a week. But who knew what toxins would thaw out of the frozen flesh.

"No, Lennock," she says. "You can't eat it. Maybe the Nama Singers can compost it for their gardens."

Lennock spits at the mention of their name.

"After tomorrow's conference," Crawthis says. "We will give it to them."

The hunters take the fish carcass away to pack it in ice.

She is light and shadow, but above all, she is memory.

⋙

Peatro winces as he scrapes at the mixture of ice and mulch at the base of a gnarled walnut tree. Once the soil is roughened, he opens the sack his mate gave him and dribbles out a bit of the nama.

"You don't need to go with them," Mary says.

He rakes the nama into the icy soil and spreads it around the base of the tree.

"I'm a True Person as much as I'm a Nama Singer," he says. "That will help."

"They don't see you that way."

"I'm going."

Peatro lifts the sack and limps to the next tree. She can see the bruises beneath the fur of his ribs, and the shudder he tries to hide with each breath. He scrapes at the frozen soil with an ancestor's shoulder blade lashed to the end of a bamboo pole.

"Anolea needs you here," she says. "The conference could last days. You need to work the fields, hunt, whatever it takes for your children."

"I know what I must do for my children," he says. "I'm going with them tomorrow morning."

Mary sighs. She floats away from the young man, toward the grotto. A handful of Nama Singers are out in the fields, pruning and weeding and attending to the pathetic crops. She glides over to the nearest entrance into the grotto and descends toward the drum room.

Every ice bench is full of men and women singing to pouches of nama; with so many people singing in such close proximity, they stick their heads into the pouches and draw the edges closed around them, so that the nama won't be distracted by others' songs.

Anolea has her face in one of the sacks. Mary waits for her to finish. The air is filled with muffled nama song, so many being sung at the same time that Mary can't identify any individual song.

After several minutes, Anolea finishes and takes her head out of the sack. She seems surprised to see Mary there.

"I thought you were with Peatro," she says.

"I was," Mary says. "But that man is stubborn. Is there anything you can say to keep him here?"

A young boy walks over to Anolea, takes her sack, ties it shut, and walks down an ice corridor with it.

"Once Peatro's made up his mind," the girl says. "It sets firm as the oldest ice."

Another boy walks over to Anolea and hands her a new bag of unsung-to nama.

"Quite the operation going on down here," Mary says.

"Your news has catalyzed us," Bora says. She shuffles up beside Anolea and places a hand on the young woman's shoulders. "Before the elders leave tomorrow, I wanted to ensure our workers had everything they need to convince the gardens to grow while we are conversing. Come, let me show you our efforts on the surface."

"I've been to the surface," Mary says. "I wanted to talk to your Singers. I have an idea that may help. A new song."

As she speaks, she concentrates on the song Anolea has started to sing to the fresh sack of nama. After a few bars, Mary recognizes it.

"Why does she sing the Song of Gasping Breath?"

Bora points her good ear at the young woman.

"Is that what she's working on?" Bora says. "I have them singing so many songs. The Gasping Breath is to chase our pika from their holes. Our domestic herds hide beneath the ice. Some of our wranglers are going after them now if you'd care to watch."

"You must be careful with it," Mary says. "In the wrong hands, the Gasping Breath can kill."

"Naturally, Old Mother," Bora says. "We have to be very careful in these dark days. Now come, I don't want to distract my singers. If you don't want to go to the surface, my knees won't complain."

The Eldest leads her down a corridor where people no longer live. Hoar frost coats abandoned sleeping cubbies and debris accumulates under foot. Once the sound of the drum room is lost in the windings of the tunnel, Bora slumps onto a bench carved into the ice.

"Now tell me your idea, Old Mother."

"The pika sleep for weeks during the coldest days of the winter," Mary says. "With a few changes, the Song of Gentle Repose could help the people sleep away the harshest time of the year. Metabolic rates would drop; it would save food. More people would survive."

Bora whistles the first few bars of the Song of Gentle Repose.

"That could work," she says. "Where would you make the changes?"

※

The True People line the stairway carved into the ice of the Col Sera. Bora and Peatro and the elders of the Nama Singers walk between the True People, a collection of wheezes and creaking bones and runny eyes. The elders all carry small sacks of nama. Gifts, Bora says, to be opened at the conclusion of this conference.

At the peak, Mary waits beside Crawthis, who stands tall and proud in his best furs. Lennock stands beside his father and sneers at Peatro.

When she arrives, Bora bows to the Chief. He returns the bow and then clasps her hands in the fashion of the Nama Singers.

"It's good to see you, Craw," the Eldest says. "But I can't say you're looking well."

"You've had better days yourself," he says.

The Chief leads them to his tent, which is made from the hides of his fathers. The Nama Singer elders sit in a semi-circle, the True People family heads sit opposite them. Peatro sits at one intersection of the two people. His heritage is more evident here: he has the thick fur of Nama Singers, but it is striped like many of the True People; his nose is as large as Crawthis', his eyes hooded like the elders. The brother of Peatro's long-dead father is one of the family chiefs. He nods to Peatro, who doesn't return the gesture.

Mary sits beside Peatro, across from Crawthis and Bora.

"Thank you all for coming," Mary says. "Both peoples face one of the hardest decisions they will ever collectively make. The fact that you've all come here to find a peaceful resolution fills me with hope."

"Together, we will find a way," Crawthis says. "Let us begin the ceremony with an offering."

He opens a gutsack and pulls out a squirming pika. With a quick motion, he cuts the little animal's neck and drains its blood into a skullbowl at his feet.

"We thank the god-world for its bounty," he says, his eyes closed. "Even in these dark times when the god-world tests us, he is still merciful."

He passes the skull-bowl to Bora, who takes a sip before passing it back to Crawthis.

"Tasty that," she says. "Though I hope the meat is going to people who'll have more use for it."

"Are things that bad among the Nama Singers?" Crawthis said.

"I saw more ribs than bellies among your people."

"We aren't here to compare who's starving more," Mary says. "Soon everyone will starve. If we plan properly, we can minimize the losses."

Lennock laughs.

"Their elders are starving," he says. "Their farmers are runts. Our elders feast on pika. We already know who will survive to the next season."

"We agreed to meet with the Nama Singers," Crawthis says. "We did not bring them from their homes to taunt them." He stares at his son until Lennock looks away, then he turns to Bora.

"Mary has explained the threat we face, Eldest. I understand it, if my son does not. Our god-world will only provide enough food and warmth for one hundred and fifty of us to survive. The rest shall perish. We recognize that some True People will be among the dead. We enter these negotiations as partners in peril. Now let us consider how best to face this grave challenge."

Soon they are weighing lives. One of the True People suggests drawing lots as a means to choose who will survive. A Nama Singer elder recommends choosing those who've already proven they can produce many children. There are suggestions to preserve the best hunters, the best farmers, the best singers, and the best cooks. Lennock says the strongest should survive, as it has always been.

Several hours into the discussion, Crawthis gestures to Peatro.

"You have the blood of both people in your veins," he says. "What insight does that grant you?"

Peatro hesitates. He looks at Bora, then at Mary.

"Old Mother," he says. "You've lived thousands of years, you've seen many other peoples. How did our cousins in the other worldships handle situations like ours? How did the old people deal with scarcity?"

Mary thinks before she answers. The people of the *Savanne* never had to the chance to decide what to do about scarcity; an asteroid ripped a hole in the side of the greatship and made atmosphere a vanishing resource. The lost *Borealis* might have faced a similar situation, but she hadn't spoken to them in seven thousand years. The *Himalayan* made it to its destination without ever having to face such a dilemma. Disease offered no choices to the people of the *Arcticus*.

Mechanical failure of the *Saharran*'s heating system left no options either. And the *Amazonian*, still crawling across the void, functioned well, its children fat and happy.

That left the old world.

"On Earth, the old people didn't do well in the face of scarcity. Those who had resources hoarded them, while those without grew increasingly desperate. People starved while others grew fat. Wars resulted. Even at the end, when there was so little left, they chose to fight, to destroy each other, rather than sit down and make difficult decisions."

Mary smiles.

"You are already well ahead of the old people."

"So very far ahead," Peatro says.

And the conference resumes. Sometime during the long discussions, Mary discusses her idea: the Song of the Long Sleep. It isn't perfect, she knows, but it will skew those dreadful fractions in her children's favor. Three in ten will change to four or even five in ten surviving.

As she describes her plan to have people hibernate through the worst of the winters, the hide flaps at the entrance of the tent part and a young man, one of Peatro's friends named Erol, steps through, panting.

"Sorry to intrude," he says. "But the midwife told me to run. Peatro, it's Anolea. She's gone into labor."

"It's too soon," Bora says.

"You must go to her, Peatro," Mary says.

"I have to go, too," Bora says. "No one's brought more babies into the world than me. I'm sorry, Crawthis. We'll have to continue this tomorrow."

Bora grabs her cane and starts to rise.

"No," Mary says. They are handling these discussion better than she could have hoped. Peatro and young Anolea are another matter. "Stay, Eldest. I'll go with Peatro. Once the children and their mother are safe, I'll return."

"We need you here, Old Mother," Bora says.

"No you don't," Mary says. "That's clear to me now. This is your decision to make; you don't need my help. Come, Peatro."

Mary floats with the two young men, lighting their way along the path she marked out the day before. The distance from the grotto to the Col Sera is long, a five kilometer spiraling path along the interior of the *Pacifica*, and by the time they get to the fields of the Nama Singers, both young men are panting.

The fields are crowded. It seems all the farmers on this side of the world are out tending their crops. Those nama sacks Anolea and the other singers were filling the night before are everywhere in the gardens. Mary hasn't seen this many people working the fields since she arrived. Bora had said that they would convince their gardens to grow.

When they descend into the grotto, Mary hears Anolea's low moan of pain. She floats ahead of the men, toward the agonized cries.

She is light and sound and memory. And those memories can do more than just give weight to her inconsequential mass; they can help babies into the world.

"Get her something to drink," Mary says to Peatro and Erol. "And thick hides. Something sweet to put in the water."

The two men run at her bidding. She floats beside Anolea and the midwife.

"Don't worry, child," she says. "Everything will be all right."

⁂

The shuttle takes her children closer to the gargantuan cylinder in orbit about the moon.

Blue-green light from Earth reflects along the *Pacifica*'s length.

The children aren't paying attention to her lesson. Who could, when their old world and the new both loom in front of them? Still, she must teach them. They must perfect their skills if their offspring are to survive the millennia.

"Four notes, four base pairs," she says. "When the algae hears those four frequencies, its modified ribosomes transcribes it to either adenine, guanine, cytosine, or thymine. With those four notes, you can build any gene you want."

One of the children, a young boy who will remind her of Peatro, practices the notes. He sings well; he has perfect pitch and he can sing quickly.

"Good," she says. "The rest of you could learn something."

The boy stops singing.

"Any gene?" he says.

"Any."

"Could someone sing a whole genome?"

"It would be a long song," Mary says. "So long that you would need many lifetimes to sing it."

"But conceivably, someone could sing a person."

"I suppose," Mary says. "But no one could memorize that many notes."

"We couldn't," the boy says. "But you could. One day, when I'm long gone, can you sing me, Mary?"

She floats beside the boy, wordless.

The other children in the shuttle are finally paying attention.

⋀⋀

Three hours later, Anolea bleeds onto her great-grandmother's ragged hide. Other hides that once belonged to grandparents, aunts, and uncles prop her up so that she can push. The midwife kneels between her legs, confirms what Mary already knows; her contractions are minutes apart and Anolea has only dilated four centimeters. Peatro stands at his wife's side and tries to get her to drink from a gutsack filled with sweetened water.

"Tell me again what you've given her?" Mary asks the midwife.

"Nothing," she says. "Just the water."

"You know the Song of the Soft Breeze?"

"Certainly."

Anolea lets out a terrible sound.

"It's time to sing," Mary says. "She can't take much more of this. Peatro, sharpen your knife."

The midwife runs to the drum room to fill the empty nama sack she carries, her footsteps echoing back to them. It is the only sound in the grotto other than Anolea's moaning: they are the only people beneath the ice. All the other Nama Singers are in the fields, working. Mary is thankful for this; she doesn't want a crowd around the struggling mother-to-be.

After another moan, Anolea reaches for Peatro's hands; she claws at him as if drowning.

"What have we done?" she says. "They aren't ready."

"Quiet," Peatro says.

"We'll lose them all," Anolea says.

"Quiet, woman."

"What does she mean?" Mary says.

"She's delirious," Peatro says, but Mary doesn't believe that.

The midwife returns, carrying a gutsack full of nama.

She left with an empty sack, Mary remembers.

"You said you gave her nothing," Mary says to the midwife. "Yet you carried an empty nama sack."

The midwife looks at Peatro, who will not look at any of the three women who surround him. The midwife provides no answer either; instead she starts to trill a nama song.

"What was in the nama sack?"

None of them answer.

In the silence, Mary hears something. Sounds too dim for a human ear, yet they are human sounds. Cries of pain. Roars of rage. A bone cudgel breaking living bone.

Without realizing it, she floats toward the nearest stairway.

"Wait, Old Mother," Peatro says. "We need you here."

On the ice, the sounds are clearer. Grandfather knives cutting through skin. Children weeping for mothers, and the sudden end of that weeping. Skulls and ice colliding. And beneath all that, people struggling for breath.

The fields are empty, only wind walks beneath the trees in the orchards. All the Nama Singers and the heavy sacks of nama they carried are gone.

"Don't go," Peatro says.

He's followed her onto the ice.

"They're dying," she says. "My children are dying."

"Seven in ten must die," he says. "It was either us or them."

The Song of Gasping. It wasn't meant for the pika. And she marked the path for the Nama Singers to cross the ice. She led the elders with their sacks full of poison.

"I can stop it."

"You can save some, maybe," he says. "But if you go to them, Anolea and my children will die."

And then she realizes: they wanted her here, away from the Col and the True People.

Bora must have planned it from the moment Mary told her of the hardship to come. Maybe even before that.

"What was in the midwife's sack?" she says.

"The Song of Quickening."

To induce Anolea's labor.

"But why, Peatro?" she says. "They are your people, too."

He shakes his head.

"There is only one people now," he says. "Bora gave me a choice: if I agreed to help hide the attack from you, my children would be of the people; if I refused, my children would never be born. Help us, Mary, so my choice won't be for nothing."

He turns, back toward the hole in the ice where his young mate lets out another agonized cry. From across the ice, on the Col Sera, she hears the sound of slaughter. Of genocide. She is light and shadow, sound and silence. Peatro is right, maybe she can save some of the True People, but what then? How will the two peoples continue?

Before he descends, Peatro says: "We are no better than the old people. You had to know that."

No better and no worse. She has kept them human, even after all this time.

She floats above the ice, staring down the dark cylinder of the world. She is memory and absence. She will remember it forever, for however many more thousands of years she will endure. Life or death, birth or genocide.

But she can choose what will be memory and what will be absence.

⋀

She roams far and wide across the ice, but never near the Col.

A darkness clings to the Col, a shadow Mary doesn't want to brighten. The Col hangs from the roof of the world above the fields and orchards, the ice of the Col dark and stained; a constant reminder of events no one admits to remembering.

Only half the Nama Singers who departed for the Col returned, but they don't call themselves that anymore: they are just the People. They always were. Neither Bora nor any of the other elders survived; they perished when they opened their sacks full of the Song of Gasping and incapacitated the True People's strongest hunters. The People still number more than the one-hundred and fifty that the *Pacifica* claims it can sustain, but they are working on the Song of the Long Sleep. Already, some sleep beneath the ice.

She isn't sure what she is looking for as she floats across the ice, wrapped in silence and shadow. Survivors, maybe. She finds none.

Four of Anolea's five infants survived the birth and three still suckled the last time Mary visited. That was many days ago. She found the grotto overstuffed ever since the People returned from the Col. They brought meat with them. Pika meat, they called it, cut and portioned so that no one can claim it was anything else.

Mary finds it much too crowded in the grotto.

So she roams the ice. She's been roaming for days. She still has a long time before the *Pacifica* throws her across the void to the empty desolation of the *Savanne*, but that day can't come soon enough.

Then one grey morning, she spots two huddled forms leaning into the wind.

Peatro carries two children on his back, Anolea a third. They each also drag a sledge loaded with hides, bones, bamboo, mats, tendons, gutsacks, and two nama sacks.

"Where are you going?" Mary says.

"We can't stay down there," Peatro says.

"Our children have True People blood in them," Anolea says.

"When times get rough again," Peatro says. "They'll be next."

"But you can't survive on the ice all alone," Mary says.

"We can try," Peatro says.

They keep walking. The *Pacifica* is dark, the sunbeam a sick grey slash against the curving walls of the world. Peatro prods the ice ahead of him for crevasses.

Geoffrey W. Cole

She floats in front of him.
"Let me light your way."

Two from the Field, Two from the Mill

One foot of snow fell in Vancouver the night before all the dogs disappeared. Made the roads hell and me late for practice. The doggy daycare chick was out shoveling as I skidded into the parking lot. When I opened the back hatch of my SUV, I found Bruno floating on the ceiling.

"What are you doing?" I shouted. "Get down or Renford will kill me."

I wrapped my arms around Bruno's neck and tried to haul him earthward. I can take down anyone on the ice, even that huge Swedish chick who plays for Regina, but Bruno lifted me right off my feet. I slipped, caught hold of his collar. He shrugged out of it, dumped me in the parking lot, and the cold snow down the crack of my ass knocked the morning's blinders off.

Dogs floated out the open door of the day care. Feet-first, tails wagging. They all looked so damn happy as they soared up into a cloudless sky. They weren't alone. Canine shapes filled the sky all across Vancouver, rising higher and higher, until they faded into the cold blue.

At some point I realized I was still telling Bruno to get down. At some point I realized the stringy daycare girl had curled up on my lap and was weeping all over my jacket. I set her down in the snow.

I got into my SUV and sat there, trying to make some sense of what I'd seen. My teeth started to chatter. *Who's the big girl?* Papa's voice said. I could see him standing on the pond behind the old house, shouting down at me. *I'm the big girl.* I shouted it into the empty SUV but it didn't shut him up, so I turned on the radio and drove.

It wasn't just here. All the dogs were gone, and not just dogs. Coyotes took off from rural farms. Wolves soared over mountains. Foxes floated out of their dens. Australia's dingos wouldn't eat any more babies. All the wild dogs in Africa went too. Who knew there were so many damn animals related to dogs? Culpeos, maned wolves, jackals.

I parked in the alley behind my apartment and listened to the experts and their so-called explanations. Aliens. A miracle. Gas leak. Collective hallucination. The start of the Rapture. Mayan calendar bullshit. Weapons testing. Dogs had never actually existed. That one made me so angry I tore the knob off the radio trying to shut it down. Bruno had existed, dammit. He was the best damn thing there ever was.

I couldn't go home. Papa's voice would be too loud in my empty apartment. I went walking instead, the same hour-long route I did with Bruno every morning. It was heavy going. The snow was a thick wedge of butter spread across the city. After I'd made one round of the circuit, I could just walk in my boot prints.

The second time around, I found a family kneeling in the snow outside their home. They prayed in a quiet that matched the stillness of the snow-muted city. Mom and Dad and twin boys around eleven. *Perfect family like that,* Papa's voice said. *You can bet they're hiding some dirty little secret.* Neither Mom nor Dad looked at me as I walked past, and the boys pretended not to watch as they prayed. Their words fervent as they talked to God.

Oh shit. I had been walking an hour and a half or more. I shifted Bruno's collar to my other hand and called Renford.

"It's the first practice I've ever missed, and I know that's no excuse."

That's as far as I got. The snow around me practically melted from the fury pouring out of my phone, but he cooled down when he ran out of ways to call me an idiot.

"You're not the only one," my coach said. "Don't let it happen again."

Renford gave us Wednesday off so that we could get our acts together, but we had the season opener against Montreal in two weeks and he told me I better be in skating shape by then or I could stay home for good.

"Don't let this throw you off," he said. "We need you out there, Nadezhda. You're the damn wall."

Sure, coach. Whatever you say, coach. Suck a skate full of taint sweat, coach. I kept walking, punching down the snow in my boot prints.

On the third lap I spotted a bent woman propped-up between two ski poles on the sidewalk ahead. Patrice the Pug's owner. I crossed the unplowed road to avoid her. Eyes brimming with squirrel-like intelligence stared at me from beneath her wide-brimmed hat. When Bruno was a pup, he took a bite out of Patrice the Pug's ear. The old bat had never forgiven him or me.

No sign of her on my next lap, but the family was still kneeling on their front lawn. They looked colder. My belly was growling. I hadn't eaten since breakfast six hours earlier.

After the lap, I cracked the door to my basement suite. The dog bed seemed huge in one corner of the room. Bruno's bowls sat beside the dishwasher, surrounded by congealing puddles of saliva and prescription kibble. The couch corners shredded. The table ends chewed. Quartered chew toys. And everywhere, his smell. That wet-dog funk. I couldn't take it.

You don't need a dog, Nadezhda, Papa's voice said. *You need to practice.*

Out on the street, it was getting warmer, the snow heavier. When I came around to the family praying in the snow, I asked them what they were doing.

"He took the dogs as a sign of His mercy," Dad said.

"It's irrefutable proof that God exists," one of the twin boys said.

"He'll take the faithful next," Mom said. "Pray with us."

The boys shivered in the snow.

"I'll stick to walking," I said.

I must have done twelve laps that day and the family was out in the snow right up until the very last. It was near midnight, the half-melted snow resolidifying. Mom and the boys were going back inside, but Dad was still there, shivering and praying. Crazy bastard.

I crawled into my SUV and went to sleep.

Ⰼ

The seat belt jabbing me in the ass woke me up. I had to stop doing this. It had been two weeks since they all disappeared and I still hadn't slept in my apartment. Coffee, for the love of God, coffee. My left leg gave out as I hobbled toward the house. I tumbled into a drift and filled it with curses.

"There's a better way," an ancient voice said from the alley. Patrice the Pug's owner hovered between her ski poles. In that ancient wool jacket, I bet she smelled worse than Bruno after a downpour. "I know how hard it is."

"You don't know nothing, lady." I brushed off the snow.

"There is a place we're building, where we can remember them. Where we can talk to them."

"Save your hippy bullshit for someone who cares."

"He'll forgive you. All you have to do is ask."

I slammed the door behind me and hung Bruno's collar on the knob. It was quiet, his smell not quite so strong.

Into the kitchen, start the percolator, find the grinds, soak his kibble, freshen his water, add a little Cheese Whiz to the kibble, even though the vet told me to quit it, pour myself a glass of water, some Vector with soy milk and bananas. As I was putting the Cheese Whiz away, I saw what I'd done. I dropped the Cheese Whiz jar and started to cry. *Here I thought you were a big girl*, Papa's voice said. I shut the tears off. Two weeks is long enough. I'm playing hockey tonight in front of twelve, maybe thirteen thousand paying customers. *I'm the big girl.* The wall.

I trashed it all. The dog bed, the murdered toys, the bowls, the half-finished bag of diabetic kibble, the leash, the tennis balls he'd never chase. Then I vacuumed. I found whole dogs worth of fur under the bed and the couch. Once it was all gone, his smell seemed to go with it. In its place was the thank-fucking-God aroma of coffee.

I sat down in my clean basement suite and drank. Only then did I notice his collar, still hanging from the door knob. Why couldn't he take the cats? Or the birds? Or all the fish in the goddamn sea? I got it, I guess. Love unconditionally. Wasn't that what all the world's religions taught? And there they were, doing a better job of it than us even as we kicked them and starved them and snipped off their balls and left them alone all the live-long-day. But why take Bruno? A few tears broke through the wall, but I snarled and I pushed them back across the blue line.

I had to get ready for the game.

She checked me hard into the boards. The crowd howled. The end of the world might be upon us but the stadium was full. I slid to a stop somewhere behind our net. A blur of Winnipeg blue and gold went past. Number 39, Monroe. What did she just say? I scrambled back to my feet and got some steam up. Monroe was waiting for a pass at the blue line and I swear she grinned as she saw me coming. The whistle blew. Off side. I deeked to avoid leveling her. As I blew past I said: "Say it again, bitch."

We lined up across from each other as we waited for the puck to drop. She was missing as many teeth as she had brain cells.

"Little baby lost her puppy?" she said in a thick French Canadian accent.

I dropped my gloves and knocked out a few more teeth for her. The crowd roared. The refs blew their whistles. Ladies aren't supposed to fight, it's against the league rules. I got her helmet off and landed two more punches before she managed to get me once. Three more quick jabs to her mean little mouth and she was down. I got on top of the bitch and kept wailing, punch after punch until my girls dragged me off.

They threw me in the penalty box, and after the ref reconsidered, they tossed me right out. The crowd booed and spat.

My fists ran red under the sink in the locker room. More her blood than mine. After the first period, Coach Renford came in and laid down a verbal beating almost as bad as the one I'd given Monroe. Told me I was likely suspended, maybe for the rest of the season, and that he wouldn't fight it.

When I got back to the SUV, Bruno's stink was still there. Fainter, but still there. Gobs of his fur clung to the upholstery. His collar sat on the seat beside me. I stared at my wrecked fists on the steering wheel, and past them, to the glowing logo on the side of the arena.

Rain spattered on my windshield. The roads were going to be hell.

※

Patrice the Pug's owner hobbled over the icy sidewalk, her ski poles barely keeping her upright. Most of the snow was gone, but here and there hard patches of ice slicked the road and walkways, invisible in the morning gloom. I caught up to her in front of the house were Dad was still praying on the frozen front lawn. Two weeks plus a day now. No sign of Mom or the boys.

I offered Patrice the Pug's owner my arm.

"Very kind of you," she said, her fingers like sparrow claws. "Offering a little old lady your formidable arm."

Her sweater smelled as bad as I imagined.

"It's been hard on all of us, okay," I said. "I didn't mean to snap at you yesterday."

"You don't need to ask me for forgiveness."

"I don't need anyone's forgiveness."

"Save it for them. The pilgrimage will make everything clear."

"Pilgrimage? Lady, I just gotta say goodbye. It's wrecking my life."

"The pilgrimage will help you rebuild. Trust me. Start at the foot of Lynn Creek, the old off-leash trail, and walk against the water's flow."

Her sparrow claws released me and she walked on ahead, only skittering once on the ice. On the lawn, Dad was looking at me, an expression on his face I couldn't quite figure. He got his phone out as I hurried home.

※

Lynn Creek was fat with snowmelt and its roar filled the forest, drowned out even the sound of the highway traffic. Usually packs of dogs ran wild all over these trails, their owners watching from within their rain-soaked jackets. Today there was no one, but that wasn't just what made the place feel different. Candle lanterns hissed in the rain where they hung from tree branches. Sopping wet prayer flags fluttered in the breeze. Laminated pictures of dogs hung in the bare trees. Cheesy as hell, if you asked me.

Something big rustled in the brush opposite the creek. Shouldn't the bears be asleep? I looked for a rock to bash it with. A man crawled out of the woods. He smiled, wiggled his butt, and loped on all fours up to me.

"Whoa," I said. "Back off."

He tried to sniff my crotch. I shoved him away. He wore tattered jeans and a filthy dress shirt. Burrs clung to his week-old beard. His teeth chattered. He came at me again, rump wagging, and I raised a fist. He cowered.

"Buddy, I did not come here for your shitty performance art."

He used his teeth to pull a card from his breast pocket and dropped the card at my feet. In unsteady black felt-tip, it read:

These are the last words I will ever write or speak. Blessed be the Lord, for He has shown us the way to Salvation. There is no more Faithful, Loyal, or True creature than the Hound. The path to Heaven must be trod on all Fours. To serve as a Hound is to be close to God, to be a Hound is to serve Man. Let me serve you.

As I was reading, he snatched Bruno's collar out of my pocket and ran off with the stinky old thing clasped in his jaws.

"I demolish chicks bigger than you for a living," I said.

He skipped to a stop, turned and crawled back toward me. He still clenched the collar in his teeth. I grabbed it but he wouldn't let go. His ass wagged even harder when I tried to pull it free.

"Drop it." He dropped the collar at his feet, then rubbed his head against the collar. He was trying to put it on. I snatched it away and stuffed it into my pocket. He let out a howl.

I kept walking. He followed on all fours, the skin on his fingers raw and bloody. That made two of us. He dropped a stick at my feet that I refused to toss for him. He drank straight from the milk-colored creek, and once he was finished he crawled back up the bank, raised his leg, and pissed his pants.

"Oh, dude," I said. "Get out of here. You're disgusting. Get out. Go. Go!"

He whined and turned in a circle and wouldn't look at me. I gave him a shove with my boot and he landed butt-first in the snow and started to weep. Great wracking, coughing tears.

"Hey," I said. "Hey. Don't cry. I didn't mean it." He clasped his head in his hands.

"I try so hard," he said.

I knelt down beside him. "Maybe you need, like, professional help."

He looked up at me, brown eyes, the filthy beard, the chattering lower lip, torn skin on the heels of his hands.

"Dogs don't sit like that," I said.

He smiled, let his tongue hang out and shifted onto all fours. Ass wagging again. I picked up a stick.

"You're not my dog, but that doesn't mean you're not a dog." I threw the stick far into the woods behind us. "Go get it, boy. Go on."

He darted off into the woods after the stick. I hurried on up the trail.

There was a log structure ahead, down by the bank of the swollen creek. Decorated trees formed a kind of colonnade leading to what I could only think of as a temple. People moved beneath tinsel-laden branches. Christmas ornaments glittered in the candle light. In the cool beneath the trees, some slushy snow still remained in wet patches.

I passed a cairn of carefully placed stones, and as I did, I recognized the place. The dog shrine. There were old laminated photos of dogs on the cairn, and urns with what I assumed were the ashes of cremated pets. Bruno liked to piss here. But the place was transformed. Three more cairns had been erected in the two weeks since the dogs disappeared, and they ringed the entrance to the temple.

A big old cedar formed the living central pillar of the temple. Eight thick logs radiated out from the cedar to other trees and people were weaving sticks and twigs between those logs to form a roof. At the base of each tree, shrines were covered in laminated photos, leashes, dog toys, canine sweaters, well-loved teddy bears. People knelt at some of those shrines, praying or meditating, others talking in that unmistakable childish tone that is only used to speak with dogs. Others worked on the structure. I hovered in the entrance, trying to take it all in.

"You look strong," a man on a ladder said. "Can you give me a hand?"

He was working on the anchor for one of the main roof supports. Not bad looking for a skinny guy. Dark hair, nice smile, clean shaven, expensive Arcteryx jacket. I went over and boosted the log into position. He drilled through it and bolted it to the tree. I passed him up the tools. Once it was done, he climbed down and shook my hand. I asked him if he'd seen the filthy guy on the path who acted like a dog.

"Steve?" he said. "He's harmless. Thanks for the help. We could use more of it. Do you have time?"

"Too much."

He put me to work. His name was Richard and he'd had two German Shorthaired Pointers: Gretchen and Olga. He came up here the day after they ascended, his term for it, and had started work on one of the new cairns. He'd needed to do something, and working with his hands helped. It helped me too. He put me to work on the roof. Natural materials only, they'd decided, and some of it had to be open to the sky so we could see where the dogs went. We gathered up more thatching and carried it over to the roofers.

"Now I know where I've seen you before," he said. "You play for the Ravens, right?"

I shrugged. "At the moment, no."

"Oh yeah, the fight," he reddened beneath his hood. "Sorry, didn't mean to bring it up."

"It's fine," I said. And it was. With the weight of the wood, the cold rain, with all these other people going through the same thing I was, it was like I had a team again. "Really, it's fine."

Hours passed. I got soaked but I didn't care.

൝

"So you did come."

The stink of wet wool wafted in under the roof we were thatching. Patrice the Pug's owner stepped into the temple. I was up on a ladder, driving a spike into a tree that we would use to hang a lantern. I came down to greet her.

"This place really is special," I said.

Her sparrow-claws dug into my arm. "Have you asked forgiveness yet?"

Richard watched from beside a cairn where he was mixing mortar to fill the voids between stones.

"I told you, I don't need forgiveness."

"Oh yes you do."

She dragged me toward another cairn. There was a photo of a pug on the top of the cairn. A pug with part of its ear missing. I remember Bruno clamping down on that little ugly head, biting that ear. Richard was still watching.

Patrice the Pug's owner knelt down in front of her pet's shrine. "Hello my little lovey-dovey," she cooed. "How is my little scrunchy-poo? I have someone here for you. Remember that mean lady who let her nasty beast bite you? Do you remember, scrunchy-poo? She's come to ask your forgiveness." She looked at me. "Hasn't she?"

I tried to step away but she dug her claws into me. "Lady, I'm not asking forgiveness from your stupid dog."

There was a gasp from the other people in the temple. Patrice the Pug's owner bared her teeth.

"Take it easy, Nadezhda," Richard said. He came over and stood beside us. "If you need to make amends, this is the place to do it. Our dogs are watching."

"I'm not making amends for her dog's stupidity," I shouted. "Get your claws off me."

"Didn't I tell you, scrunchy-poo?" Patrice the Pug's owner said. "No control. She is vile. But you'll still forgive her, won't you darling?"

I wrenched my arm free. Patrice the Pug's owner went tumbling into a pile of slush at the temple's edge. Everyone stopped working and stared at me like I was the crazy one.

"Nadezhda, please," Richard said. He held his hands up, like he really thought I was gonna start wailing on some soggy grandmother. "This isn't a place for fighting."

"She's nuts," I said. "You're all nuts. They're gone. They were better than any of us. Even stupid Patrice. But they aren't saints, they were just dogs. Who the hell knows why they were taken? All that matters is that they are gone."

I turned to go but the trail leading out of the temple was blocked. At least a dozen people were standing in the rain, huddled under umbrellas. Many of them carried Bibles. The man and woman standing at the head of this gaggle were Mom and Dad from the frozen front lawn. Their twin boys waited in the crowd behind them.

"She's right, you know," Mom said. She had the soothing voice of a sports medicine doc. "The dogs aren't saints. They should not be worshiped."

"Blasphemy," Dad said. He was shaking. Mom put a hand on his shoulder.

"The dogs were a test," Mom said. "The Lord has given us concrete proof of his omnipotence. Now we must be stronger than ever in our faith."

Several people in the temple snorted. I'd had enough. I walked toward Mom and Dad and their crowd. Patrice the Pug's owner crawled out of the slush. Richard walked with me.

"Out of the way," I said. "I've had enough crazy for one day."

Mom gave way, but Dad blocked the trail.

"Please, daughter, I've seen your suffering. You can walk all day looking for answers, but you won't find them." He held out his hand. "The Lord is the only true path to salvation."

"Leave us alone," Patrice the Pug's owner said. "Your tired faith has no place here."

I tried to get around Dad, but he blocked me at every turn. His wife was trying to calm him down, but he wouldn't listen. Behind me, Patrice the Pug's owner was shouting, getting more hysterical by the second, and more of the temple-worshipers were taking up her cause. They berated these trespassers and belittled their religion, like they weren't out in the woods praying to dead dogs.

"Let me past, Dad," I said. "I'm not going to ask again."

"Violence is unacceptable here, Nadezhda," Richard said.

Big girls think of their team, Papa's voice said.

"Let her go, honey," Mom said.

"The Lord will see I am pure in my faith," Dad said.

I lifted him and moved him out of my way. A snowball hit one of the people ahead of me.

In an instant, more snowballs flew between the temple-worshipers and the gathered missionaries. With the snowballs came snarls of rage, vicious names, sputtered curses. Patrice the Pug's owner was a little whirlwind, her ski poles abandoned as she hurled mud and slush at the intruders. Dad climbed onto a cairn and trampled the photos and mementos so carefully placed there, all the while shouting scripture at the crowd. Richard and Mom were trying to calm the mob, but their efforts only seemed to further infuriate them.

I was about to leave these crazy bastards to their little war when a dog started barking. The crowd hesitated. Steve the man-dog ran on all fours from the woods and into the center of the temple. He barked and snapped and charged at anyone showing aggression, until the whole crowd was quiet. Then he sat, ass wagging, in the slushy snow.

"Good boy," I said from the temple's edge.

"What is this devilry?" Dad said. He was still standing on the cairn and looked down on Steve as if he was a rotting fish. Dad had a large cairn stone in one hand.

"He's a nasty little joke," Patrice the Pug's owner said. She limped over to Steve. "Shoo. Get out of here, you nasty little man."

Steve snarled at her, lowered his head.

"Hey," I said. "Leave him alone. The fighting upset him."

Patrice's owner grabbed one of her discarded ski poles and poked at Steve. "This is a holy place. A place for real dogs, isn't that right scrunchy-poo? Shoo. Get."

"Hey," I said again. I rushed over and knocked the ski pole down. "I said that's enough."

Steve calmed and sat back down. Patrice's owner cursed my name and knelt to retrieve her pole.

"He is a demon," Dad said.

He hurled the cairn stone. It struck Steve in the side of the head and knocked him into the slush. The slush stained red. Without realizing what I was doing, I charged the cairn. Took Dad out at the knees and sent him flying. He thudded to the ground and I was on him before he had the chance to get his head up. *Only dumb dogs fight.* Gloves off. Pinned his arms down with my knees. I realized I was screaming: "He's just a dog." Dad wept, and tried to wriggle free. "I'm the big girl." Nose bloodied, lip split. And I wanted more. I wanted to bite his ear off. I wanted to grab the cairn stone and bash his skull open. I lifted the cairn stone. Dad pleaded for his life. "He took everything." Mom was holding onto my arm, trying to stop me, but she was nothing, just a wisp, and I shrugged her off. "I'll show you what happens to people who hurt my dog."

A warm tongue licked the hand clutching the cairn stone. Steve, the man-dog, crawled over and licked my other hand, the one wrapped around Dad's neck. Blood wept from the cut above Steve's eye and he was panting hard, but he kept licking my face. Little pleading whines came from his damp lips. I dropped the cairn stone into the slush. Dad rolled out from under me. Steve licked my face a couple more times, and then he vomited a wad of kibble and fell onto his side. His legs made little jerking motions.

"Call an ambulance," Richard said.

"I already have," Mom said. "But they can't get up this path with the ice and slush."

Dad's followers gathered around him and lifted the man up between them. I heard him weeping, asking for forgiveness. Whether it was from me, or Steve, or his followers, or God, or the dogs above, I couldn't tell you. Richard and Patrice the Pug's owner and the other dog worshipers gathered around Steve and I.

"It's fine," I said. "I've got this."

I lifted Steve up. He was heavy despite his thinness. I couldn't go as fast as Mom and Dad, but I was the big girl. Richard and Patrice the Pug's owner and the rest of the dog worshipers tried to follow me but I shouted them off, and they were scared enough by now to heed my warnings.

The ambulance waited in the parking lot. When the attendant saw Steve, they said they could take him too.

"It's not as bad as it looks," I said. "I'll drive him."

I lay Steve down in the back of my SUV. He was panting, eyes closed, his tongue hanging out. I draped Bruno's old blanket over him. The ambulance pulled away. Steve looked so bad. When I was searching for my phone to call the vet, I felt something in my pocket.

Bruno's collar. I loosened it and slipped it over Steve's head. He breathed easier. I stroked his shoulder.

"Good boy. You're a good boy."

I closed the hatch and drove.

☾

Steve moaned in his sleep on his new dog bed. The vet said he had to keep the cone on day and night and he hated it, kept scratching at the thing. I couldn't sleep either, not when I was expecting the police to call, but it was near three and no call yet. Dad threw the first stone. If he pressed charges, we'd both go to the penalty box. So long as the cops didn't call, there was a chance I could play pro hockey again.

Steve bolted upright, eyes unfocused. "Liddy? Amanda? Mel?"

"Shush," I said, as I stroked his back. "Easy, boy. It's okay. You're going to be okay."

He touched the collar at his throat and prodded his dog bed. Then he looked up at me, huge brown eyes wet.

"There you go," I said. "You're okay, Steve. Go to sleep." He turned in a circle, sniffed the bed, and lay back down. "Good dog."

In minutes, my dog was snoring. *Big girls think of their team*, Papa's voice said. For the first time in a long time, I agreed with him.

When it grew lighter, I leashed Steve up and took him out into the cold morning for a walk.

Captured Carbon

The shape on the ice floe looked like a woman but Jeje Dhillon knew that was impossible. He floated half a kilometer off the coast of Tuktoyaktuk and as far as he knew he was the only person dumb enough to be stuck out here. He lifted his diving mask for a better look anyway. Maybe it was a walrus or a seal or oil in the shape of a woman. Jeje hyperventilated to prep for the dive. Oil, that made the most sense. The news sites said the slick was still twenty kilometers from Tuk, but the news sites were the lying mouths of the oil companies, and if the woman-looking shape really was oil, that meant the coral was in trouble.

Jeje used the buoy line to pull himself down the seven meters to where the reef grew above the bubbler pipe. Thousands of tiny tentacles extruded from the calcified carcasses of their ancestors and greeted Jeje with their usual enthusiasm.

Hey fellas, he thought at them. *What a lousy day to say goodbye, huh?*

He used hand-holds the coral had grown for him to move across the reef to its easternmost edge, and he took water samples as he went. His boss wanted to make sure the phage they had injected into the bubbler feed line was dispersing all the way across the reef. The phage would splice in some genes that should make the coral a little more resilient if and when the slick made it to Tuk.

Gotta make sure you all get a taste, he thought. *Don't want the crude making you sick.*

The coral usually loved the wild currents he stirred up with his gesticulations, but today they were straining to taste the current coming from the North. They were worried for their little ones.

His lungs were starting to burn. He moved back along the reef and ducked into a grotto the coral had grown at his suggestion. Three little pods grew at the center of the grotto, each pod filled with thousands of coral planulae. He couldn't remember whose idea it had been to grow the pods — his or the coral's — but it had been his idea to sell them. At fifty thousand dollars a pod, how could he refuse? That was enough to get him back to balmy Halifax.

I'll find a safe home for your babies, he thought as he snipped the base of each pod and placed them in his Otter box.

You take care of yourselves, alright? I'll miss ya. He climbed up the anchor line to the surface.

The ice floe had drifted closer, and when Jeje lifted his diving mask, there was no longer any ambiguity: the woman-shaped smudge on the ice wasn't a walrus or a seal or an oil slick. He swore. Tony was supposed to meet him after her shift, and she promised she'd have the cash for the planulae in hand. One hundred thousand NAU dollars. He could be on a plane tomorrow.

The woman lay on her side, as if she'd fallen asleep on the ice. Five degrees below freezing, and she was out here wearing nothing but overalls. Jeje swore again and started to swim.

When he pulled himself up onto the ice, her face was the same deep blue as the ocean below. It took him a second to realize he'd seen a much less blue version of that face plastered across all the news sites reporting on the spill. *You're supposed to be dead.* He pushed his finger tips into the frozen skin of her wrist like he'd cops do in the movies. *Oh. Maybe you ain't.*

∿

"… is committed to preventing any oil from reaching the coast line. Arctic Energy crews are seeding the affected areas with Petronome, an organism custom-designed by Atrifor to deal with Arctic oil spills. Petronome is a smart-bug, designed to seek out and metabolize any crude oil in its environment. Petronome will —"

The advertisement had been running on Elvis' music feed all morning, and he was thankful when his phone interrupted it with an incoming alert.

– *Message from Jeje: Need pick-up now. OMG.*

Elvis Jacobson turned his boat around and opened up the throttle. Last time Jeje had sent a text like that, it was because he'd thought the coral were depressed. Turned out one of the calcium and CO_2 bubblers had been blocked, so he hadn't been totally off the mark. This time, though, Elvis feared the kid had found something worse. Smoke darkened the northern sky where the fire boats were still trying to put out the flames on the *Beaufort Endeavour*.

I did the best I could, Anaak, Elvis thought as he steered his boat toward the other end of the reef where he'd left Jeje to collect samples.

He had a good view of the entire nine kilometer expanse of his leasehold as he weaved his way through patches of sea ice. Though there was nothing but neon orange-painted growlers to mark the reef, he could see the shape of the reef below in his mind. Twenty years now he'd been watching it grow, and all it would take was a few days for the oil to kill his livelihood.

Several ships prowled the waters on the northern horizon. Clean-up crews, no doubt, that were dumping the Petronome that Arctic Energy kept blathering about in their advertisements. Elvis worried about that too. From what he'd read, the Petronome was an unknown; neither Arctic Energy nor Atrifor had released anything about the smart-bug they were dumping by the tonne into the ocean. As far as he was concerned, both the oil and the Petronome were a threat to his reef.

I'm leaving everything to you. His Anaak's words came back to him as he reached the mid-point of the reef. *Do something smart with it or I'll haunt you until the day you die.*

He'd thought about going South, like his parents had done, but Anaak had raised him here. Going South didn't seem right. His cousin Randy had purchased a leasehold near Katovik and loved to brag about all the money he got for growing carbon-fixing coral, so Elvis had done the same. The first few years had been good. They were always growing new methane collection systems out in the permasludge back then, and the generating stations where they burned the methane for power were paying good money to capture their waste carbon. But Klomad's licensing fees for their custom coral kept going up, faster than Elvis could bid on more capture contracts. Then the winter ice started coming back a few years ago and he had to buy an upgrade from Klomad to further modify the coral so they could withstand months under the ice. Now he could barely afford to pay the kid.

He hated to admit it, but a small part of him hoped the oil would ravage his reef. The lawsuit would take years, sure, but they'd give him a big payout and he could retire. Go south. Anaak would understand, wouldn't she? He'd stayed long enough.

He could see Jeje on a big slab of pack ice now. The kid was kneeling over the prone shape of a woman lying on the ice. That was odd, but it meant the kid wasn't worried about oil. His reef was safe, just in time for another licensing payment. With a mixture of relief and disappointment, he pulled up along the ice.

"She alive?" he shouted. He tossed the kid a toe line.

"Think so," Jeje said. The kid pulled the boat and the ice floe together.

The woman's skin was blue, her hair looked like sea weed, and her coveralls were frosted with ice. If she was alive, it was a miracle.

"Tie the line under her arms," Elvis said. "And we'll haul her into the boat."

Jeje tied her off. He was good with knots, and with the coral. Really, the kid was good with anything that didn't involve talking to other people. Elvis liked that about him. They worked in silence as they tugged and pushed the woman to get her into the boat.

Elvis found an irregular pulse at her neck.

"She's breathing too," Jeje said as he climbed over the gunnel.

"We gotta get her out of those clothes," Elvis said. The kid swallowed hard, the brown skin at his cheeks darkening. "Don't be modest, kid. She'll die if we don't warm her up."

They dragged her into the boat's small cabin. He dug out an old survival suit, blankets and some chemical heating pads, then the two of them peeled the woman out of her coveralls. It was like peeling the clothes off a corpse. The coveralls were burned and torn along her left side, as were the long underwear she wore beneath the coveralls. When they stripped her out of the long underwear, Elvis found the kid staring at her, his eyes wide.

"Never seen a pair of tits before?"

Jeje shook his head, and pointed to the skin on the left side of her body. "It healed."

While the rest of her was shades of blue, the skin along her left arm and most of her left side was pinkish and raised, like road rash that had three weeks to heal. Jeje pushed back the damp hair from the left side of her face and there was more of the weird healing skin there too.

"Three days," the kid said.

"Three days what?" Elvis said as he pulled the survival suit over her legs.

"She's been in the water for three days," the kid said. He slid the woman's arms into the suit. "Don't you recognize her?"

Elvis looked at the woman's face as he zipped her up, and sure, she looked kind of familiar, but he couldn't place her.

"The engineer that ran the *Beaufort Endeavour*," the kid said. Jeje packed the heating pads under her armpits. "Marion Lombardo, that's her name."

"Didn't the news say she died in the explosion?"

"If she did, she got better."

Elvis wasn't sure if the kid was joking. He never could tell with anyone under twenty-five, it was like they were a different species. They propped Marion's head up with a life jacket. She still looked dead, despite the slight flare of her nostrils and the bumpy skin along the left side of her face.

"We better call the coast guard," Elvis said.

Elvis reached for the radio. The woman moved faster. Her fingers were ice claws on his wrist, and her eyes were clouded, like Anaak's in the last few years before the cancer took her.

Marion spoke with the voice of a drowned man: "No."

M

Thirsty, so damn thirsty. Marion downed the bottle of water the older of the two men offered her but it did nothing to slake her thirst. The water sat heavy in her gut and after a moment she spat it all up. That worried the men. The older one looked ready to go for the radio again.

"No coast guard," she said. "No cops."

"You're sick," he said. "We need to call someone."

She shook her head. "I'm alright. I just need to warm up. Please."

The two men looked at each other, confusion plain on their faces. She could understand that. She was confused about so many things, but she knew that the authorities could not get involved. If they did, they would try to stop her.

"Give me a minute, okay?" she said as she leaned back against the life jackets. The older of the two led the younger man back out onto the deck.

She waited until the two men were deep in conversation before she started to move. The boat smelled so good. There had to be something she could drink in here. As she looked for anything to quench her thirst, she disconnected the radio the older man had been trying to use to contact the coast guard, and when she was sure he wasn't watching, she grabbed the phone in the glove box and the back-up battery for the radio and dropped them both out a porthole. The younger one probably had a phone on him; she'd have to get rid of that as well. She'd seen him tapping on something when he'd found her on the ice.

The ice. Marion looked down at her hands, and when she did, memory overwhelmed her. She tumbled into the seat behind the steering wheel.

The sea ice had been thicker than anyone expected. All those years capturing carbon and reducing emissions had finally brought ice back to the Beaufort Sea, and the ice had laid siege to her rig. Alarms rang in her memory-high pressure in the suction line, temperature alarms across the rig — and anything they did only seemed to make it worse. The sound was so awful. She was supposed to be at her daughter's birthday party back in Kitchener, but she'd put off going home to deal with the ice. She'd always hated the sound of children's parties, but the alarms were worse. Then the explosion. She was flying through the air. No, not flying. *I'm falling. And I'm on fire.* Flames consumed her left arm from fingertips to elbow. *Minnie's birthday party. Blow me out, Minnie. Blow me out.*

Then she'd awoken on the ice with this terrible thirst. The fall should have killed her, let alone the burns or the ice-cold sea, yet here she was. She remembered the years of crystalline ambition and hard work that had led to the engineer's position on the *Beaufort Endeavour*, but those memories were like watching a film of someone else's life. She had other memories too, disjointed sensations: the taste of blue, the urge to split, the relief of death. But that too belonged to someone else. The sound of alarms, the hot shame of missing her daughter's birthday, even questions surrounding what should have been her death, all of it paled compared to her thirst.

Her nose found it for her. The bottle sat in a milk crate with several other plastic containers. She unscrewed the lid and drank. The taste made her gag but she forced herself to keep drinking. As she swallowed the final drops, for a brief second her thirst was satiated. With a new clarity of mind, she looked back over at the men on deck. The older of the two was still gesturing at her, then at the line of orange buoys out on the water, while the younger one seemed preoccupied with a yellow Otter box that hung from the belt of his dry suit. He kept touching it, like he had to reassure himself it was still there.

Killing them wouldn't be hard. The old her, the one who remembered Minnie, recoiled in horror at the thought. *You wouldn't dare.* The new her ignored the revulsion. She needed their boat to get to the next rig. The older man wouldn't let her take it without a fight. One quick shove and the ocean would take care of him. The younger man didn't care about the boat, but she couldn't get a good read on him. This kind of analysis was new to her. Before the explosion, she'd bent her mind to the task of how to most efficiently pump oil from its hiding places deep in the Earth. The new her had to master a different calculus, and the young man was an unknown variable. Best to bludgeon him to death with the gaff hook to take him out of the equation.

Her thirst came back with a vengeance. She found another bottle, this one had a different taste but provided the same sense of satiation. She was chugging it when the older man came back into the cabin.

"Jesus Christ," he said. "You're drinking gasoline."

⁂

Jeje wished the coral could talk to him up here. They would know what to do.

Gasoline ran out the corners of Marion Lombardo's mouth. She lowered the jerry can, a look of total amazement on her face that Jeje didn't buy for one second. He felt like he could almost understand the woman, like he'd felt with the coral before he finally started to understand their gestures, but she still eluded him.

"Gasoline?" she said. She wiped her mouth and looked at the container as if for the first time. "Oh my God."

She fainted to the floor. Elvis ran over to her. "Coast guard," he said to Jeje. "Now."

Jeje tried the radio but the power line was cut and the back-up batteries were missing. Elvis' phone wasn't in the glove box either. That meant using his phone. Shit. He didn't have a voice plan — too expensive — and a call to the coast guard would put him back several dollars.

"What's the hold up?" Elvis said.

"Your radio is busted," Jeje said. "And I can't find your phone."

The woman moaned and tried to sit.

"Lady," Elvis said. "I think we need to make you throw up." He turned back to Jeje. "I used the phone two minutes ago when you messaged me. It's in the glove box."

Jeje looked over at the woman. Marion stared up at him with her cloudy eyes. *That's how you know a person*, his father had said when the deputies came to deport his parents. *The eyes let you look deep into a person. Not to their soul — there's no such damn thing — but past all the bullshit we wear to hide our true selves.* A thin film sat between Marion's true self and the outside world, but those eyes were staring at the phone in its dry bag strapped to Jeje's wrist.

"She chucked your phone," Jeje said. He held up the cut power cable on the radio. "And she cut the radio."

Elvis blinked in confusion. Jeje liked his boss, Elvis was kind and generous as he could afford to be, but the man could be slow at times. Too slow. The woman lunged for the gaff hook hanging on the wall. Jeje grabbed his boss and hauled the big man away from the woman as she spun around, the gaff held like a baseball bat.

"What the hell?" Elvis managed as Jeje threw him to the deck. The woman lunged at them.

Jeje slammed the cabin door shut and locked it from the outside. She screamed at them from within, then hammered the door with the butt end of the gaff.

"What is wrong with her?" Elvis said. He got to one knee as the woman smashed out one of the tiny windows in the door. She tried to crawl through the too-small opening. "Call the cops, Jeje. Now."

Jeje looked down at the phone strapped to his wrist.

"I'll pay for the call," Elvis screamed.

Jeje took the phone out of its case and flicked it on. Tony's message waited for him: – *Got the goods?*

"Hold on," Marion said. She'd cut her forearm trying to get through the window and viscous pink liquid seeped from the wound. "Please, I'm not myself." She looked ready to weep. "Something happened to me after the rig exploded. I don't want to hurt anyone."

Elvis didn't look convinced. "That may be the case, but we're still gonna call the cops." He looked over at Jeje and gave him the nod.

Jeje brought up his dial pad.

"What's in the Otter box?" Marion said.

Jeje felt his mouth go dry. The coral would know, he was certain. They would feel that their planulae were in danger. "She's crazy."

"He's been protecting that thing ever since he found me," Marion said. "Why's it so important?"

Elvis looked skeptical. "What's she talking about, Jeje?"

Jeje wanted to retract into the calcified carcass of an ancestor. Elvis wasn't supposed to know about the planulae pods. "Nothing, Elvis. She's crazy."

"Elvis," Marion said. "If there's nothing in the box, why won't he show it to you?"

The big man shook his head. "I don't know what the hell is going on here, but I think I oughtta know what is in the box."

Jeje fought back tears. He put his hand to his mouth to try to stop himself from talking, but it was no use. The coral below must be shuddering in disappointment. "The coral wanted me to do it," he said in a whisper. "They wanted their babies to be free."

"Oh Christ no," Elvis said. "You're stealing from Klomad?"

"Coral want to colonize," he said. He edged closer to the side of the boat. He wouldn't be able to get the life raft out before Elvis could stop him, but he could swim. It wasn't that far to land. "How could I deny them their most basic urge?"

"Fuck that," Elvis said. "You're not stealing them out of the goodness of your heart. How much you getting?"

His buttocks bumped against the edge of the boat. Thirty minutes of swimming, forty max. There was no way Elvis would leave his boat in the hands of this crazy woman. He could swim back to shore, get Tony the planulae and be on a plane back to Halifax tomorrow morning. But Elvis had been good to him all these years. Jeje could make him understand, if only he could explain it right.

"Fifty thousand per pod," he said. "But I'm only gonna sell two. The third I'm gonna raise back home."

"Know what Klomad will do if they catch you?" Elvis was moving closer, like he knew what Jeje was planning. "Selling their proprietary organisms will land you in one of their private prisons. Jesus, Jeje. You've been living under my roof for three years. You know better than this."

The water below the boat was dark. He didn't have his hood up, the first dunk into the Arctic Ocean would be awful.

"Give me the box," Elvis said. The big man put out his hand. "I'll get rid of them, pretend this never happened."

Jeje cradled the Otter box. "I've got a buyer. I don't know what she'll do if I don't have the product."

Elvis went for the Otter box. Jeje tried to fight him off, but Elvis was twice his size, all muscle and instinct honed over a lifetime on the permasludge. "Give it to me, boy. Now." He tore the box off Jeje's belt.

The boat pitched beneath them. Jeje was already off-balance, and his feet slid out from under him, the grey-blue sky inverted, and he fell toward the Arctic waters.

Elvis caught the kid by the ankle as he was tumbling over the gunnel. The kid's head dunked in the water and the drag nearly pulled them both in, but Elvis wedged his knees under the rail and hauled with all his strength.

"Ungrateful little puke," Elvis shouted as he tossed the kid onto the deck. Jeje lay sputtering, seawater pouring out of his nose.

Elvis would deal with the kid later. First he had to deal with the woman sitting in his seat, piloting his boat. She'd tried to toss them both into the ocean with that little maneuver. The anger that took him then had been buried for decades. He was thirteen again and his parents were explaining how they were gonna move South to make money that they promised they would send home, but never did. *Anaak will take care of you now.* His blood was liquid fire, his fists granite. Anaak's inheritance had bought him the boat; he'd be damned if this woman would take it away from him.

He flicked open the latch and shoved the cabin door, but it didn't budge. She'd wedged the gaff into the jam. Elvis reached through the shattered window to tug the gaff free but she moved faster. She cut at him with his filleting knife. He felt a sting at his right wrist and the knife flicked away, a smear of crimson along its honed edge.

"Stick your hand in here again and I'll chop it off," Marion said. She went back to the wheel.

"You're gonna pay for this, lady," Elvis said, but his voice sounded hollow. The old anger was already seeping out of him. She kept jerking the boat from side to side to keep them off balance. That had to be what was making him lightheaded.

"Oh no," Jeje yelled. "No, no, no."

The kid was scrambling around the deck, looking for his Otter box no doubt.

"It went overboard when you did," Elvis said. He sat on the deck to try to get his sea legs back. "Keep pissing me off and I might chuck you in after it."

Jeje shook his head. "Not the box. My phone. I was holding it when I went over." Terror twisted his mouth into a trembling rictus. "We're all alone out here."

The last of the fury drained out of Elvis. He had lived off that rage for years, it had kept him up at night and woke him up in the morning, but it had hollowed him out. The past twenty years without it had almost been enough to fill him up again.

"We're not alone," Elvis said. He forced himself to breathe. Three years he'd housed and employed the kid. Sure the kid had made a mistake, but hadn't he made his fair share of dumb moves at that age? "We got each other."

"She's taking us out into the open ocean," Jeje said.

Elvis' vision was a little spotty and cold sweat poured down his neck, but he still knew where they were headed. Tuk crouched on the coastline between the deflated bulk of the pingos that Anaak claimed used to guard the bay. They were heading toward the dark smear of smoke from the still-burning *Beaufort Endeavour*.

Elvis' guts roiled. He hadn't been sea-sick since his first year growing coral. What the hell was wrong with him?

"You're bleeding pretty bad," Jeje said. The kid was looking at Elvis' arm where the woman had sliced him. It had only been a little cut, he thought. Elvis pressed his fingers to it and was surprised when they came away dripping.

"Holy shit."

Jeje shook his head, and pointed into the cabin. "There's a first aid kit in there. We just gotta get in."

"She'll slice you to ribbons, kid," Elvis said. "No way you can get in there."

"Maybe I can get her to come out."

Elvis pressed his hand to the wound. He had to stop the bleeding or he really might pass out. Then it would just be the kid alone with that woman, and the kid didn't stand a chance. He tried to get his belt off to tie off his wrist but his hands were too slick with blood.

The roar of the motor cut out. Jeje stood over the outboard motor with the disconnected fuel line in one hand. "Now she's gotta talk."

The cabin door burst open. Marion walked onto the deck, gaff hook in one hand and a bottle of lubricant oil in the other.

"Take it easy," Jeje said, his voice trembling.

"Reconnect that line," she said. She took a long pull of the oil, then gestured at Elvis with the gaff. "Or I'll put this hook through his skull."

"Listen to the lady, Jeje," Elvis said. An awful taste filled his mouth, like that medicine Anaak had given him when he came down with scarlet fever in the eleventh grade.

Jeje hesitated beside the motor. He was fiddling with it, but Elvis' vision was swimming too much for him to see what the kid was doing.

"Put the gaff down," Jeje said. "Or the motor's going to the bottom of the sea."

The clamp on the motor's mounting bracket: the kid had loosened it right off.

"Not bad, kid," Elvis said. His words were slurring. Blood welled up between the fingers on his arm, and no matter how tight he squeezed, it wouldn't stop. "Not bad."

Elvis wanted to say more, but his mouth was too dry. He was losing it. Shit, he was going to leave the kid alone with this cloudy-eyed wacko. *I'm sorry, kid*, he tried to say. *So sorry.*

The older one's head hit the deck with a wet thump. Marion stepped over him and moved closer to the younger man who trembled beside the disabled motor.

"I ain't kidding," the younger one said. "Take another step, and I'll strand us here."

"Do that and your friend will die. He's already lost too much blood."

The younger one's hands shook. "Please," he said, his voice shaking as much as his hands. "We gotta talk this out or we're all gonna regret it. Why do you want this boat so bad?"

Listen, said the her who should be dead. *You don't need to hurt anyone else.* But the thirst was still strong. *Talk to him,* the dead her implored. Why not? she thought. It would buy her some time. She lowered the gaff.

"I need to get to the next rig."

"The next oil rig? Which one? The *Beifang Dipinxian*? *Hercules 22*?"

"*Beifang*. Then *Hercules*."

"Are you going to blow them up too?"

"Blow them up?" Marion said. And she started to laugh. The sensation was a novel delight. "No. I didn't blow up the *Beaufort*: I was born from its ashes. You wouldn't understand what I plan to do with the *Beifang*."

The younger one held her gaze. His eyes were a dark brown set deep in his thin face and they didn't blink. Like he was looking into her. Understanding changed his expression from fear to wonder. "You want to feed."

Her thirst was still there and the smell from the fuel line the young one held in his hands was enough to make her salivate. "Not the way you think."

His excitement grew. "The most basic urge. Just like the coral, but you aren't coral. You're something else."

"I remember being less than I am now," she said. He wanted to come closer to her, she could see it in his expression. *Keep talking to him*, the old her insisted. *He just wants to know you.*

"The Petronome," he said. "Artificial protists created to metabolize crude oil. They are what healed you, right? They are what changed you. You're a hybrid."

The older her was drowning again beneath the ocean of her thirst, but Marion needed her now. *Can we trust him? We can try.*

"I'm thirsty," she said. She tossed the gaff hook into the water. "Now will you let me slake my thirst?"

He shook his thin head and gestured past Marion. She'd forgotten about the old one: why bother thinking about something that was almost a corpse?

"You can heal him," the young one said. "The same way you healed, well, yourself."

Her hand had been on fire and now it was almost whole. The parts of her that were many recalled the metabolic pathways they had hijacked to seal up her wounds: the old one's injuries were trivial by comparison. "Healing him will change him."

"He'll die if you don't," Jeje said. "We'll take the life raft and you can have the boat."

She could still kill him. *Why risk losing the motor?* The old her whispered from her tomb. *Give him this and no one else need die.* No, she thought to herself. Give him this and we will live in the old one too.

She sliced open her left arm at the wrist. Pink fluid dripped onto the wound the older one still clutched with his unthinking fingers. While a thin strand of fluid connected the man's wound to her arm, she knew the man's pain. She heard a name — Anaak — and she felt an old, ashen fury. When that viscous line of liquid severed, she lost contact with him, but she knew a part of her lived on within him.

"It will take some time for him to come around," she said. She pointed the knife at the motor's mounting bracket. "Will you reattach my motor?"

The young one went to work, though he never took his eyes off her. The dead her was quiet in her grave. Once she had the motor idling again, she helped him lower the unconscious older one into the self-inflating raft that the young one ejected into the water beside the boat, then she helped him down into it.

He held onto her wrist as after he'd stepped into the raft. His eyes were full of wonder. "You really are new."

She shrugged him off. "He's going to be thirsty when he wakes up."

She went back into the cabin. In seconds, the life raft was a tiny spot on the waters behind her. She emptied a spray can of WD40 into her mouth, and in the calm after drinking, the roar of the motor and the splash of icy water against the hull seemed incredibly quiet. For a moment, she wished for the mechanical quiet to be replaced by the sounds of a children's birthday party. It wasn't the dead her wishing it: this was the new her. The real her. More than anything, she wanted to hear children laughing.

It didn't last long. Soon, there was only the thirst.

The Way of the Shrike

Every time their potbellied house demon admitted another guest to her birthday party, Marjormam hoped it would be Pranny. Every time it wasn't, Marjormam fed her disappointment another hors d'oeuvre. The house filled with friends from school, teachers, aunties and uncles whose names Marjormam couldn't remember, all of them telling her how proud they were that she would be joining her father on the spike. I'll never go on the spike, she wanted to tell them, but their plan was a secret, so Marjormam kept her mouth stuffed with pigeon-meat pastries.

Then it was time to put on their show and Pranny still hadn't arrived.

"Can you do the show on your own?" her father asked from outside the washroom in which Marjormam had locked herself.

"It's a two-person musical, Dada."

Out in the entryway, the house demon growled in welcome.

"Relis, Franco, Pranny," her father said, loud enough that Marjormam could hear. "So glad you could make it!"

Marjormam daubed at her eyes with her lace sleeve and slid out of the washroom as if she'd never heard of the place.

"Sorry we're late," Pranny's father Relis said. "Pran couldn't decide what to wear."

All the careful nonchalance Marjormam had composed fled when she got her first look at Pranny. The dark black dress Pranny wore was so tight it might have been painted on.

"Hey kiddo," Pranny said, wrapping Marjormam in a chaste embrace. "Happy Childhood's End."

Perfume drenched Pranny's bare neck, hiding something sour beneath the musk.

"Everyone's in the living room, girls," Marjormam's father said. "Think we can start?"

That snapped Marjormam out of her Pranny-haze. She dragged Pranny past the guests crammed onto couches and dining room chairs, and they slid behind the stage the house demon had unfolded in front of the fireplace.

"What took you so long?" Marjormam whispered behind the stage. "There are a few scenes I wanted to talk —"

Pranny kissed her and Marjormam's complaints melted away. She moaned in delight as Pranny's tongue slipped into her mouth, but as she ran her fingers along the hem of Pranny's dress, Pranny released her and launched into her vocal warm-ups. The taste of hot wine lingered on Marjormam's lips.

Pranny passed her the Dread Baroness puppet and whispered: "Our audience awaits."

"Pran," Marjormam said. When she slid the puppet onto her hand, the panicked thrill of the impending performance set her heart racing. "It's really happening. By this time tomorrow we'll be on the road."

Pranny tucked a piece of paper into Marjormam's sleeve. "A few more things to pack before we go. If you can't get them all by the end of my shift, that's okay, we can wait another day or two."

No, Marjormam wanted to say, she couldn't wait another day or two — tomorrow night would be her first on the spike — but Pranny raised the Brother Daedledoo puppet into the ghost-light and launched into the old revolutionary song that was the opening number of the musical they had written together. Well, not entirely together. Marjormam had wanted to write an autobiographical show, but Pranny insisted on performing history like all the other amateur puppeteers around town. Once they were on the road, Marjormam was sure Pran would listen to her ideas.

Forty-five minutes later, the felt Dread Baroness loomed over the wounded Brother Daedledoo and Marjormam pronounced the verdict: "For trying to steal the land of my ancestors out from beneath my feet, yours shall never touch it again. I condemn thee to eternal torment on the Spike."

The living room erupted in applause. Marjormam hated performing for relations: you never knew if the adulation was sincere or simple flattery. The road would be the true test.

᠕

After the last of the guests filed out, Marjormam's parents insisted she go to bed.

Marjormam handed Olbert the house demon a pair of sticky ice wine glasses. "I'll help Olbert. I don't think I can sleep yet."

Before Mama could protest, Dada put a hand on his wife's shoulder. "They call it Childhood's End for a reason, dear. She gets to make her own decisions now." He patted Marjormam's cheek the way he'd done since she was a little girl. "You're on spike 12,492 at 7 p.m. It's far, but you'll be promoted closer in no time with your acting skills." He gave her a warm embrace. "You're going to do so well."

Only after the sounds of her parents' bedtime routine quieted did Marjormam open the note Pranny had given her. The list was extensive. More food, more wine than Marjormam imagined they could carry, and there, at the bottom of the list, a pair of matching corsets. Corsets.

Even the finest corseterie in the City required a couple days to complete their craft after they had taken measurements.

Marjormam crushed the list in a sudden fury. After Take Your Kid to Work Day, almost four years ago now, she'd sworn she would never mount the spike. Even then, she'd known she wanted to be a puppeteer. Pranny knew that better than anyone. Pranny had her first shift two months ago when she turned seventeen, and every time they got together, Pranny told her how awful it was. How much she wanted to get away. Yet Pranny's list practically guaranteed Marjormam would be on the spike tomorrow.

Olbert handed Marjormam a handkerchief. She thanked the twisted creature and enlisted his help in folding up the stage and loading it with supplies. Once loaded, she hefted the stage onto her back. The straps dug into her shoulders, but it wasn't that bad, and there was room for more.

Find matching corsets, she thought as she lay in her childhood bed for what she told herself was the last time. Find corsets, and then we're free.

ᚠ

The City's ten thousand vultures circled down through the fading daylight to roost. As the clock ghosts moaned six o'clock, Marjormam staggered under the weight of the stage onto the Way of the Shrike. She didn't have long: Pranny's shift ended at seven, and they planned to hit the road from there.

On either side of the Way, men and women writhed on their spikes. As a new Spikeperson, union rules dictated that Pranny was impaled far outside the city, almost four kilometers from the gates. Omnibuses took Spikepeople out to those distant sites of perpetual torture, but Marjormam had spent the last of her coin on the matching corsets that were carefully strapped to the outside of the folded stage, so she had to walk.

Marjormam pulled her cloak over her head as she approached her father's spike. She would have said goodbye to her parents if she thought they'd let her leave. Instead, she'd left a note with Olbert with strict instructions to deliver it tomorrow when she failed to return from her shift.

It seemed much longer than an hour later when the clock-ghosts moaned seven. Pranny's shift was done. Marjormam swore, and started to run as best she could under the weight of the folded-up stage. She crested a hill and spotted Pranny, still impaled on spike 10,957 on the roadside ahead.

The spike had erupted through the soft flesh above Pranny's right breast, tearing the skin that Marjormam so adored. She hung pale and trembling beneath the gore-covered shaft, her legs kicking in the air a hand-width above the gravel. Marjormam was about to run the last few paces when she noticed the girl standing at the base of Pranny's spike. A few years older than either of them, the girl wore fishnet stockings, cap, and corset, her entire outfit stained and torn from a shift on the spike, though her flesh was whole.

"It's okay, Pran," the girl said. Pran? Only Marjormam called her Pran. "The barbers will be here soon. You're almost done."

Jealousy burned hot down Marjormam's veins. She slid the stage off her shoulders and ran to Pranny's side. As she was reaching out to touch Pranny's twitching legs, the older girl said: "Don't touch her."

Marjormam pressed her hands to the cold, tacky skin of Pranny's thigh. "It's going to be okay."

Pranny's eyes widened in alarm. "Don't touch me!" she screamed.

Marjormam reeled away as if struck. She pressed her hand to her mouth, tasted Pranny's semi-congealed blood, and almost vomited. Everything happened so fast after that. A young man in a red and white striped shirt arrived at the base of Pranny's spike, and when he squeezed a few drops of a clear fluid onto her tongue, she went slack. Now the older girl touched Pranny's face, brushed the sweat-damp hair out of her eyes, and whispered things Marjormam couldn't hear.

A twisted little demon that looked like a hairless goat who'd had its forelimbs swapped with a monkey's cranked a mechanism at the base of the spike. Over half a minute, Pranny rose up the length of wood she'd spent a cruel thirteen hours descending. When she neared the top, the older girl and the barber leaned a ladder against the spike and, working together, carried Pranny down to a waiting leather bedroll. The barber poured an aubergine-colored liquid between her lips. Seconds later, the wounds marring Pranny's shoulder and fundament closed up, the color seeped back into her flesh, and her breathing came easy. She sat up.

The older girl produced a wineskin that Pranny pulled on for a long moment. The older girl offered it to Marjormam, but she refused.

"Sorry," Pranny said. "It's very hard at the end."

"It doesn't matter," Marjormam said. "You won't ever have to mount the spike again. I've got everything ready. Even the corsets. They're off the shelf, but we're about the same size, and they fit me well. We can put them on when we get to the campground at Flayton."

Pranny exchanged a glance with the older girl. Marjormam felt her chest tighten. Pranny seemed about to say something, then stood and brushed flecks of gravel off her gore-stained clothes.

"We can't go yet," she said, speaking more to the older girl than to Marjormam. "I have to get changed before we hit the road."

Marjormam patted the side of the stage. "Our clothes are packed. We'll stop at the first waystation and you can wash up there."

Again, that considering look with the other girl. "And I have to collect my pay." Pranny took the stage and swung it on to her shoulders. She made the whole operation look so easy. "We're going to need all the money we can get. Come on, Marjie, we can take the omnibus back into the City."

Pranny offered Marjormam a blood-flecked hand. Marjormam looked back down the Way of the Shrike with its forest of impalees toward the City Infernal. This was the furthest she had ever traveled without her parents. A part of her whispered that if she turned back now, she would never leave again.

"We can try on the corsets once I'm cleaned up," Pranny said.

But that was a silly thought. She had walked this far, surely she could do so again. Marjormam took Pranny's hand.

❦

A serving demon tottered down the aisle of the omnibus carrying a multi-layered tray of confectionery and beverages. The older girl, who'd introduced herself as Seferia, bought bladders of wine for her and Pranny, bubble tea for Marjormam, and a sack full of pastries they all shared. Covered in icing sugar, full of caffeine and alcohol, Marjormam and Pranny sang bits of songs from their show for Seferia, who clapped after each snippet. The dread that had taken root in Marjormam's belly as the omnibus rolled back into the City was easy to ignore when she was in the company of these two beautiful women, the weight of the folded-up stage no longer digging into her shoulders. They would still leave, she kept telling herself, in the quiet moments between bursts of song and laughter.

"Why don't you get off at Chiropractor Square," Pranny said. "The paymaster's is another few stops further on. I'll come back and meet you there."

"Like the old song," Marjormam said.

"'Met my love 'neath the Gallows Tree,'" Seferia sang.

"'I was swinging,'" Pranny and Marjormam sang in harmony. "'And she was free.'"

All three of them exploded into laughter.

Seferia put a hand on Pranny's forearm, the touch so intimate that Marjormam barely registered what the older girl said: "I think you need to tell her, Pran."

The bubble tea went sour in her gut. "Tell me what?"

The bell rang and the conductor demon called out "Chiropractor Square! All connections."

"That this is your stop," Pranny said. "Hurry, Marjie, or you'll miss it."

Marjormam ran to the door and had stepped down the stairs when she realized she'd left the folded stage on the bench.

"The stage!" she shouted at Pranny and Seferia. "I forgot the stage!"

She argued with the conductor to get back onto the omnibus, but the driver was already whipping the dromedaries into action. As the great vehicle pulled away from the curb, Pranny appeared in the doorway, stage held awkwardly in front of her. Marjormam took it, staggered under the weight, and fell away from the omnibus to land with a thud on the hard cobbles. Wood cracked. A peal of laughter echoed from behind her, as if everyone in the Square found her misfortune hilarious, and embarrassment ignited the jealousy coursing through her veins as she rolled out from beneath the stage.

But the laughter wasn't for her. A crowd was watching a puppet show on the far side of Chiropractor Square and they now booed as a puppet who had to be the Wild King Daedledoo pranced about the stage. The omnibus disappeared down one of the City's cavern-like streets. Marjormam hoisted the stage up, and swore as bundles of smoked pigeons tumbled out of a crack in the frame.

She dragged the stage over to a bench beneath the soaring limbs of the Gallows Tree and tied a strip of ribbon around the cracked frame. Dead criminals hung from the branches of the old tree, and the carrion monkeys who called the tree home feasted on the thieves and back-alley circumcisers and false prophets who had met with the Dread Baroness' justice.

Marjormam ate one of the smoked pigeons, hoping the food would calm her, but with every bite, she imagined the declaration Pranny had left unspoken. Was Pranny planning on leaving with the older girl instead? Or perhaps she wanted to propose? Maybe she wanted to perform as the Dread Baroness and relegate Marjormam to the First Spikeman role. Yes, that had to be it.

Marjormam watched the puppet show from the bench. She squirmed at the similarities between the play and the one Pranny had written. Pranny's show treated the history of Daedledoo's Revolution as the most serious drama, whereas the performers across the square turned the whole thing into a farce. Despite herself, Marjormam laughed at a few of the jokes. Thousands had died during the revolution and in the centuries of impalements that were its legacy, it shouldn't be funny, but the crowd lapped it up too. They should try to make their show funnier, Marjormam decided.

She rested her head against the bench as she watched and didn't even notice when exhaustion dragged her down into sleep.

※

"Shoo!" a woman's voice woke Marjormam. "Get away, filthy things."

Marjormam blinked as she sat upright. "Pranny?"

"Oh thank the countless stars," the woman said in a Wildlander accent. "We thought you was dead." The woman standing above her was older even than Seferia, and had sad green eyes that shone in the ghostlight. "It's late, child. You ought to be getting home."

"I'm not a child," Marjormam said. "And I'm not going home. I'm leaving the city tonight."

"The monkeys may have ruined those plans."

The stage lay on its side, its contents spilled across the dirty cobbles. In the dark branches of the Gallows Tree, dozens of monkeys clutched pieces of food, clothing, bottles, and puppets.

"Pranny, my girlfriend, was supposed to meet me here," Marjormam said, as she stuffed the few supplies the monkeys hadn't stolen back into the stage. "She mustn't have seen me sleeping on the bench." The monkey's chittering sounded like laughter. "Did you see her? A beautiful girl with short-cut blond hair?

"I was behind the curtain," the woman said, gesturing across the square where the puppeteers were packing their supplies onto a wagon drawn by a geriatric camel. She picked up the Dead Baroness puppet and brushed dirt off her felt armor. "This is good work for an amateur. Did you make it?"

Marjormam snatched the puppet from the older woman's hands. "Pranny made that one. We planned to spend the night at the campground in Flayton. I bet that's where she's headed, don't you think?"

"I could not say," the woman said. She found a sack of boiled drake eggs behind the bench and handed them to Marjormam, "But if you need work, we are always looking for new crew."

Marjormam looked across the square at the small team of men and women wrapping up their show. She imagined Pranny and her in a few year's time, a crew of their own working for them, back in the City Infernal for three nights in Chiropractor Square. Her parents and Pranny's fathers in the audience, aglow with pride. The ovation would startle the carrion monkeys right out of their foul tree.

"She'll be in Flayton," Marjormam said, taking the eggs. The stage made an empty thudding sound when she hoisted it onto her shoulders. "She has to be. I really liked your show!"

Ghostlight chilled the city as she crossed its deserted streets. Tired manwhores called to her from beneath shaded doorways, and though they offered nothing but fleeting pleasure, they seemed to Marjormam to be the insidious whisper of the City itself. *Why fight it?* The City said. *Pranny won't be in Flayton. She's galavanting through my streets with Seferia even now. She doesn't want you, but I do. Take your place on the spike. Stay with me.*

"She'll be there," Marjormam said to a surprised manwhore, and she ran for the City's gates.

When she reached the Way of the Shrike, the impaled scolded her for running with such a heavy load on her back. How she wanted to laugh at that. Her stage was empty. Weightless.

Her toe caught an upraised cobble and she hit the Way with a crunch. The scolding calls changed to shouts of concern. Marjormam laughed in dismay. The impact had smashed the stage into a dozen jagged pieces.

The Dread Baroness puppet lay amidst the wreckage. She picked it up and carried on down the Way, but she couldn't run anymore. She tried to hold on to that image of her and Pranny returning triumphant to the City, but it seemed as unreachable as a monkey in the upper branches of the Gallows Tree.

One puppet, that's all she had left, but it was enough, wasn't it? The felt eyes of the Dread Baroness stared up at her. Good work for an amateur, the puppeteer had said. Marjormam had always thought their Dread Baroness was perfect, but the puppeteer was right: the eyes were different sizes, the black armor had been poorly stitched, and the whole thing stank of monkey shit. It was amateur garbage, just like the overly-serious play Pranny had written. No audience would ever give them an ovation, much less coin. They would starve on the road and be back in the City within weeks, begging for a post on a spike.

Without quite realizing it, Marjormam noticed she was reading the plaques at the base of each spike: 11,999. 12,301. 12,450. As she drew closer to her spike, she found herself slowing until she stopped at spike 12,492. Thirteen feet of sharpened absence against the star-filled sky. A ladder propped on the spike invited her to climb.

Marjormam was still standing there, staring up at the spike sometime later, when Pranny called out to her. "It's not so bad as you think."

The omnibus clattered past, and there was Pranny, standing at the omnibus stop a few spikes down. At the sound of her voice, Marjormam dared to hope again, just for an instant, but Pranny wasn't dressed for the road. She wore stockings, corset and cape, just like Seferia had been wearing, and she had a wine skin slung over one shoulder.

"Where's your girlfriend?" Marjormam said.

"She's just a friend."

"You're supposed to say that I'm your girlfriend."

"Maybe I can call you that again." Pranny unslung the wine skin, and handed it to Marjormam. "The puppeteers in Chiropractor Square told me you were heading for Flayton. I'm glad you came to your senses. They call it Childhood's End for a reason."

Marjormam took the wine skin and drank before handing it back. The stuff tasted like vinegar and left her feeling slightly nauseated. "Why didn't you tell me you didn't want to go? We've been planning this for months."

Pranny squirted a bit of the wine into her mouth. "I thought you'd get over it. And I was right, wasn't I? We can still put on the show. I'll get us a gig at one of the open nights at Rind's."

Marjormam showed her the filthy Dread Baroness puppet. "Won't be much of a show."

"We'll make new ones on the weekend," Pranny said. She handed Marjormam a small tin of cream and a folded straight razor. "Rub it on the tip of the spike and your —"

"I went to the orientations," Marjormam said. She tucked the Dread Baroness puppet into her belt and took the tin and the razor. "Hold the ladder."

Marjormam started to climb. From the top of the ladder, she could see the thousands of Spikepeople working their trade by ghostlight, all the way from the City's gates to the far horizon. Did she really think she was so special that she deserved something more?

Marjormam smeared cream on the tip of the spike and reached into her traveling trousers to rub it on herself. The cream left her numb. She unfolded the straight razor. Ghostlight reflected blue across the blade. Marjormam took a shuddering breath and reached between her legs to make the insertion cut.

"I'll stay through your whole shift," Pranny said. "I promise."

Marjormam was about to shut her eyes against the pain when she saw movement on the Way. Between the writhing Spikepeople, a single old camel dragged a cart piled high with props and stage dressing. Pranny gazed up at her, an expectant look on her face, but the cart was drawing closer. Marjormam snapped the razor shut.

"Everything okay?" Pranny said.

"Yes," Marjormam said. "I'm done with your promises." She took the Dread Baroness puppet and drove it onto the tip of the spike, then hurried down the ladder.

"What are you doing, Marjie?" Pranny said. "You don't get paid if you don't get skewered."

"Then I won't get paid," Marjormam said. She planted a kiss on Pranny's rouged lips. "Goodbye, Pranny. Tell my parents I'll be back in a few weeks. A month at most."

Beneath the mismatched eyes of the felt Dread Baroness, Marjormam ran to join the puppeteers leaving the city.

Three Herons: Great Blue

The fish taste of diesel
The frogs are runny,
eggs not quite poached.

What use is perfect stealth in a world so loud?
Engines chew the air where once we ruled
Petroleum erupts in combustion chambers
Every human screams into the slabs they press to their ears
They mate they compete they nest they hunt
And every act is cacophony.

There are no new streams
Nowhere left to fly
I could wear bells on my ankles and a whistle on my beak
The fish wouldn't notice.

What use is a face hammered into a spear
When the fish are so fat and sick
A gargantuan man on a collapsing plastic chair
Can pull them by the bucketful from my river
With a flick of his arthritic wrist?

Why fly? Every stream is just as loud, just as filthy
So wait
As quiet as a shadow
Until they consume themselves.

River of Sons

The German Imperial Army had been marching through Brussels for twenty-nine hours when the mandarin duck flew into Imke Tison's apartment, landed beside her breakfast, and tapped an SOS on the china with a webbed foot. Imke offered the duck, her former mentor Monsieur Pilo, whom she hadn't seen since the invasion began, chalk and slate. He snatched her cigarette instead.

After a long drag, Pilo took the chalk in his bill and wrote: "Bind hex."

"A soul binding?" Imke said.

He pointed one wing toward the street.

"Show me."

Imke tucked Monsieur Pilo under one arm and ran out the door. Beneath the rising August sun, German infantrymen marched in an endless grey column down the Boulevard Waterloo. The lockstep precision sounded to Imke like the churning gears of a vast, hungry machine.

Pilo honked and nipped to direct Imke through the city. As she dashed around a corner, she ran into a cart piled high with what looked like the contents of an entire home. Dirty Flemish refugees formed a defensive ring around the cart. The sight of them, exhausted and terrified, shook Imke. The last time she had seen her parents had been beside such a cart, though these people had saved more of their belongings than her parents had escaped with. But unlike these refugees, her parents had only stayed in the city long enough to deliver seven-year-old Imke to the Fellowship before they had pushed their cart back out into Flanders, never to see their daughter again. Imke found herself touching her right temple, where a lock of her hair had turned snow white on the night her family fled their farm.

"Anything you can spare?" said the dirty matriarch, her gaze lingering on Monsieur Pilo.

Imke drew Pilo in closer, mumbled an apology to the woman, and squeezed past the cart.

Scraps of song echoed from the Boulevard, "Der Hohenfriedberger" sung in clear, young voices. Imke ran beneath large posters that had been pasted to the walls of the city mere hours before the occupation. Surrender. There was to be no resistance. Brussels was an open city. The Kaiser's city.

Pilo led her to his apartment. Using the key he'd given her not long after his transformation, she let herself in. The housekeeper must have fled on one of the first trains out of the city. August heat trapped the stink of duck shit and cigarettes. Pilo nosed through the arcane tomes scattered about the place, tomes that should have been in La Tour Noire. Imke, desperate for air, unbuttoned her suffocating jacket and leaned out the south-facing windows, which offered a bird's-eye view of the Boulevard Waterloo.

An Ottoman cavalry unit moved down that great concourse, at least one thousand centaurs, lances held over their right shoulders as if they were off to a tournament to joust with French cavaliers. The thunder of their steel-shod hooves sent the city's songbirds into worried murmurations.

Pilo pecked at her ankle. He had dragged over an old tome, open to a page of dense script titled "Rise, Ye veils, and Revealeth". If he was right about the soul binding, all Imke had to do was cast this spell to identify it.

"I'm a researcher, Monsieur," Imke said, repeating the excuses she'd been giving him since before he had been transformed into a mandarin duck. "You know how I feel about performing magic."

Pilo bit her. With a yelp, Imke lifted the book. She hadn't performed any magic since she'd cast the series of spells necessary to qualify as a Yeoman Fellow. Magic terrified her. It was an uncontrollable force, a whole planet of magma, and she was the volcano through which it wanted to pass. When he noticed she wasn't reading yet, he hissed and came in for another peck.

"Give me a minute," she said.

Soul binding was foul black magic, prohibited by both the Fellowship and by city's new arcane overseers, the German Zaubererkorps. If the German sorcerers were to discover that the souls of their soldiers were being bound by some rogue necromancer, Imke shuddered at what they might do to her city.

Imke read through the "Rise, Ye Veils, and Revealeth" incantation on the page Monsieur Pilo had opened for her. The spell was tricky, but not beyond her. All she had to do was cast it, confirm Pilo's suspicions, and bring the matter to the Head Fellow. Then she could return to her research.

She struck a match, lit his cigarette, and began to recite the incantation.

The tome was written in a strange dialect of the Ur-tongue — Minoan, she suspected — but she had no trouble with the pronunciation. Each word dipped into the source of her power and drew streams of arcane energy into the world. For the first half of the incantation, it was as if she were in her exams again, her power contained, exact, but as she moved into the second half, she slipped. A bubble of energy pulsed through the delicate streams she was drawing forth, then another.

As she incanted the last stanza, she knew she'd drawn too much. The scent of cloves filled the apartment. Her sense of time stretched out: the metronome precision of the centaur unit slowing until minutes passed between hoof-falls. From high overhead, a metal cone the size of a church bell screamed toward Brussels. With the certainty of dream-logic, she knew this was an artillery shell, one of the huge ones that had so devastated the forts at Liège. She also knew the shell was a vision brought on by the bungled Revealeth spell. An omen tracing a terrible parabola across the sky. Soon the dream-shell would burst and it would turn the centaurs and Brusseleers and Flemish refugees and her and Monsieur Pilo to horsemeat.

The duck latched onto her ankle. She swore and took control of the overflowing streams of magic. Time resumed. The dream-shell vanished. Duck-shit and stale tobacco replaced the scent of cloves. But her vision hadn't entirely returned to normal.

Spanning the entire width of the Boulevard Waterloo, like a vast hide stretched for tanning, hung a taut membrane of scintillating green necromancy. Every centaur marched through the membrane; and as each one came out the other side, their soul was bound to whomever had cast the hex.

Monsieur Pilo let out a desperate honk.

"This is an abomination," Imke said, scooping him up again. "We'll go to the Head Fellow. She'll know how to end it."

*

"Stop that, Pilo!" Imke shouted at the duck as he swooped through the rafters of the Trithemius Library. Pilo ignored her and dive-bombed a white-bearded German officer who was loading books onto a cart. Until recently, the Library had housed the most prestigious collection of occult literature this side of the Bosphorus. Most of the collection had departed with the other members of the Fellowship as they fled Brussels, but the white-bearded officer had been looting those volumes that remained when Imke and Pilo found him.

"Please, Monsieur Pilo," the officer said in broken French. "I am only doing as I was told."

Imke was not surprised the bearded German knew Pilo's name. Everyone knew of the Neanderthal mandarin. Two years ago, Pilo had traveled to a cave system near Aquitaine to decipher petroglyphs painted by a long-dead neanderthal. The archaeologists scoffed at Pilo's claim that the red-ocher images were in fact a primitive conjuration ritual. Thaumaturgy was as far beyond a Neanderthal as calculus was beyond a rhesus, they insisted. Pilo had only partially proven them wrong. The glyphs were arcane, but they were a transubstantiation ritual, not a conjuration. Neanderthals could indeed perform magic, and for a reason no one including Imke could understand or reverse, they liked to transform themselves into mandarin ducks.

The door to the library creaked open, admitting a diminutive Bavarian officer in a hauptmann's horse-hair hat who appraised the scene with calm precision, then turned to the hulking fusiliers who followed him, and said: "Seize that bird."

The fusiliers jumped and grasped at Pilo, who swooped away from their clumsy attempts, veering back down to peck an ear or throw off a felt cap. One of the fusiliers, a man so young his moustache looked like little more than golden down pasted by sweat to his upper lip, unslung his rifle and fired. Imke screamed in surprise, while Pilo flew into the upper rafters of the library.

"I said seize him, fusilier," the Hauptmann said. "Not shoot him."

Another person stepped into the library, this one much taller than the Hauptmann. Magda Vandroogenbroeck, Head Fellow of the Arcane Fellowship of Magicians, Conjurers and Astralnauts, Brussels Chapter, looking as ancient as the Ur-tongue itself, fixed her gaze on the bird perched above. To call the Head Fellow severe would be an understatement; many an apprentice had claimed she could paralyze them with a glance.

"Come down, Monsieur Pilo," the Head Fellow said. "Now."

While he fluttered down from the rafters, the Head Fellow's fingers moved in quick, stuttering gestures at her side where Imke could see them. In the secret sign language of the Fellowship, she said: *What is this?*

Came to discuss urgency, Imke signed back, trying to remember the right gestures. *Duck angry. Book stealing.*

The Head Fellow blinked twice at that, then turned her attention to the Bavarian officer in the ridiculous horse-hair hat. "Hauptmann von Lepske, if you would be so kind as to ask your men to stop shooting at my Fellows?"

"The duck was assaulting my officer," said the Hauptmann.

"Your officer was stealing," Imke said, as the white-haired German pressed his fingers to a duck-nipped ear. "The terms of the surrender clearly said there would be no looting."

The Hauptmann had a magician's eyes: they were bright and blue and much too young for the pale wrinkled flesh in which they sat. "Count von der Goltz has authorized a two-hundred million franc levy on the city to fund the transition of power." He gestured toward the book cart. "Consider this part of the Fellowship's contribution."

Pilo hissed and advanced on the Hauptmann.

What urgency? the Head Fellow signed. Like the Hauptmann, she too had eyes much too young for the paper-thin flesh that surrounded them. Though she appeared to be a woman well past her hundredth year, she was only fifty-three.

Soul bind, Imke signed. *All soldiers. Still active.*

The Hauptmann laughed as Monsieur Pilo fanned out the red and green crest at the back of his head and pecked at the Hauptmann's boot.

"Senior Fellow Pilo," the Hauptmann said, the laughter never leaving his voice. "Show a little more respect! As your apprentice noted, the terms of the surrender are clear. If a single German soldier is attacked, then his attacker and every male member of the attacker's household is to be shot. I could have you killed for the blood you've drawn, and your apprentice put into bondage."

"Imke Tison is a Yeoman," the Head Fellow said. "She passed the tests and is a full member of the Fellowship."

The Hauptmann whirled on her, his huge hat flopping to one side as he did. "The point is I could give you and your baby-faced Yeoman over to my soldiers for their sport for the crime your duck committed." He straightened the hat. "But I quite enjoyed the lecture you and Monsieur Pilo gave at the conference in Prague five years ago, so as a professional courtesy, I will forgive this one trespass. Now if this matter is settled, may we continue our transition planning?"

Need breaking spell, Imke signed. *Stop binding.*

The Head Fellow considered Imke for a long moment, then seemed to come to a decision. "Not yet, Hauptmann. I believe my Fellows have something they need to share with us. Fellow Tison, what has brought you to La Tour Noire this morning?"

Imke gazed in apprehension at the Germans with whom they shared the library. With a quick gesture, the Hauptmann dismissed his two fusiliers and the duck-bit officer. Clearly, the Head Fellow and the Hauptmann had some history, but Imke was still nervous as she beckoned the Hauptmann, the Head Fellow, and a simmering Pilo into one of the library's reading rooms. There, Imke took out the slate and chalk. While Pilo sketched, she described what they'd seen.

To the untrained eye, the hex appeared to be several harmless wards — vermin banes, gentle repose, a ward against nightmare — but when Imke performed the Revealeth ritual, she had seen its true nature. Pilo completed his handiwork: he'd drawn a cross-section of the Boulevard, with the hex stretched across its entire width. Two corners of the hex were pinned on the upper floors of buildings on opposites sides of that great street, while the other two corners were pinned in opposing cellars, forming an invisible sheet through which everyone using the Boulevard must pass.

"How many soldiers have marched through Brussels since the occupation began?" the Head Fellow said.

The Hauptmann didn't seem to hear her. He brushed at the lapels of his uniform as if it had been soiled. "My men and I marched along that route last night. I sensed something was amiss."

"How many?"

"Two hundred thousand souls. At least. Imagine the sorcery one could perform with that many souls for fuel."

Pilo honked and drew a crude skull on the slate.

"Not until they die," Imke said. "The hex binds their souls, yes, but whomever created this hex can only claim each bound soul at the moment of death."

"Those soldiers march to the front," the Hauptmann said. His gloved fingers worried at the edge of the table. "This is an act of war, Head Fellow. I would be within my rights to execute half the city for this affront."

The Head Fellow spoke in measured tones. "Necromancy is as abhorrent to us as it is the Zaubererkorps. To even be admitted as an apprentice, our members must vow to only ever spend their own life to power their art. Whoever cast this blasphemy is no Fellow."

Pilo hissed again, though not at the Hauptmann this time.

Imke knew what upset him. "They might not be a Fellow, but this is no hedge magician. The illusion they used to conceal the binding is the kind we learn in First Year."

The Head Fellow swore. "One of our failed apprentices, perhaps? Your soldiers have not been kind to the people of Flanders."

The Hauptman's ancient skin twisted into a mockery of a smile. "Nothing they didn't deserve. If this is the work of a failed apprentice, then a Yeoman and a diminished Senior Fellow should be enough to undo it. Tison, Pilo, have the hex removed by noon, then find whoever cast this abomination and bring them to me."

"With respect," Imke said. "I am a researcher, not an active practitioner. I'm not the right Fellow for this task."

The Hauptmann slapped his palm on the table as if he'd heard a great joke. "I would have my subordinate whipped if they refused an order like that."

"We are civilians," the Head Fellow said. "We don't whip anyone. If Yeoman Tison wants to refuse, she is within her rights to do so. However, the three of us are all that remains of the Fellowship in Brussels, and I must supervise the collection of the levy."

Silence fell in the little reading room. Imke felt panic rising at the thought of again opening herself to the sea of incandescent magic.

"I will send two of my soldiers to help, should any locals prove troublesome," the Hauptmann said.

"You must also find the animaquary," the Head Fellow said, apparently taking Imke's silence as acquiescence. "The object they've prepared to contain the bound souls. We can destroy it here."

"We won't be destroying anything," the Hauptmann said. "The animaquary is the property of the Zaubererkorps. We will keep it for further study."

The refusal Imke was still trying to formulate died on her tongue when she realized what the Hauptmann really wanted. Once the soldiers began to die, the animaquary would contain incredible power.

He must not have it, the Head Fellow signed to Imke.

"As you command, Hauptmann Von Lepske," Imke said.

Aurochs pulled artillery wagons down the Boulevard Waterloo. Imke sympathized with the great shaggy beasts as they endured the whippings from their drivers, the August heat, and the immense weight of their cargo, for she too carried the fate of the city on her shoulders. If Imke didn't bring down the binding hex, the Hauptmann might order these very guns turned on the city she so loved.

"I still think this is a mistake," Imke said to Pilo, who was smoking a cigarette in the crook of her arm. "I've spent the past two years trying to decipher Neanderthal petroglyphs. All I have to show for it is the bit at the end that makes your transformation irreversible. I don't see how that will help in annulling a soul binding."

Pilo squirmed out of Imke's arms and flew up to alight on the eave above a boarded-up confectionery. One corner of the soul binding was pinned on the upper floor of the closed shop.

"I don't see any magic," said one of the two soldiers who escorted Imke; he was the moustachioed young man who had tried to shoot Pilo.

"It is well disguised," she said. "But keep your focus on the uppermost window of the confectionery and you will see it."

A moment later, the soldier gasped. One couldn't look at the binding directly, but if Imke focused on the building instead, she could see a faint shimmer in her peripheral vision that could be mistaken for heat rising off August cobblestones.

Imke led her escorts to the back of the shop, careful not to go anywhere near the binding, where Pilo fluttered down to meet them. Another group of refugees crowded into the courtyard at the rear of the confectionery. They stank of smoke and horse manure, and all of them watched Imke and her German escorts with the huge eyes of cornered animals.

The door to the confectionery was boarded over.

"Remove these," Imke said to her escorts in German.

"Collaborator," one of the refugees said in Flemish. The speaker was an old woman clutching a wicker basket just like the one Imke's mother used to collect kindling. She leaned across the nearly empty basket and spat on the cobblestones between them.

"We are on official business sanctioned by the Burgomaster," Imke said. "This is for the good of the city."

"Give us the duck," one of the other refugees said, a man in his late fifties too old to fight but holding a hoe as if he planned to take on the entire German Imperial Army with it. "The children haven't had anything to eat for days."

Pilo hissed at the refugee. Imke scooped him up and joined the soldiers, who had finished prying off the boards.

"See that we are not disturbed," she said.

On the upper level, the only light came from gaps in the boards that had been hammered over the windows. Dust danced in those blades of light, and the walls of the buildings shook with the weight of the passing guns. The entire floor had been used as storage for the shop below, but the shelves had been cleared of sugar and flour and tins of sweets in haste, and were now all bare in the near dark.

Pilo pecked at Imke until she lit him a cigarette.

"Those can't be good for you," she said. He made a dismissive honk and waddled beneath luminescent glyphs painted on the ceiling near the outer wall.

To the untrained eye, the glyphs were a vermin-bane. Though Imke could not see the forbidden characters yet, they radiated foul necromancy.

Pilo hissed in alarm. Imke felt it too. A presence in the far corner of the room. All the blood ran out of Imke's legs, replaced by ice. Plaster crumbled out of the wall, and the wood of the shelves began to warp, making terrible popping and crunching sounds as it expanded outward.

Pilo nipped her ankle, but Imke barely felt it. As the wall bulged further outward, taking on the rough outlines of a man, Imke fell into memory. She was a child staring out the window of their farmhouse at the torchlit faces of her neighbors. They cursed her and her family as they advanced with their fire and their lamp oil. Her mother's panicked packing. Father's hands shaking as he took the musket down from above the hearth. A great swelling of magic in her belly that would give the neighbors all the more reason to burn her for a witch.

Plaster and wood and brick shaped like a German soldier stepped free of the wall. A soul, a part of Imke knew, enslaved by whomever had bound it. The soldier worked the bolt on the long piece of wood in the form of a rifle. That wild, uncontrolled magic still rose in Imke. She thought of the crop circle she'd made as a child that had drawn their neighbors to her home — she had flattened every fence, farm animal, and piece of foliage for a mile around — and now she pictured the same here in Brussels.

Pilo flew up and pecked her between the eyes. It was a gesture he'd done so many times when he was a man; one stubby finger tapping against her skull.

"You control your magic," she could hear him saying. "It does not control you."

She raised the warding glyph moments before the rubble-soldier fired. The impact still knocked her over, but the glyph had taken the worst of it. Pilo darted at the soldier as it fixed a foot-long nail as a bayonet. Imke rose to one knee.

"Beware all ye who hide in darkness," she said, the old recitation starting as a whisper. "For I wield the light eternal. I speak the Ur-tongue. I see with blinded eyes." With each word, she felt herself leaving that frightened child behind. "To oppose me is to stand before the flood."

The rubble-soldier raised his rifle, ready to impale. The Ur-tongue poured out of Imke, syllables she had memorized years ago that came back to her with perfect recall. *For the Banishment of Constructs and Other Aberrations.* The magic poured through her, molten and consuming, but she held onto the streams, shaped the scalding tendrils to her will.

Stone and timber crumpled into a pile where the soldier had stood. Pilo skittered away to avoid being buried.

Imke released the magic and dropped, gasping, to the ground beside Pilo. She felt scoured out. "Are you alright?"

He stretched out one wing, then another, seemed satisfied with the result, then waddled over and nudged her with his shoulder. Another gesture from his human days. One of the first spells she'd ever successfully completed, a simple transubstantiation that turned a stone into a cabbage, had elicited that exact same response.

But this was no time for wet-eyed reminiscence. Imke straightened, her joints aching, and said: "Come, Monsieur, we have work to do."

Before she spoke the words of the Revealeth spell, Imke took a moment, seeing the words in her mind. She was more careful as she spoke the Minoan-inflected verses, and this time she knew she'd done it right.

The vermin-bane melted away, leaving only the soul binding glyph etched onto the ceiling. Imke drew a pentagram and circle in chalk on the floor beneath the glyph and stepped into the circle. Still raw from defeating the rubble-man, she took hold of the magic again. She recited the breaking spell the Head Fellow had shown her. Jagged syllables of the Ur-tongue poured out of her, and with it, the magic consumed the minutes and hours of her life. The glyphs resisted, fought to survive the onslaught of her breaking, so she poured more of herself into the task.

She expected more when the invocation finished, but the soul binding simply belched oily smoke for an instant before disappearing. Out on the Boulevard, the binding would be a triangle now, one corner pinned in the lower level of the Carmelite Church two buildings away. Once it was removed, the soldiers and Brusseleers and refugees would be safe. Imke and Pilo could clear the other two corners of the binding at their leisure.

"That wasn't so bad," Imke said, kneeling down before him. "You ready for three more of those?"

He nuzzled for her cigarettes.

"I suppose you've earned it."

In the light of the match, Pilo let out a honk of surprise. He reached one wing up to touch her left temple. The hair there felt strange, yet also familiar. She held up a lock and saw to her dismay that it had turned as white as the bolt at her right temple. How much of her life had she traded for the power she had just wielded.

Days? A week? More? The match burnt down to her fingers. She let out a yelp as she dropped it, and was about to light another when a great commotion erupted at the base of the building. People yelling in Flemish, an anguished wail, and angry German responses.

The morning brilliance blinded her as she ran out the door. She reached a hand up to shade her eyes, but before her vision could adjust, somebody tackled her to the ground. The woman stank of unwashed underclothes and ash. Arthritic fingers clawed at Imke.

"Collaborator!" she screamed. "Did you help them burn my orchard? Did you?"

Pilo honked in rage. The other refugees were shouting and begging for food.

Imke tried to push the crone away. "I didn't touch your orchard."

"Five beautiful trees," she said, her breath rancid. "Chopped down in the fullness of their fruit. You did it, collaborator. You cut down my trees!"

The fusilier with the golden moustache threw the crone off. She landed beside her empty kindling basket, weeping. Pilo flew over to reprimand the old woman.

Imke was about to thank the fusilier when he snatched Pilo out of the air and, with a quick twist, broke the duck's neck.

"Here," the soldier said in stunted Flemish. "Feed your children."

He threw Pilo's body to the refugees.

Imke heard herself shouting incoherent pleas as the refugees fought over Pilo. Bright green and orange feathers drifted above the scrum. Her friend, her teacher. And these monsters were tearing him to pieces.

That childish rage flared in Imke. She couldn't bottle it, not this time, but she could channel the streams of magma. She spoke the Ur-tongue. An old spell, the first that came to mind. Precise and controlled. All her fury poured into it. As she finished the last syllable, the fusilier and the refugees tearing at Pilo disappeared. Only the old crone and the other soldier remained. Empty clothing fell into heaps on the cobblestones. Nesting at the center of each bundle was a leafy green head of cabbage. Eleven, Imke counted. Eleven piles of clothing, eleven heads of cabbage.

At this, the old crone cackled in delight.

Imke fell to her knees, staring in horror at what she'd just done. In her mind, she leafed through all the spells she'd ever read, looking for anything that could undo this — some of the cabbages were much smaller than the others — when the other soldier drove his rifle into the back of her skull.

As she fell, a dozen pieces of kindling appeared in the old woman's wicker basket. No, Imke realized. Not a dozen.

Eleven.

⁂

Iron-shod boots marching on cobblestones. The sound a terrible storm washing away the peace of one hundred years. Imke smelled sun-warmed brick and the stink of the woman who had attacked her. Her eyes were covered in rough fabric, her arms bound behind her. She reached for her magic, but it was as if a great stone floor had been built between her and the depths from which she drew her power.

"I don't think we have long, Imke," the Head Fellow said from somewhere nearby.

In the darkness behind the blindfold, Imke watched Monsieur Pilo's body tumble end-over-end toward the starving refugees. The rage that had gripped her then found her now, and she was glad that she couldn't reach her magic.

"Oh Madame," Imke said, choking on the words. "I did something unforgivable."

"Unforgivable only in that you were so inefficient in your sorcery," said Hauptmann von Lepske in his perfect German. "You've aged two years in the span of an hour, Fellow Tison. Is this how you teach magic, Vandroogenbroeck? It is no wonder your country fell so easily."

"Damn you, von Lepske," the Head Fellow hissed, and she began to incant.

"Tutt, tutt," said the Hauptmann, as if scolding a child. "I've etched a circle of negation around you both. There will be no vegetable surprises here. If you have any last words, don't waste them on the Ur-tongue."

Rough hands lifted Imke to her feet. They pressed her back to a brick wall, the very walls of La Tour Noire, she was sure. The Head Fellow was positioned arm-to-arm beside her.

"This isn't right, Hauptmann," the Head Fellow said. "One of our Fellowship was murdered. Imke was only defending herself."

"By turning a soldier and a dozen refugees into cabbage?"

"Bring them here and I will turn them back. Please, Ernst. Extend me another courtesy."

"It is too late for that," the Hauptmann said. "I went to the scene of the crime. All evidence of the partisan attack had been harvested. No doubt my fusilier and your refugees have already been stewed."

Imke let out a sob, realizing now what was to come. "Head Fellow Vandroogenbroeck had nothing to do with this, Hauptmann. I was the one who cast the spell. Only me."

"Quiet, girl," he said. "By the authority granted to me as a representative of Count Von Der Goltz, I hereby sentence you both to death by firing squad for the killing of Fusilier Borke."

"Please, sir," Imke said. "I found the apprentice who cast the binding." She thought of the basket filling up with kindling; those had been the souls of the people she had vegetated. The old woman who carried the basket must have cast the binding. "At least defer my punishment until we have stopped her."

"Justice cannot be deferred," the Hauptmann said, raising his sabre. "May God have mercy on your souls."

"No," Imke shouted, but she was drowned out by the thunder of the fusillade.

Hundreds of birds taking flight at once. A sound like a bag of groceries falling to the floor. Imke couldn't understand why her heart still beat. Was this another vision? Was this death? The air was hot and tinged with gunsmoke, blood and piss.

Gloved hands removed her blindfold. She blinked in the August sun. The Head Fellow lay to her left. They had shot her beneath one of the Burgomaster's posters: "Brussels, Open City. Offer No Resistance." Both the wall and the poster were stained with her blood. Twenty paces away, the soldiers were checking their rifles. Starlings roiled in a great black cloud across the sky.

"Head Fellow," someone said.

Two fusiliers dragged the Head Fellow's body by the ankles toward a cart. All that knowledge, all that power, lost to the world when they needed it most.

"Head Fellow?"

"The Head Fellow is gone," Imke heard herself say.

The Hauptmann took her chin in his gloved hands and turned her face so she was looking into his too-young eyes in that ancient, weathered face. "You are the most senior Fellow remaining in the city, so the post is yours."

Imke flinched away from him. "There must be an election."

"Consider your appointment provisional!" the Hauptmann snapped. "I have spared your life, Head Fellow. Show me a little gratitude. Attacking the fusilier wasn't wrong — he murdered a man we both respected — but justice wasn't yours to exact. With this, I have returned balance to our relationship. But I want you to remember your place. Defer to the authority of the Kaiser. You will not get a second opportunity to walk away from the firing squad. Do you understand?"

He looked up at her, demanding an answer. All Imke could manage was a nod.

"Good. Now, I understand we have some necromancy to annul. As you are short-handed, I will assist you in completing this task. Shall we?"

He indicated back toward the Boulevard. The marching song was unintelligible from this distance. Imke took out her slate. Much of the map Pilo had drawn was smudged beyond recognition, but it helped to hold it, to have this thing that had so connected her and her mentor.

"Here," she said, pointing to the Carmelite Church. "Our next stop must be here."

"Excellent."

The Hauptmann put a silver whistle to his lips and blew, though it made no sound.

Hooves rang on the cobblestones. When Imke saw the unicorn canter into the courtyard, it was all she could do to stop herself from weeping. It was a mare the same brilliant white as the horsehair plume atop the Hauptmann's hat. When it knelt before him, she felt sick. Nothing so beautiful should debase herself before such filth, yet the creature did not flinch as he climbed onto her back.

He extended a gloved hand to her. When she hesitated, he said: "There is much I can teach you, Head Fellow. You are powerful, of that I have no doubt, but your methods are sloppy. Inefficient. As we unravel this binding, I will teach some German precision." He waited, his hand out. "Don't make me ask again."

Repressing a shiver of revulsion, she took his hand and climbed onto the unicorn.

As they rode, Imke choked down her bile. In the space of an hour, she had watched both her mentor and the head of her order killed, and she had committed an atrocity. For the first half of that ride, clutching to the perfumed coattails of the man who had ordered the Head Fellow's death, Imke wished she too had been shot. But as they rode through the city, passing hundreds of refugees who did a poor job of hiding their fear and hatred, Imke's loathing found a better target. The Hauptmann. He wanted the animaquary and the power of the hundreds of thousands of souls it would gather.

He must not have it, the Head Fellow had told her. So Imke wouldn't let him have it. As penance for those she'd killed, she swore she'd stop him.

They dismounted before the Carmelite Church. Another blast of the Hauptmann's silent silver whistle sent the unicorn back to the dream-realm it called home. A unit of bergmonch marched on the Boulevard Waterloo. Twice the height of any man, they wore vestments cut from the same grey cloth as the rest of the army.

Walking in pairs, they carried massive cannons between them and did not sing.

Brusseleers and refugees waited in a long queue near the church, at the end of which a silent nun handed out bread. Once Imke was done with the Hauptmann, she would leave this place, go somewhere where she couldn't hurt anyone again.

Imke spotted the old woman in the line, her basket of kindling on the ground before her.

A dozen twigs filled the basket, every one of them a captured soul.

Leave here, Imke signed to the woman, hoping there was enough left of the old crone that she remembered her early lessons.

Surprise shone in the woman's mad eyes. Her fingers moved slowly on the rim of the basket, and a smile twisted her chapped lips. *Hate now them also yes?*

Orchard will grow again, Imke signed.

"There a problem?" the Hauptmann said, as he reached the doors of the church.

Imke shook her head, and made a final, desperate gesture toward the crone. *Please go.*

The silent nun tried to bar the Hauptmann from entering, but the soldiers moved her out of the way. He posted a pair of soldiers to guard the door and two more inside the cavernous nave to keep watch while they descended into the crypt.

Imke followed the Hauptmann and another pair of soldiers into the stone-walled chamber. Dust rained from the ceiling onto a dozen stone coffins in time with the marching bergmonch outside. The stink of damp rot filled the place, and the only light came from the Hauptmann's sword, which he held aloft, the blade spilling a gentle white luminescence.

One of the soldiers, a young man of no more than eighteen, crossed himself.

"Easy, boys," the Hauptmann said to the soldiers. "Nothing here can harm us."

Imke approached the soul binding where it had been etched onto the wall. The glyph was disguised as a curse on those who would disturb the dead. Imke wondered if the mad old woman had seen the irony in that.

"Juvenile work," the Hauptmann said. "This shouldn't take more than a minute. Show me how the Fellowship prepares its Yeomen."

A lump rose in Imke's throat when she took out the chalk, but she forced it down and began to trace the pentagram and circle on the stone floor beneath the glyph. There was no room for error here. The Hauptmann's young eyes in that ancient face watched her every move. To deviate at all would condemn more of her countrymen. So she pictured Monsieur Pilo there beside her. Though he was human in her imagination, he had green and orange mandarin feathers in the brim of his hat, and he could only speak in honks and hisses. With him there with her, she could control her magic.

"With your leave, I'll begin the invocation?" she said. Be docile, she thought. Be meek. Be conquered. And be ready to act.

The Hauptmann waved her toward the pentagram. As she stepped into the circle, the church echoed with three quick gunshots, then silence. Shouting from above, another volley, a sound like a small avalanche.

"Is this your doing?" the Hauptmann said.

"You've been with me this whole time," Imke said.

"Begin the breaking," he said. "If this is the failed apprentice, I'll put an end to them. Be ready, boys."

But he didn't need to warn the soldiers who stood with them; both already trained their rifles at the simple wooden door that sealed the crypt. It began to rattle in its hinges, as if a steam engine was trying to shake it to pieces, then the vibrations ended as quickly as they'd begun. The two soldiers exchanged terrified glances.

The quiet that followed was broken only by dual incantations from Imke and the Hauptmann, and the ceaseless march of the army above.

"Show yourself!" the Hauptmann shouted.

The door exploded inward as if struck by an artillery shell. Vicious lengths of shattered oak impaled both soldiers, but the largest chunk was aimed at the Hauptmann. The heavy timber should have crushed him, but he held his sabre before him, and the door splintered when it touched the sabre's point.

The crone stepped in through the doorway, dragging her basket with her.

"You," she said to the Hauptmann. "You burned my orchard."

She whipped one of the pieces of kindling out of the basket and snapped it in two. Imke recoiled, sickened at the violation the crone performed so casually. The soul she'd just shattered released a roiling torrent of raw magical energy, and with a few hurried syllables, the crone wrestled that energy into the stone floor.

A soldier made of rubble began to crawl up from the stone and soil beneath, but the Hauptmann kicked it with his polished boots, and the rubble-soldier fell to pieces before it could be born.

The Hauptmann laughed in derision. "All that power, and the best you can do with it is summon a bodengeist?" He made a fist with his free hand, and the stones that had been trying to form into a man flew across the crypt and slammed into the crone, knocking her off her feet.

Imke stuttered in her incantation.

"Keep working, Head Fellow," the Hauptmann said, not looking behind him. "I'll handle this hedge-witch."

The crone moved faster than seemed possible for her ancient, wrecked body. She broke another stick. Tendrils of pale smoke flowed from her fingertips into each of the stone coffins that filled the crypt. Bones moved within, and the lids of the coffins began to slide open.

"Five beautiful trees," the crone said. "In the fullness of their fruit."

The Hauptmann raised his sabre with both hands and uttered three short syllables. Every coffin slammed closed. When he brought down the sabre with a swift cut, vines grew up from the stone floor, enveloping the coffins and sealing them shut. Imke marveled at his precision.

"Trees?" the Hauptmann said. "Surely you haven't done all this for a few spindly pear trees." The crone hissed and cursed him, and the Hauptmann laughed. "You don't remember, do you? Whatever ungodly amount of yourself you spent on the binding burned it out of your ill-trained mind. Perhaps I can remedy that."

He pointed his sabre at her and sang an ancient lullaby. The crone, who had been ready to break another twig, fell onto her side and pressed her gnarled hands to her mouth. The sound that came out of her silenced Imke. It wasn't weeping; this was a woman's soul being torn to pieces.

"Not pear trees then," the Hauptmann said. "Where were your sons stationed? Liège? Namur?"

He took a step toward the crone, so intent on her that he didn't notice that Imke had changed her incantation. She took up the slate on which a few lines of Pilo's map still remained.

"Liège," the crone said through her tears. "I brought each of them into this world — five beautiful boys — and in a single day — one wretched day — your army took them all from me."

"An unfathomable loss, Madame," the Hauptmann said, raising his sword. "Let me send you to them."

Imke poured magic into the slate as the Hauptmann brought down his blade. The slate flew like it was fired from a siege gun, glowing with the red heat of her fury. It struck the Hauptmann square in the back, knocking him across the crypt and into the far wall.

She ran to the crone, but it was too late. The Hauptmann's sabre was embedded halfway through her neck. Those eyes, no longer mad, were still weeping as the light went out of them. The stick she'd been holding fell from her fingers.

Imke let out a scream. The church shook with her rage.

"Perhaps I do not give the Fellowship enough credit," the Hauptmann said. He'd hit the wall with enough force to knock him senseless, but he simply brushed the dust off his uniform and held up his hand. His sabre made a whistling sound as it soared back across the room to its master. "That caught me quite by surprise."

"I won't let you have their souls," Imke said, standing between the Hauptmann and the basket full of kindling. "That much power can never be yours."

The Hauptmann laughed as he stepped toward her. "Then try to stop me."

The blade flew at her in a blinding spray of light. She only had an instant to draw up a ward. The impact knocked her backward, but she stayed on her feet. Every spell she'd ever read leafed by in her mind's eye: she picked one she thought he might not anticipate.

The floor around the Hauptmann turned to liquid stone, and he sank up to his shoulders. But even as the stone solidified around him, he spoke the Ur-tongue, and his body melted into gauzy smoke that flowed out of the tomb she'd made for him, reforming into a man a few paces away.

"Creative," he said. "But you are being too gentle. This is a duel, Imke. Only one of us will walk back into the light."

He drove the point of the sabre into the ground, and the blade emerged under her left foot, driving up through her boot in a gout of blood. Imke screamed and fell to the flagstones beside the dead crone. Her foot was pinned as if she were a beetle on display. He barked one of his little giggles and left his sabre driven into the stone while he walked toward her.

"That was entertaining," he said. "I'll give you that."

Imke tried to reach the slate, which lay a few paces ahead of her, but every movement sent bolts of agony coursing through her. She collapsed against the stones once more. As she tried to push herself upright, her hand closed over the piece of kindling the crone had been holding.

When she swung the stick around, the Hauptmann paused, a look of true worry on his face for the first time since she'd met him.

"The Fellowship abhors necromancy," he said.

"There is no more Fellowship," she said.

She snapped the stick in two. For a moment, as the soul's energy poured into the crypt, she could see a human form in the maelstrom. Someone's son. But the shape disappeared as Imke took hold of the chaos. She spoke a few quick words of the Ur-tongue, and poured the soul's energy into the Hauptmann.

He writhed in agony. His mouth and nose stretched out into a snout, the bones snapping and creaking like old floor boards. Already his fingers were shrinking, twisting, turning to useless claws. Coarse white hairs punched out along his jaw and neck and he let out a shrill, animal scream. The stink of an old attic filled the crypt, his shrinking head slipped beneath the neck of his jacket, and he collapsed to the stone floor. The white horsehair hat landed upright on top of empty grey fabric.

Imke trembled for a moment in the sudden stillness of the crypt, then emptied the contents of her stomach across the flagstones. When the retching stopped, she pulled her foot off the Hauptmann's blade. The sight of all that blood threatened to set her retching again, so she spoke quick words of healing and leaned up against a coffin to catch her breath.

As the army thundered by above, the Hauptmann's horsehair hat wobbled once, twice, and then a pink, whiskered nose emerged from beneath the brim.

"That's quite enough," Imke said.

She lifted another twig from the crone's basket and snapped it in two.

⋙

Imke felt nauseated in the crone's clothing. She'd kept her dress and jacket on beneath the filthy rags, but that had been a mistake.

Four carts of books sat in the courtyard outside La Tour Noire, all that remained of the Fellowship's once great library. One of the German officers who had collected the books was marching over to her, lecturing in broken Flemish that she was not allowed here.

Imke snapped one of the twigs. The nausea sharpened, but she didn't retch, which was good. If she were to be an effective necromancer, she couldn't go around throwing up each time she performed black magic.

Every single German in the courtyard collapsed into separate piles of empty uniforms, and from each one of those piles, a starling took flight. They flew confused and alarmed, some flying straight into the wall still stained with the Head Fellow's blood, but others flew with ease. The natural starlings who called the tower home squawked in protest at these new arrivals.

Most of the books were useless, but a few contained magics that Imke might need. She put them in a sack, then she undressed. She tossed her skirt and jacket onto the carts, then tore down the blood-stained Open City poster and used it to set the carts aflame. She pushed each burning cart into La Tour Noire.

With smoke rising behind her, she dragged the basket out of the courtyard, but it had grown heavier. Dozens of sticks materialized in the basket every few seconds. The German Imperial Army must have made it to the front.

The silver whistle she'd taken from the Hauptmann's empty uniform was warm to the touch. She wiped it off before bringing it to her lips. When the unicorn cantered toward her, she knew that it would be impossible to move through the occupied territories astride such a conspicuous beast. A quick snap of a twig, and the unicorn transformed into a mule with a snow white tail.

"I'm sorry," she whispered to the beast, who snorted in alarm. "But the transformation is permanent. An old trick I learned from a Neanderthal."

She tied the basket to the mule's back and took out the little metal cage she'd shaped from the Hauptmann's sword. Within it, a snow-white rat with brilliant blue eyes chewed at the silver enclosure.

"I know you intended me to learn German precision," she said, as she tied the silver cage above the filling basket "But you've taught me something much more valuable: Belgian rage. It is a lesson I intend to teach your armies."

The Hauptmann rat squeaked in protest.

When she reached the Boulevard Waterloo, a collection of baggage carts being pulled by grumpy aurochs was trudging through the city. After they passed, only a hot wind filled the great thoroughfare. Brusseleers and refugees took tentative steps out onto the cobblestones to reclaim their city.

Imke waited until the afternoon heat passed, then followed the army out into no man's land.

'Ti Pouce in Fergetitland

On the last Somday in Novembuary, 'Ti Pouce pulled the stunt that set us to starving. Pers and Mamons and we seven and 'Ti Pouce was lined up outside Lor Gerol's palazzo to procure vittles. The smerf fam ahead of us, distant cousins of Mamons, was giving their gifts to Lor Gerol's cliquo, when 'Ti Pouce leaned in close to us at Danley.

"Watch close, my brothers and sisters," our wee big brother said. "Today I will secure enough vittles for the journey across Fergetitland."

"To what place?" we said.

"Think of any place," said he, and we did. "That place is better than here."

"Quiet, children," Pers said. "'Tis our turn with the cliquo."

Pers sent we seven hopping up to the cliquo Gerol with what we scavenged from the waste: a block-o-cinds, a tyre, pillow stuffing, an action figure, one bucket, a rake handle, and a ratty corpse. All good rawmats we could have turned into vittles, but we gifted them to the cliquo Gerol instead.

"Seek you a blessing?" the cliquo Gerol said.

We said what Mamons always taught us: "We're blessed as we are."

The cliquo laughed at that. "Little spider thinks they're blessed. They live in a hovel!"

"Our hovel suits us finely."

That seemed to stoke their mirth further.

"Ignore them, my brothers and sisters," 'Ti Pouce whispered to us at Margerine. "'Tis the last time you'll go begging from them."

"Be cautious here," we whispered back, and he stepped up ahead of us.

"Generous cliquo Gerol," he said in a voice five times larger than his slight stature. He reached into his pockets and took out a big clod-o-ground in one hand and a lovely if stale cakelet in the other. "I offer thee this fine clod-o-ground."

He gifted the clod to the cliquo Gerol, then he lifted the cakelet to his lips.

"We could offer a much finer blessing if you were to gift us that cakelet," the cliquo Gerol said.

The cliquo smacked their seven fat mouths. They were surrounded by fine gifts that could be transformered into vittles, enough for hundreds of those cakelets.

"I can see you are ahungered," 'Ti Pouce said. "And I know 'tis a hardship for a cliquo to walk to the fabupot for your vittles. I think I see a remedy. Trade me what my brothers and sisters gifted you, and this cakelet is yours."

The cliquo Gerol tossed everything we gifted them right back at 'Ti Pouce and soon they were fighting over the cakelet.

"Don't know about this, 'Ti Pouce," Pers said.

"Squarefair was the trade," 'Ti Pouce said.

'Ti Pouce dragged all the regifted gifts through the door into Lor Gerol's throneplace. Pers and Mamons and we seven followed him in.

Mamons' cousin was getting vittles from the Lor. The cousin dropped the rawmat he'd brought into the fabupot and Lor Gerol rized up from his throne and had to scrunch so his headbone didn't crack the ceiling. Fingers like mallets punched the codes and the fabupot beeped like a happy animal. The rawmats rattled and splorked as they was transformered and out the other end slopped twin bowls of icyscreamy, a mound of cakelets, a bucket of poulet frittes, a bottle of medicinals for the cousin's sickly wife, and a sack of wine slurpee. Lor Gerol punched codes to make the fabupot stop, and he kept the slurpee to himself. We seven's bellies grumbled as the smerf fam walked away with that fine haul.

It was our turn.

"Vittles please, your Lorship," 'Ti Pouce said. He opened the bag with all the regifted gifts, plus the rawmats we brought for the fabupot.

The door to the throneplace opened behind us and the cliquo Gerol waddled in, all seven of them covered in cakelet crumbs, them wailing like one of their heads was dead.

"Whatever's the matter, me darling cliquo?" Lor Gerol said.

"The weency one tricked us, Dada," the cliquo said. Fourteen fingers accused at 'Ti Pouce. "He made us give up our gifts for a lone cakelet."

"This true, Pers Moyer?" Lor Gerol said.

Pers dropped to his kneebones. "Your cliquo traded squarefair with my 'Ti Pouce."

Lor Gerol roared like a waste train. "I ask so little for providing the vittles. No tithe, no tax, only gifts for my darling cliquo. Yet your runt tricked them." Lor Gerol pounded the ceiling with a fist like a boulder. "From this day and each one after, you are barnished from this here palazzo, Pers Moyers. Step feet on this stone again, and I will wipe yer kin from this Earth."

The yellow light atop the palazzo shined dim and sickly against the grey of smoglight.

Pers whipped 'Ti Pouce in front of the other smerf fams waiting outside. We thought he deserved more, it was his fault we was ahungered, but Mamons had enough and told him to cease.

The palazzo sits atop the tallest hill in the waste, and on most Somdays while we walked home we seven admired the fine views of the trenches and the excavations and the Clavement waste rail line and the scattered hovels that fill the valley Lor Gerol renamed after himself, but that Somday the view was of a deadland, and we was doomed to soon add our grave to the countless graves below.

On the walk home, we seven fell into a hole where other smerfs had excavated rawmats too close to the road and Pers and Mamons and 'Ti Pouce had to pull us out. After, 'Ti Pouce said it remembered him of the day we seven was spawned: all of us spilling out of Mamons, one after the other, each fused to the next at the kneebone.

"The nursing went on morn, smoglight and dark," Mamons said as we got to walking again. "A cliquo of seven. You were adored."

She grew quiet then, but we knew the story well. We were the first clique-de-sept anyone ever heard of, and for a while we was famous. Smerfs from across the valley would come and gift us in exchange for a touch. Blessings of health and fecundity, Mamons said those touches profited upon the gifter, until a month after we was spawned, when Lor Gerol announced one of his wifes had spawned his own clique-de-sept. He declared his cliquo to be the only true provider of blessings, and the gifters ceased their pilgrimages to our hovel. We was first, though. We thinks Lor Gerol had a hate on for us ever after.

Mamons had some vittles tucked away in the hovel for just such an occurrence. Dryish cakelet, molded frittes, battered butter, and handfuls of chewing gum. Filled us up, it did, but the next morn we was ahungered again. Mamons begged round the neighboring smerfs but none obliged. Lor Gerol had sent the crier out: any smerf fam spied feeding Moyers would be starved out same as us. With no soda or latte to bev, we got mighty thirsty too.

Pers had heard of another town other side of the Lorenshen Fergetitland that had a fabupot, so he packed sacks for travel.

"Let me adjoin yourself," 'Ti Pouce said to Pers. "I'm useful."

"Unambiguous no," Pers said. "You are the speaker for the Moyers until my return."

Pers returned two days later with a crusty stump where his left arm used to hang.

"Cancanlupan took it," he said as he tumbled to the floor.

We knew some medimangling from some paperwords we regandered once, and with the few medicinals in the hovel, we patched Pers up. Three days after that, Pers was feeling well enough to swear, and we was all so ahungered that we ate dirt. He and Mamons was in conference all day and well past dark. We seven slept on our stitched together mattresses and 'Ti Pouce lay lengthwise at our eight feet.

Pers shook us awake with his one remaining hand. "Up get, me cliquo, and me runtling 'Ti Pouce. The stork-o-fortuna flied by in the dark."

"We're leaving for a new place, aren't we?" 'Ti Pouce said.

"'Tis what you've been waiting for, me runtling," Per said.

"Why doesn't Mamons join us?" we said. We didn't like that Mamons hadn't packed a thing.

"She'll join us before dark," Pers said. "She wants to say goodbye to her cousins."

He had us pack what we hadn't traded to Lor Gerol for vittles and marched us into the gloom-o-morn. Mamons waved from the window of the hovel, she holding a rag facewise.

"We're going through Fergetitland?" 'Ti Pouce said.

"The stork-o-fortuna showed me the way," he said. "We going Oowest."

We gripped the hand of our wee big brother.

"Picture it, my brothers and sisters," 'Ti Pouce said. "No Lor to bend knees to, no queue for vittles. 'Tis the day we been waiting for."

"'Tis the day you been waiting for."

We walked for hours, Pers saying nothing, 'Ti Pouce telling every joke he knew. His excitement couldn't infect us, and the laughter from Pers' sounded false. For a shortish while we knew the landscape — trenches cut into the waste for rawmat, hovels like the hovel Moyers, bones of old buildings, graves and graves and graves — but soonish it changed. Spindly black things sprouted from the dead earth. Fogclouds seeped up from slick pools. Things like living ropes twined and teased along the ground, tripping us up. Fergetitland.

Near dark we arrived at a riverlet flowing with clouded waters. The slopes steepened on either side of us and then they grew sharpish and cliffy, and the waters went from clouded to clearer.

"Take a pause and breath a bit," Pers said. "While I regander ahead."

Pers disappeared round a bend in the creek. A cancanlupan howled its code.

"Danley, Staniel, Raggity Anne, Allan, Paul, Saul, and Margerine," 'Ti Pouce said, singing our names like he always does.

"Oui?"

"What for does the cancanlupan howl?"

We shrugged our seven shoulders.

"Wouldn't you be crying if you was living in Fergetitland?" He howled at his joke.

"Nothing about this is amusing, 'Ti Pouce."

"We're going to a new place," he said. "Cheer yourself!"

"Then why is Mamons still homewise?"

Pers showed his headbone from the top of the cliff.

"Me cliquo, 'Ti Pouce," he said, his voice aquivered. "Me and Mamons is regretfilled, but we got nothing more to feed you. Better to try out here then see you starve at home. This be your place now and evermore. Bev the water, mash the growing tings. You're better off here."

That flat headbone disappeared. 'Ti Pouce climbed up the cliffside while we seven hollered bellow.

"There's no track nor trace of him," 'Ti Pouce said. He slid down the cliffside. "But badness isn't the entirety of it. We're free, my brothers and sisters. We can find some better place as we please!"

We started crying at Allan and it caught all around.

"Whatfor's the matter?" 'Ti Pouce said.

"Our hovel."

"What of it?"

"At the palazzo Gerol, when you told us to think of any place, that's the place we thought of. We want no other."

'Ti Pouce paced upstream a ways, and for the moment between the howl of a cancanlupan and the answer of its echo, we thought he might leave us, but he returned.

"Your brother will right things," he said. "Regander this." Metalbits glinted on his grubby palm. "I left the metalbits so Mamons could find our path. Looks like we'll require them now."

'Ti Pouce showed us his trick: during the long walk, he dropped metalbits through Fergetitland. The metalbits shined frosting-like in the moonglow.

"'Twill guideline us home."

Homeward we walked. 'Ti Pouce reconnoitred ahead, collecting the metalbits as he did, and we seven followed as fast as our legs allowed. We was still enfuried with him, but he was making things right. We whistled as we went. Our brother tried to hush us but we said we read paperwords that proclaimed whistling kept the cancanlupan and the lion-o-iron from murdering your body, so he whistled likewise. Fergetitland did not seem so terrifraiding while whistling, until 'Ti Pouce quit his whistle.

"This be a tragedy for which I am unprepared," 'Ti Pouce said. He scuffed the ground.

"What's wrong, brother?" said we seven.

"The metalbits are gone."

"Where for now?"

He gazed into the fogclouds and up at the moon and scratched his wee headbone.

"This way," he gesticulated to the left a the moon. "I think."

We followed. His whistling was different. Rattylike. Our mouths too dry to make an accompanying whistle. We clasped our hands and his.

"For a bit of positivity," he said. "The cancanlupan no longer howls."

But we heard other tings in Fergetitland: snappings and breathings and moanings and then there was the smells, all fungicide and oil and metalblood. After a while we found a dark creeklet that smelled like the one near our hovel. We followed it, the banks slick, the mud sucking at our eight feet. 'Ti Pouce whistled, and it sounded bravish now, fierce and certainlike.

The coyoodle lept on our backside and got Margerine in its toothvice. We hollered and struck it, but the steel dentition only sunk deeper.

"They lust after metals," we shouted. "Lure them off us!"

"Hey 'oodle," 'Ti Pouce said. He shook the metalbits he'd recollected at the coyoodle. The creature looked up from where it was mauling us, beady glasseyes following the metalbits. "Want them, 'oodle? Come get em."

'Ti Pouce tossed a few metalbits at the ground and the coyoodle leaped off us to gobble the metalbits. We seven sobbed. 'Ti Pouce tossed more metalbits into the dirt by the creeklet bank, and coyoodle gobbled those up too. 'Ti Pouce tossed the last of them metalbits into the creeklet and coyoodle jumped in after them. That critter screamed like a waste train unrailing, the creeklet stripping the furs right off its bones.

More yips behind us. Three more coyoodles slinked out of the spindlies, eyes aglow, teeth slickened with bile, head furpuffs quivering, tail furpuffs wagging.

"Run, cliquo," 'Ti Pouce said. "We don't have no more trinklets to distract them."

We ran as well as we could. 'Ti Pouce broke off a basher from a spinldy and bashed the coyoodles when they got close. He splashed creeklet waters at them, and that slowed them, but still they followed. We hurt at Margerine, the blood clotty on our rags. They chased and chased us, the moon dropped lower, and when the biggest coyoodle bit through 'Ti Pouce's basher, we knew we would end up as coyoodle poop.

"This way, cliquo," 'Ti Pouce said.

We ran with him to the edge of a trench; it was the waste we was in! 'Ti Pouce held us there and whispered: "Drop when they pounce."

"Advance upon us, coyoodles," he screamed at the three beasts. "Discover what we Moyers is made from."

All three jumped as one. 'Ti Pouce tugged us earthwards. The coyoodles soared above us and clattered into the trench below. They howled and yipped as 'Ti Pouce helped us up, but they could not climb the trench walls.

"We're saved," 'Ti Pouce said.

"Not remotely," we said. We sniffed the wound at Margerine. "That'll turn to gangrene if we don't care for it soonish."

"We got medicinals at home to fix it."

"We used all the medicinals on Pers' stump. There is only one other place with medicinals."

A lone light shone in the dark of the waste: a sole yellow glimmer upon the tallest hill. With the coyooldes crying in the trench behind us, we walked toward the palazzo Gerol, bellies afull of hunger and fearbile.

The waste is almost as terrorfraidin a place as Fergetitland come dark. It was here the Dead Folks dumped all they no longer required: autos, coldboxes, metals, fakerock, mirrors, all that stuff they knew how to make and we didn't. They devoured the world, Mamons said of the Dead Folks, and left us nothing but bones. Well, not just bones. A few of their interventions survived. The fabupot was one of them. It let us turn the bones into vittles.

The palazzo light was made by the Dead Folks too. The yallow glimmer drew us up there just like a ratty corpses draws blackbills. Up and up we walked, us hurting more and more at Margerine. Many a time we considered just sitting there and dying. Hadn't we suffered enough to earn a nice long sleep in the dirt? But 'Ti Pouce wouldn't let us.

"You are Moyers," he said. "Four hundreds years our fam been mining the waste, and we never gave up then. We sure aren't going to start now."

At the top of the hill, 'Ti Pouce harangued us over to a fakestone bowl bigger than our whole hovel and had us lie deadlike beneath it.

"You seven stay quiet. I'll slip inside, steal the medicinals, find us some vittles, and then we scamper home. Give Pers and Mamons a knock on the headbone for abandoning us. Once you are healed we can find a new place."

We listened through the sounds of the dark. Yips of coyoodles, the slow gurgle of creeklets, the moaning of collapsing trenches. 'Ti Pouce could be quiet as sleep, if he wished to. There was hundreds of times he slipped out of our bed without us awakening to go commit some prank on Pers and Mamons. Bedclothes tied to mattress coils, moustache facepainted onto Mamons with sooties, Pers' wig replaced with a ratty corpse. It was just like one of those nights, we told ourselves even as we moaned at Margerine.

The roar must of awakened all the smerfs in the valley. The palazzo's front door opened and out ran 'Ti Pouce, arms full of vittles and medicinal jars. 'Ti Pouce was halfway to the fakestone bowl where we quieted when a huge shadow rolled out of the palazzo. Lor Gerol stood upon his seguer, another contraption of the Dead Folks, and he raced down upon 'Ti Pouce. The Lor snatched up our brother in a fist almost as fat as 'Ti Pouce was tall, took back his vittles and medicinals, and stuffed 'Ti Pouce in a sack. We stayed deadlike, even as Lor Gerol rolled around in front of his palazzo, sniffing at the air like a cancanlupan.

He was rolling back into the palazzo when we whined at Margerine.

"Do you misunderstand the meaning of barnished?" he said as he scooped us up at Danley and stuffed us into the sack with 'Ti Pouce. "I gave you a chance, you wretched cliquo. Now you are mine."

He dragged us into the pallazzo, the smell all frosting and frying fat and chocolate and sugarcake and citrus treats.

"'Tis all your fault, 'Ti Pouce," we whispered.

"Hushem," he said. "I'm working on listening."

Lor Gerol dropped us onto the ground hard enough to make each one of our mouths yowl.

"Awaken, me darlings," Lor Gerol's vocals roared. "And see the toys your loving father has procured for you."

The sack shook and out we tumbled onto the polished fakestone floor. A cut of light appeared as Lor Gerol pulled back curtains. The Dead Folks' light shone yallow and into that wedge of sickly illumination slipped seven fat faces.

"These seven plus one are yours until the first crow of the blackbill," Lor Gerol roared. "Come morn, they'll be breakfast for the whole clan. The little one I won't even feed to the fabupot. Him I'll pickle in slurpee and suck his meat off his bones."

Doormetal locked behind Lor Gerol. Those fat faces squealed with delight. We tried to axesplain that we was injured, that we required assistance, but they cared none. They started right into their fun. They had we seven do jigs for them, while they stuffed their faces with cheesiepuffs and cakelet. They made 'Ti Pouce swing from the curtains.

"Kindly cliquo Gerol," 'Ti Pouce said after his performance. "'Tis the last night of repose my seven brothers and sisters will ever see, and they never slept on a true bed. Could you find it in your seven beating hearts to offer them this one terminal kindness?"

The Gerols thinking looks awful like the Gerols eating, probably on account of they were eating while they were thinking.

"We've come upon our conclusion," they said. "Tell us seven jokes, cliquo Moyers, and provided each joke be funnier than the previous, you shall sleep your last upon our bed. Don't think we need to axesplain what'll be the outcome should laughter not be tickled from us."

"Would it be impertinent of me," 'Ti Pouce said. "To ask to serve you vittles while my cliquo amuses you?"

"'Twould be impertinent for you not to feed us."

'Ti Pouce served vittles while we tried to remember what jokes 'Ti Pouce had favored us with over our years, and then to rank them in order of hilarity.

"Whatfor does the cancanlupan howl?" we said, starting with the unfunniest.

"Dunno."

They groaned at the puncher.

"Better be funnier next one," the cliquo said around mouthfuls of cakelet.

Next one was this: "Why did the blackbill fly over the creeklet?"

"Unknown to us."

"Cause if he'd waded through his legs woulda melted off."

That seemed to tickle them.

"How about that longish joke," 'Ti Pouce said. "The one about the waste miner who discovers a magic auto?"

We knew it, but it was long, longer than it takes for the moon to transverse our bedroom window, but if 'Ti Pouce asked it, there was a reason.

"There was once a waste miner name of Orfeo," we started, and on we continued with the long joke. The cliquo Gerol had their fourteen legs dangling sidewise from their bed, the legs swinging and kicking. They was still beving slurpee and mashing vittles, but as we unspooled the joke, they slowed. Each mouthful took minutes to swallow. Six of their fourteen eyes was closing, and we was terrifraid they would find this joke no funnier than the last. Our telling slowed too, but 'Ti Pouce whipped us on with: "And then?" and "Whatever happens nextish?" and "Continue, cliquo!", so on telling we went.

Now we arrived at the puncher: "The magic auto drove off and left Orfeo's head at the crossroads."

Not a chuckle or guffaw to be heard. Nought but snoring. Our marrow ran cold. Then a laugh did start in the dark, the laugh of our wee big brother.

"You done it, my brothers and sisters!" he said. He pulled back the curtains and the yallow glimmer shone on seven faces asnoring on their huge bed. 'Ti Pouce held up a cakelet: a single medicinal pellet was pressed into the thick frosting. "Now out we go!"

We started for the door when out on the waste a blackbill squawked. Our telling had taken too long.

"Yer time is at an end, cliquo Moyer!" the Lor roared. "Finish up, my darlings. I'll porridge them soonish."

'Ti Pouce stood by the door terrifraiding. "We're to be transformered."

"Maybe not," said we, for an idea had been passing between our seven brains and we spoke it now. 'Ti Pouce laughed again and we went to work, going as fast and as quiet as we could. We dragged the cliquo Gerol to the floor where the Lor had tossed us. 'Ti Pouce shredded their bedsheets into ropes and we tied their legs together, transformering the cliquo Gerol from a fourteen-legged creature to an octopod like us. We then climbed onto the bed, a more comfortable experience we never knew, while 'Ti Pouce snapped off bedposts and headboard and we added six leggies to our eight. He stuffed raggies into the mouthbits of the sleeping cliquo Gerol.

"But the yellow glimmer," we said. "The Lor will see 'Tis his cliquo on the floor and us bedwise."

'Ti Pouce crawled out the window and in a blink it was dark all round the palazzo Gerol.

He squirmed back into the bedregion and shuttered the window as the Lor's footsteps echoed outside the door.

"Hide under the bed, brother," we whispered.

'Ti Pouce shook his head. "The Lor is expecting a weency one as well as a clique-de-sept. You hear the fabupot, you run. Your brother will caretake of himself."

That door opened and the stink of Lor Gerol, all glazing sweet and slurpee-wine sour, filled up the bedregion.

"For the sake of all the Christlings," Lor Gerol roared. "What has happened to my yallow glimmer?"

"Take them away, Dada," 'Ti Pouce said, throwing his voice so it seemed to come bedwise. "We hate having the mean cliquo with us in the dark."

"Hushem, me darlings. Dad will erase your troublings."

We listened, feeling sick in all seven of our bellies, as Lor Gerol stuffed 'Ti Pouce and his own cliquo into the sack. He dragged the sack out of the bedregion. We waited until we heard the beeping of the fabupot before we sneaked out of the bed, and for a moment we considered running into the throneplace to assist our brother, but then all the children Moyers would be vittles, so instead we ran out the big door of the palazzo.

A pale misty had arisen over the waste. We clattered down the road, the whole time considering whether we would ever see our wee big brother again. He'd saved us, he had, and here we were, running away from his demise. How we hated ourself.

Down we tumbled into the dust and started weeping.

"Onward, cliquo," our wee big brother said as he ran by. "Before the Lor uncovers his error."

Overjoyed, we ran after him. 'Ti Pouce carried a great mound of vittles and he dropped a pie or biggiemac on the road behind him as he ran. We wanted to eatum, but by then we knew to trust the strange exertions of our wee big brother.

"Me darlings!" the Lor roared clear enough for us to hear a klick away, and it was coming closer. "Me darlings!"

We was too slow. Our wee big brother was doomed because of our cruddy pace.

"Continue without us," we said. "We will only get us all killed."

"Never," he said. "We Moyers stand together."

We found a nearby trenchlet and tossed ourself in. "Run, big brother. Find yer better place."

He considered for long moments. The Lor's roaring was upon us: "He'll pay, the runtling will."

"I'll return for you," 'Ti Pouce said, and he ran.

The Lor roared on: "I'll flay the flesh from his bone and turn it to pork rinds."

The grind of the seguer wheels crunched down the hill and ceased near us. The sky was blotted by the vast shape of the Lor.

"Wherefor is your runtling brother?"

"We'll never say."

He roared out laughter. "He's dropped his vittles, the greedy creep has. Don't move, cliquo. I'll return for you once I've turned his testicules to gobstoppers."

The sky unblotted and the seguer wheels resumed, and soon the Lor Gerol's roaring disappeared toward Fergetitland.

We waited in the trenchlet all through smoglight, but he never returned. 'Ti Pouce neither.

It was dark when we climbed out and returned to the hovel Moyers. Pers and Mamons were overcome with weeping when we approached. Mamons kissed us on all of our cheeks while Pers checked us over from the footbone at Danley to the headbone at Margerine. Both of them was terrifraid of the wounding at Margerine, and they forced us to the mattress, where Mamons dabbed hot raggies on the wounding while Pers digged out on the yard, and returned with a vat of medicinals.

"Wherefor is my runtling?"

"Unknown," we said. The medicinals were pushing us slumberwise. "The Lor chased him to Fergetitland."

We awakened the next morning to find the hovel afull of vittles. Frittes of all kinds, cakelets, chocolates, sacks of slurpee both boozed and virginian.

"The fabupot's been running morn, smoglight, and dark," Pers said as he beved iceyscreamy. "Lor Gerol must not have stoppered it in the haste of his departure."

We feasted like never we feasted before, but it was no happy feast, for we couldn't share it with our wee big brother.

Weeks passed, then months, then seasonings. The fabupot transformered Lor Gerol's palazzo into vittles, and then started on the hill on which it stood. The days was filled with feasting on account of our liberation from the tyrant Gerol, but that was no consolation, for the Lor took 'Ti Pouce with him. Pers and Mamons tried to cheer us with jokes and vittle combinations, and they enfattened like we never seen them, but it was no use.

A year to the day of the Lor's disappearance, the smerf families in the Valley Gerol organized a festival to celebrate the overdue arrival of the stork-o-fortuna. Pers and Mamons begged us to join them, but we wouldn't go.

From the hovel, we could see what remained of the hill where the palazzo Gerol once stood. Now it was just a pile of vittles. Pers and Mamons walked down the road, her fat arm on his stump.

A coyoodle yipped in Fergetitland. It made the old wound at Margerine ache. We returned bedwise and lay there, entroubled, when we heard a sound we could never unremember: seguer wheels on hard ground.

It was Lor Gerol, we knew with certaintude, arrived to devour us. The raggies parted and a wee figure stepped in.

"My brothers and sisters!" said a voice five times larger than its owner.

We leaped from bed and snatched our wee big brother up in all our arms. Near crushed him and soggied his fine new shirt with our weepings.

"Where you been?" we seven said.

'Ti Pouce told all.

When Lor Gerol dumped the sack containing his own asnoozed cliquo into the fabupot, 'Ti Pouce danced and quirmed to stay out of the transformering hole. The Lor returned to his bedchamber, and only then could 'Ti Pouce slide out of the sack. He scooped up medicinals and vittles that had once been cliquo Gerol and ran until he found us. After we jumped into the trenchlet, Lor Gerol followed the trail of medicinated vittles 'Ti Pouce left for him into Fergetitland. When 'Ti Pouce dropped his last vittle, he hid way up in a spindly. Lor Gerol rolled in on his seguer not long afterwise. The Lor leaned that machine up against the spindly where 'Ti Pouce was acowered, and he sat his giant sitbones in the dirt. "Turn your blood to slurpee wine," was the last thing Lor Gerol said before he stuffed another medicinated donut mouthwise and aslumbered.

'Ti Pouce waited longish, then hopped down from the spindly and stole Lor Gerol's seguer. 'Ti Pouce is wee and Lor Gerol hugeish, but the seguer's controlpole shrunk right down for 'Ti Pouce and off he rolled into Fergetitland.

"Why didn't you return to us?" we said.

"Why was you aslumbered upon my return?" he said. "It was the night after we fled the palazzo. You was sleeping on your stitched together mattresses, Pers and Mamons weeping over you. Everything regandered correctish, so I departed."

"Where for?"

"The world, me cliquo." And with that, 'Ti Pouce gifted us a sack. Inside was orange stickies and reddish lumps. "Carrots and apples. Real vittles, not fabbed. Eatum."

The carrots was dry, but the apples crunched and juiced most wondrously. 'Ti pouce stood still in the door raggies.

"You're departing, aren't you?"

"Come with me," he said. "There's so many places and things to show you."

We regandered around our hovel: the chair where Pers sat to think, the washbasin where we washed ourselves, Mamons' stack-o-magazines, all our paperwords on a rack, and at the base of our stitched together mattress, the weency 'Ti Pouce-shaped indentation.

"Here is where we belong."

"I was affeared to hear it, but 'tis not unexpected. I'll return at least once yearly. I'll bring gifts for my brothers and sisters."

"And tales. Bring us tales."

We regandered from the hovel as 'Ti Pouce rolled into Fergetitland. The wind had never felt so cold, nor the waste so empty.

We was still there some time later when a smerf fam wandered up the road from the festival. The young patron and matron carried a waifish child with a stunted leg between them.

"You the cliquo Moyer?" the matron of the smerf fam said.

"Seen any other clique-de-septs around here?"

They placed some vittles from the festival and a hand-wound rope at our feet.

"Could we ask your blessing?"

The cold still afflicted us, but the wind didn't seem so frigid.

"Take up your things," we said. "We are blessed as we are."

We touched their child upon her stunted leg and gave her blessings of health and growth, then gave them instructions to care for the girl we remembered from old paperwords.

It was dark when Pers and Mamons returned from the festival. We never told them of 'Ti Pouce's visit, not that one, nor the others that followed over the years. For certain they asked about the gifts gifted to us, but we said it was from the fams who pilgrimaged to our hovel for blessings and medimangling.

As the seasonings change, we sit out front of the hovel on a special chair 'Ti Pouce brought for us, listening for the sound of seguer wheels in Fergetitland. We have to listen hard, for further down the valley the fabupot churns and churns as it transformers the world into vittles.

Desolation Sounds

A kilometer from the Nanaimo marina, Priscilla Patel's fiancé pulled the truck to the curb, took off his bandanna and blindfolded her.

"Got a surprise for you, baby girl," he said, catching her hair in the knot.

"You know I love surprises, Daddy," she lied, and sipped her can of Chardonnay.

"Are you two going to be this gross the whole trip?" said Evan, her future son-in-law, from the back seat.

Darren laughed. "You ain't see nothing yet, kiddo."

Her stomach sloshed as the truck lurched into motion. Old rock and roll on the radio. Darren smelled like Eaux-de-White-Man-on-Vacation: cigarillos and beer. Eighteen-year-old Evan put out a miasma of Axe body-spray and unwashed socks. She could barely smell the smoke coming in through the vents.

"The McKenly's called," Darren said. "They won't be able to join us."

"Oh no. Why not?"

"Guess the insurance on their Whistler place doesn't cover wildfires. Diana said you gave her the heads-up."

He waited, and in that silence she guessed what he was thinking: how did she, the oldest waitress working the loudest bar on Vancouver Island, know anything about wildfire insurance?

Priscilla could smell the case-law books in the Nahum Gelber law library at McGill, could hear Rajesh chewing his pen as he studied. But no. Those weren't her memories. They belonged to that other girl, who had that other name, and that girl had been gone a long time. She was Priscilla now, and Priscilla was a party girl.

"Saw it on Insta. Too bad they can't come — Diana is so much fun!"

"Better that way." Darren sounded relieved. "We can celebrate your birthday just the three of us. Our first real family vacation. Hey, we're at the marina. Time for the surprise."

Darren helped her out of the car and led her by hand. The smoke smell was brighter here, astringent, like plastic was burning along with all those trees. Dozens of boats made gentle knocking sounds. Not popping sounds, she told herself.

"Ready?" Darren said.

The bandanna came off with a chunk of her hair.

"Shit, sorry baby."

"Got a little problem here," she said. She couldn't open her left eye. The bandanna had gummed up her false lashes and she had to get Darren to help her peel them off. When she could see again, she found Evan was doing his best Vanna White beside the shittiest sail boat in the marina. It was smaller than all the rest, the paint along its sides was peeling where it wasn't covered in grime, and even from here, she knew it would stink.

"I know we planned on renting," Darren said. "But I bought us a whole boat for less than it cost to rent for one week. What do you think?"

She thought it might not make it out of the harbor. But that was the old her. Party Girl didn't care.

"I love it."

"I even had it renamed."

On the back of the boat, stenciled in curling black letters was "Coffee and Cream," complete with the silhouette of a naked woman reclining on a shark.

"I'm the cream," he said, big and sunburnt and smiling like an idiot.

"I'm your coffee."

"And I never want to start another day without you." He swooped her up in his arms. She laughed, amazed by his cheerful obliviousness and unwavering adoration. He spun her, pressed tobacco-tasting lips to hers, set her down, and handed her a bottle of Prosecco.

Pop, pop, pop, she thought. The scars on her palms itched.

With the speed of long practice, she peeled off the foil and was twisting off the cage holding the cork when he grabbed her wrist.

"Not for drinking, baby. For the boat. For luck!"

She barked the dumb-girl laugh he liked.

The *Coffee and Cream* was a little too far from the dock, so Evan and Darren held onto her belt while she leaned over the water.

"I christen thee good ship *Coffee and Cream*," she said, and swung the bottle. Fibreglass crunched. The bottle didn't break: it punched into the hull and wedged in the hole it made. She windmilled her arms, about to fall into the cold Salish Sea, when her men pulled her back to steadier ground.

"Looks like someone fired it from a cannon," Evan said.

Darren laughed, Priscilla joined in, and soon the three of them had tears streaming down their faces.

Darren inspected the bottle and the wound it had punched in the boat.

"Looks ship-shape to me," he said. "Let's see if we can find some wind."

Priscilla danced in the smoke-haze at the front of the boat. The engine chugged behind them, spewing more fumes into an atmosphere already rebelling against hundreds of years of industrialization. No, she forced herself away from those thoughts, tried to lose herself in the music pumping from the Bluetooth speaker clipped to the guardrail. Party Girl doesn't give a shit about climate change. Party Girl wants to dance.

And dancing felt good. Though it was a little chilly, she wore her bikini for Darren, who was grinning around his cigarillo from behind the wheel, looking happier than she'd ever seen him. She blew him a kiss. Then the speaker chirped twice, announced its batteries were dead, and went silent.

She swore, and when she bent to try to coax it back to life, found Evan looking up at her from the hatch leading down into her cabin. How long had he been watching her dance? She pulled Darren's old BC Lions hoodie over her shoulders.

Evan jabbed a finger out of the hatch. "Is that the fjord Dad's talking about?" he said. Beyond the boat there was only smoke. "You can just see the shape of the mountains."

They were motoring away from Vancouver Island toward the mainland. The big fire crawling toward Whistler had turned the horizon a uniform smoker's-lung beige. Straight ahead, she could make out the hint of mountains forming a rough V down to the sea.

"You been here before?" she said, but her future step-son had disappeared. Video game beeps rose from the claustrophobic space below deck.

Priscilla zipped up Darren's hoodie and stumbled over to the cracked pleather seats beside Darren at the back of the boat.

"He was staring at me again."

"Brown girl in a two-piece," he said, flashing her the grin that had so dazzled her when they met six months earlier, she mixing cocktails, he buying more than he could handle for the excuse to talk to her. "I'd be worried about any eighteen-year old boy who wasn't staring."

"I'm going to be his stepmother."

"You two get along like gangbusters. Relax. Have a drink. Wine or beer?"

He flipped open the cooler beside him.

"I choose wine."

He handed her a skinny can.

"Been wanting to check out this place for years," he said. "Bet we'll have the whole bay to ourselves. Everyone goes to Desolation Sound, no one comes here." He cracked a beer, sipped, smacked his lips in appreciation. "The Salish used to hunt whales here, know that? Greys, not orcas. They'd chase a mother and a calf into the bay, block the entrance. Enough meat to feed the tribe for months."

That big toothed smile. Him looking at her like he expected an answer.

Party Girl came up with: "Fucking barbaric."

"Baby girl, you can't say that about our First Nation friends."

She took her cannabis vape from her fanny pack and had a long drag. "Killing whales is barbaric."

"They're just big fish and we're gonna eat fish all week." He slid a tackle box out from under his seat and gestured for her to open it. Fishing lures in little compartments sparkled in the smoky light. On top of the lures was a long, curved filleting knife in a yellow plastic sheath. "The rule on this boat is the rookie does the gutting and cleaning. We'll see who's barbaric."

She shut the box. Slowly unzipped his hoodie, let it fall onto her seat. "You wouldn't make a nice little girl slice up a nasty old fish, would you Daddy?"

"Get a room," Evan said.

He was staring at them from the cabin.

"Don't be a pervert," she said.

"For fuck's sake," Darren said, shading his eyes as he looked ahead.

The smoke seemed thinner as they slid into the bay, like she was looking at the scene through dirty glasses. Pine studded mountains fell to the sea at a sharp angle. At the far end of the bay, a creek flowed out over a pebble beach.

"What's wrong?"

"We're not alone," Darren said.

An old boat was anchored near the beach. Once, it might have been a high-end cabin cruiser, with two decks, a lounge at the back, but now it made their crappy sailboat look brand new. The way the derelict swayed, with its left side low in the water, made her think of Uncle Pranav at her first wedding, who'd drunk so much Chivas he stumbled at such an angle to the car his wife kept insisting he shouldn't drive. Dark grime crawled up the hull of the wreck from the waterline, like it hadn't been cleaned in years.

"Don't think we have to worry about company," Evan said. "No one's staying on that thing."

"Fucking irresponsible boat owners," Darren said. "We can report the derelict next time we have cell service." He cut the engine. The *Coffee and Cream* drifted into the bay opposite the derelict. "Let's anchor, drop the crab trap, then we'll go check out the beach, find some clams to go with the crabs."

Darren tossed the metal crab trap into the water. As it disappeared, Priscilla thought she saw movement below: swift, longer than a salmon. A seal, maybe? Sea lion? She hoped Darren didn't plan on adding one of those to the menu.

⁂

"Geez," Evan said. "What happened to the trap?"

The crab trap looked like it had been crushed by a bus. The remains of several unfortunate crustaceans twitched in the bent and twisted metal, and a stinking black substance, oil or mud, coated the cage.

"What could have done that?" she said.

"Underwater rock fall?" Darren said. Bits of crab meat splattered onto the grungy fiberglass deck. "Maybe we dragged the anchor over it?"

Priscilla didn't buy either explanation. There was no wind in the smoke; the only thing moving the boat was the tide. They'd had no better luck clamming. Everywhere they dug, they came up with cracked shellfish, the animals inside dead or dying, not a single healthy mollusc in the hundreds they'd found. Not that she would have eaten anything if they had been successful. There was a stink in the air, worse than the acrid smoke from Whistler's burning condominiums and Volvos: a sweet, rotten smell seeping from the derelict anchored on the other side of the bay.

"I don't want to stay here," she said.

The sun sat red and angry between the steep mountain walls. If they left now, they would still have some daylight to find better moorage.

"You worried about the fire, baby girl?" Darren said. "It can't get us here. Even if it crawled over all those mountains, we're safe on the water."

Priscilla regretted telling her fiancé about her fear of fires. It hewed too close to the old her, the her she never wanted him to know.

"It's not that. This place is so boring."

"I don't like it either, Dad," Evan said.

Darren held up an empty can of Phillips. "I'm already four cans in. These IPAs kick like an angry donkey. We'll set sail first thing in the AM. Evan, put some water on for pasta."

The kid grunted and ducked down into the cabin, while Darren bent over the crab trap and tried to bend it back into shape.

Priscilla squatted beside him.

"Daddy," she said in her baby voice, trailing a finger down his forearm. "If you sail us out of here now, I'll make it worth your while."

He swore, pulled his hand away from the trap. A bright pearl of blood appeared on an index finger stained black by the strange gunk. With a sick clarity, she knew what he was going to do before he did it but wasn't fast enough to stop him. Darren stuffed his bleeding finger into his mouth and sucked.

"Shit!" he said, spitting out a mouthful of bloody saliva. "Oh God, that tastes awful. Get me a bandage, would you?"

She climbed down below deck. Evan had a big pot of water going on the electric range. Video-game noises piped from Evan's tiny cabin under the stairs. She found what had to be the world's oldest first aid kit in the bathroom cabinet.

A big splash from above.

She hurried, the image of Darren falling in filled her mind, her all alone with his creepy son on this piece-of-shit boat, but her fiancé was behind the wheel, cut hand stuffed into the beer cooler.

"Chucked the trap," he said, sipping another Philips. "It was ruined anyway. Think you could rinse off the deck? My hand really hurts."

"Here," she said, sifting through her fanny pack. She handed him a cannabis gummy shaped like a salmon and took one for herself. "It will help with the pain."

He hesitated. "Those things knock me out."

"It's low dose," she lied, counting on the salmon putting him to sleep. The thought of those crab-stained hands on her body later that night made her skin crawl. He took the candy. "I'll clean up the deck. Take care of your cut, Daddy."

She grabbed a bucket from under a seat and filled it with sea water. In the smoke-reddened light, the blood and crab-bits looked black, and there was too much of it. No matter how many buckets she poured over the stains, they wouldn't come out.

~

By the time Evan finished cooking dinner, a sophisticated task that included straining the pasta over the side of the boat, opening a glass jar of grocery-store pasta sauce, and dumping it over the steaming noodles, Darren was swooning. The gummy shouldn't have kicked in yet — Priscilla didn't feel hers — but he was pale, and had a dumb grin on his face as he tucked a napkin into his shirt.

The three of them crowded around the galley table in the cabin. Darren raised his wine glass, sloshing cheap red onto the table, and said: "To my three favourite people!"

They clinked glasses, drank.

Darren dumped Parmesan from the green plastic shaker, most of it missing his plate.

"Pasta à la Evano," he said, twirling spaghetti onto his fork. Well done, lad."

Father and son tucked into the meal but all Priscilla could do was push the noodles around. Mysterious chunks in the sauce made her think of crab guts.

"What water did you cook this in?"

"Sea water," Evan said. He had a headphone over one ear, while too-fast music chirped out of the other headphone into the cabin. "Don't you like it?"

"Feeling a little sea-sick."

"Wine helps," Darren said, topping up both their glasses. "I want you ship-shape later tonight."

"Gross, Dad," Evan said, and pulled the other headphone over his ear.

Darren clapped him on the shoulder while running a foot up Priscilla's leg.

"I think you've had enough wine."

"You're right. I'm ready for dessert."

Evan picked up his bowl and carried it into his tiny cabin under the stairs.

"Time for coffee and cream," Darren said, running a finger up her forearm. Blood seeped through the bandage on his cut finger.

"Evan will hear us."

"Not over that racket." He snatched up her hand, his fingers like ice, and kissed the scars on her palms. She went rigid. "I'm gonna make you squeak."

The boat rolled hard. Darren stumbled out of his seat, a huge man in the little cabin, and landed on his rear just shy of the range, the wind blowing out of him in a boozy gale. Laughter followed. Hers too.

When she helped him up, some warmth had flowed back into his hands.

"Let's get you to bed."

She aimed his bulk for their cabin.

"I'm still good to go."

"Of course you are."

※

Darren moaned on top of her.

"Quiet."

"Kid's music is louder than a Limp Biscuit concert," he said, panting. "He won't hear a thing. Get on top."

He flopped onto the bed.

Rearranging themselves in the cramped cabin at the front of the boat made Priscilla lose whatever interest she still had in making love but Darren was raring to go. She closed her eyes and did her best.

Once he was done, he'd pass out, and she could have a little peace. Maybe watch one of those shows she'd dowloaded? She bounced in a way he loved, threw in a few "Oh Daddys." The moans below her deepened. Maybe she'd try out the shower. Have a Percocet first. It would be nice to get Darren's smell off and wash the smoke out of her hair. No, don't think about the smoke. Get this over with, then Party Girl can have her private Percocet party. But this was taking longer than normal. She opened her eyes.

Darren's eyes were bloodshot, bulging, and his face was purple. The hands on her hips spasmed with what she thought was orgasm but was something else entirely.

"Daddy?" she said, sliding off him, putting a hand to his forehead. So hot she pulled her hand away. "Jesus, Darren, what's wrong?"

He coughed. Spittle frothed from his lips. He rolled onto his side, one hand pumping his tumescent cock, the other clutching his chest.

She covered him with the duvet then lunged for her phone. It told her she had no signal and promptly ran out of battery.

"Goddamn it!" she said. She'd meant to charge the thing in the car. She maneuvered through the cramped kitchen and hammered on Evan's door. "Your Dad's in trouble. I need help!"

No answer. She went over to the radio slotted into the wall beside the electric range and started flicking buttons. She couldn't even get the power on. As she tried to work the thing, she kept shouting Evan's name, and eventually she heard him step out of his cabin behind her.

"Jesus," he said. "Put some pants on."

She was only wearing her brassiere. Swearing, she grabbed Darren's hoody, slipped it on, then said: "Your Dad is having a heart attack or something. Do you know how to use the radio?"

"It's busted. What do you mean he's having a heart attack?"

A chasm opened up inside her. Part of that was the cannabis gummy but the other part was a deeper dread: she couldn't go through this again. Not after all the work she'd done.

"Give me your phone."

He clutched his phone close to his chest. She lunged for it, held it to his face so it would unlock.

On screen, an Indian woman was sucking off a white guy.

"You little pervert," she said, swiping away the porn. She tried to call 911 as she rushed back to their cabin but an error message sang in her ear. "What's wrong with this?"

"No reception out here."

"Then what do we do?"

Darren whimpered. Priscilla and Evan both rushed to his side. He was sticky with sweat, foam poured from his mouth, pulse racing, the veins on his skull throbbed like worms were crawling beneath his skin.

The boat tilted again, this time rolling in the other direction, and all three of them were tossed about. Evan ended up on top of her, his hands fluttering over her bare legs. She shoved him off and went back to Darren's side.

"For. Fuck's. Sake," Darren said between gritted teeth.

Evan leaned over his father and took his hand, asking what was wrong, getting no answer.

But Darren's utterance had knocked loose a thought in Priscilla's mind. Hadn't he said the same thing when he spotted the other boat in this awful bay?

It was ready to sink, a derelict, but maybe, just maybe, it would have a radio.

M

The inflatable buzzed through the weak puddle of light cast by the phone flashlight. Priscilla still struggled with the steering: you had to push the handle opposite the direction you wanted to go. With the cannabis salmon swimming through her brain, she had a hard time keeping that flip switched, and it didn't help that she was steering one-handed while holding up Evan's gross phone.

The LED light only reached a few meters ahead, illuminating smoke that seemed so much thicker now than it had in daylight. Every few seconds, she cast a nervous glance over her shoulder, looking for the red and green lights on the *Coffee and Cream*. To her great relief, even when the shape of the poorly-named boat disappeared into the darkness, she could still find those twin beacons.

She should be near the derelict by now. She stopped the motor, let herself drift, swung the light in a slow circle around her, then cut it to to see if that helped. Darkness so all-encompassing it took her breath away. She could smell burning tires, feel the immense wall of heat consuming her old life. Pop. Pop. Pop. The words of a dozen therapists echoed in her mind: "Breathe through it." "Feel the pain, then let it go." "Grief is a process you have to live through." All so much bullshit. She sucked on her vape, felt the swirling reassurance of the cannabis lighting up her mind. She was Party Girl. She chose wine. She and Darren would laugh about this next month over a box of Pinot Grigio. She turned the flashlight back on.

Two brown eyes on oily, black stalks gazed at her from the water. They startled in the light, slid back below the surface, twin concentric rings spreading from the spot they disappeared. But that couldn't be. Nothing on this Earth had eyes like that. It had to be the old trauma, worming its way back into her brain after all these years.

Now a sound in the darkness. Her name.

"Have you found it?" Evan shouted.

Found what? In the cannabis and alcohol haze, she forgot what she was doing out here.

Water sloshed against the little inflatable. Creaking and the slap of waves on something else nearby. And wasn't there a stink wafting from that direction?

She turned the motor on, charged ahead.

Seconds later, the grimy wall of the derelict emerged from the smoke. She swerved to avoid it — you have to push the handle opposite the — but she never finished the thought.

The inflatable rammed into the derelict and tossed her into the dark, stinking water.

₪

"We don't need the wine," Rajesh said.

She wanted to agree with her husband, wanted to crawl into the backseat of the Toyota beside the baby, make sure Ravi was snug in his car seat. Her feet betrayed her.

"It will only take a minute," she heard herself say, and heard herself think: Rajesh, you paid fifty dollars for each of these bottles at the tastings, no way we're leaving them behind.

Waddling out of the rental home with the box of wine, the horizon burned. Hot wind carried the raw stink of the smoke. Her husband stood at the Toyota, urging her onward. Why wasn't she running? The box, with its dozen bottles, was too heavy.

You need these seconds, she shouted silently at the girl. *They need these seconds.*

The wine went into the back seat, belted in next to Ravi's car seat. Now she was in the passenger seat and they drove through the inferno. Fire ignited the pines on either side of the highway. Taillights on the cars ahead wavered in the heat. She fiddled with the air conditioning, tried to stop it pumping the black smoke into the cabin that was making the baby cry.

Screeching brakes. Her head ricocheted off the dash. And when she was next aware, she was outside the car, choking and crying in the fire-wind. One of those burning pines lay across the Toyota's hood. She didn't feel hot. She was cold, so cold. Burning pine tar dripped onto the car. She was trying to open her husband's door, the baby's door, but neither would budge. The metal steamed from the heat. Strips of her skin stuck to the handles.

People pulled her away from the burning Toyota. Strangers, trying to save her.

Watching, Priscilla remembered hating them so much. *Let me burn with my family*, she'd thought.

As they dragged her back into a stranger's car, a popping sound from the Toyota. The wine bottles. Fifty dollars each. Boiling and exploding in the heat.

Priscilla gasped out of the flames. No, not flames. An ocean so cold, so biting, it burned. Smoke and rot-stinking air. Behind her, the electric buzz of the inflatable as it shot off into the darkness. Beneath it, the pop, pop, pop of the wine.

"No," she said to the black ocean.

No.

The gentle slap of waves on wood. The derelict. She swam toward the sound, brushed against the barnacle-encrusted hull. She found no purchase against the alternating slick and cutting surface so she kept swimming until she found the lower end of the boat. Arms so weak from the cold. With a scream, she pulled herself in, landed gasping, her whole body wracked with shivers.

I won't lose another life, she told herself. *Not even this shitty one.*

She rose onto all fours. The deck was slick and treacherous in the pitch darkness. Her head swam with wine and cannabis and visions of burning tar, and at first she thought the lights swimming in the sky were more hallucination. Twinkling Diwali lights. The *Coffee and Cream*. And in the smoke-muted air, Evan was screaming her name. The pervert must be terrified. She tried to answer but was shivering too much for words, so she shrieked instead. A war cry.

She needed light. She had a lighter in her fanny pack, but when she reached for her bag of remedies, she discovered her fanny pack was gone — it must have fallen off when she hit the derelict — and with it went all of Party Girl's best tricks. She shrieked again.

Moving like a shattered crab, using her hands as antennae, she felt her way around the stinking boat. Gas tank. Cold engines. Tumbled life jackets. A discarded wetsuit. Oars. Wine bottle. Pop. Pop. "No." A surf board. Now, stairs leading upward. The captain would have sat up there. If there was a radio, that's where she would find it, but she didn't trust the stairs in this slanted darkness. She needed light.

Big doors into the main cabin flapped open. The space beyond felt larger than the cabin of the *Coffee and Cream* and it reeked of rotting fish, rotting meat. Death.

Get out of here, she thought. *Get the hell out.*

She took a last breath of the fresher air and stepped in.

If it had been dark on deck, inside it was a crypt. The reek made her gag. A faint buzzing sound from deeper within. Insects? Her antennae-hands felt ahead. A door, maybe to a bathroom.

"You call it a head on a boat," Darren's voice said, like he was there in the derelict with her.

The smell inside septic. She moved on. Felt soft upholstery. A table.

"The mess," Darren said.

"Shut up," she said. The old her heard voices, but not Priscilla. Not Party Girl.

The table was set. Fork, knife, wine glass. A plate. On it, soft tissue, wriggling maggots. She pulled her hand away, fought the urge to vomit. What was that? Rare steak? Uncooked chicken?

But when she'd pulled her hand away, she'd knocked over what felt like a candlestick. Clenching her teeth against the nausea, she reached back to the table, careful to stay away from the plate and its writhing contents. Salt or sugar was scattered across the table. She found the candlestick. Who would burn candles on a boat? Pop. Pop. She shrieked away from the sound.

Little remained of the candle but she felt around the salt-covered table, found four more burned-to-the-nub candles in heavy, mismatched candlesticks. No matches or lighter. A picture of the cabin was forming in her mind. Mess and head on one side, did that mean the little kitchen — "we call it a galley, baby girl" —

sat opposite? Crouch-walking up the slight incline to the opposite wall, her fingers found a three-ring binder open on a counter, a pencil, and there, the folded card stock of a matchbook.

With a sob of relief, she opened it. Three matches. The first flared to life, a nova in that darkness, and she brought it to the wick of the best candle. Fire, in this tinder-box? "Stop." She went back to the table.

Maggots frothed on the fine china plate. The salt had been laid out in a careful pattern, letters or symbols from a language she couldn't recognize. The chill that walked up her spine had nothing to do with the frigid waters of the bay.

She tried to light the other candles but only two would take a flame. She wouldn't have long. Back at the counter, she grabbed the three-ring binder, expecting to find maps or — a silly hope — some kind of booklet from a rental company with precise instructions on what to do in an emergency. The binder contained something else entirely. The pages alternated between photocopies of an old manuscript written in a severe, incomprehensible language and sheets of lined paper covered in handwritten notes. A translation?

She flipped to the front of the binder. In the same careful handwriting, someone had written a poem:

> *Oh Slthaulos, greatest benthic lord*
> *I offer thee flesh and prayer*
> *Crush me in your darkest depths*
> *Fill me with your cold and void*
> *Remake me as your perfect pet*
> *End this ceaseless noise*

Several of the pages were illustrated with occult images: glyphs and symbols like those written in salt on the table, the limb of a lobster or shrimp or mantis, and on the last page, a drawing of a dissected human torso. Stark lines identified organs in the cadaver.

She raised the candle, looked past the table with its salt-symbol and terrible meal, to a corridor that lead deeper into the derelict. Through one of the open doorways in the corridor, she thought she saw someone lying on a bed.

Priscilla closed the binder, slipped it into the dry bag on which it had been sitting, and tucked it under her arm. In the drug and alcohol haze, she watched herself from outside her body as she stepped toward the open cabin, where someone's leg and foot rested on stained sheets.

"Hello?" she croaked, though she knew there would be no answer. The stink grew worse. Sweet decay. Whoever was on that bed was dead, she was sure of it, even before she stepped across the threshold and raised the candle high.

The woman had been sliced from sternum to waist, skin peeled back carefully. Flies and maggots feasted. Priscilla could almost see the lines pointing to the various organs, the indecipherable script describing each. A plastic bag over the woman's head was tied tight at the neck. Priscilla hoped with everything in her that the woman had been suffocated before she'd been cut.

In that moment, Priscilla knew she wouldn't find a radio or sat phone on this boat. Whoever had done this — some idiot, evil man, she was sure — didn't want any connection to the outside world. She stepped away from the dead woman, trying not to breathe, and made for the door.

Outside, the smoke stink was worse. Wine bottles popped. Flames tickled her peripheral vision. Her candle cast a dim pool of light across the deck. There was the surf board, the cold engine, the gas tank, the pile of life jackets, the wetsuit.

But no, that was no wetsuit. Wetsuits didn't have hair. Wetsuits didn't have fine freckles down their forearms. Didn't have fingernails. But like a wetsuit, the discarded skin lying on the deck was empty. Holes where the eyes had been. A great tear along the spine where the skin had split. Where something had crawled out.

Priscilla thought of those eyes she'd seen looking at her from the water before she crashed. None of this could be real. This came from the old her. She was breaking, falling back into the dark place she'd been in for so many years.

She lifted the empty skin, surprisingly heavy, and stared into those empty sockets. It felt so real.

"Priscilla!" Evan screamed.

"I'm here," she said, a whisper. Then shouted it. "Still here. I'm coming, Evan. Stay with your father."

She let the discarded skin slump to the deck. Careful not to tip the candle, she placed it in a cup holder while she got the stand-up surf board out and tucked the dry-bag under the cargo-straps. She leaned on the long paddle and considered the dark opening back into the cabin.

Though she hated it, she knew what she had to do.

※

Kneeling on the paddle board beside the derelict, she couldn't smell the decay; there was only the bite of gasoline. She considered the binder in its dry bag strapped to the board.

"Burn it too," said a voice that sounded a lot like her old self.

"No," said a girl who was not quite Party Girl.

Whatever had happened here, the binder could explain it, and she needed to understand.

She tossed the candle onto the deck. The whoosh of gas igniting. Heat like a burning Toyota though she was still shivering.

Pop, pop, pop.

End this ceaseless noise, she thought as she paddled.

She called for Evan when she reached Darren's shitty boat. No answer save the popping. Her hands shook so badly she couldn't get a grip on the rails.

"Could really use some help here."

No help came. She tossed the dry bag into the boat and managed to pull herself in without falling.

Light shone from within the cabin but Evan had locked the wooden door. She hammered on it. "Evan! Let me in!"

"Are you alone?"

"Of course."

The door opened a crack. Peeping eyes, wide and terrified, like Darren's during his fit. He swung the door wider and she crawled past him into the cabin.

"How is he?" she said, hurrying past Evan.

He grabbed her shoulder. "It reached in through the hatch, Priscilla. It dragged him out."

"I need to see him," she said, shrugging him off.

He scrambled after her, begging her not to open her cabin. She opened it anyway. Dead-fish stink. Blood and a darker gore stained the mattress, the same black substance that had covered the crab trap, and smokey air blew in through the wide-open hatch. Darren was too big to fit through that opening. Bits of fabric, reddish-brown hair and tissue adhered to the fiberglass rim. For a second, flames licked the air above the hatch, like the *Coffee and Cream* was on fire, but she blinked and they were gone.

"No."

She climbed onto the bed, reached up through the hatch.

"Don't go back out there," Evan whined. "Please!"

Shouting Darren's name, she climbed into a world painted in flickering oranges and reds by the light of the burning derelict. No one answered her. She stumbled away from the hatch, her legs numb from cold and booze and drugs and the dread that came with the certainty she was falling again into the dark time.

"You need to relax, baby girl," Darren said from behind her.

She whirled. There was only smoke. A trail of gore led from the hatch over the side of the boat and disappeared at the water line. Pop. Pop. Pop. The stink of the Toyota's burning tires. Even after all these years, it was still burning.

"Please, Daddy," she cried into the darkness. "Please!"

The boat heaved. Evan shouted from below. She slipped on the deck, exhaled a scream of pain as she landed hard on the anchor chain, rolled onto her side, gripped the rail, and found a pair of eyes on long black stalks looking at up her from the water. The burning Toyota reflected in those unblinking orbs. She thought of the empty wetsuit skin. Holes where the eyes had been. Then the thing clicked out a long, recurved claw, plunged it into the side of the *Coffee and Cream*, and pulled itself out of the water.

She pushed away from the rail, mouth open, screaming soundlessly. Dozens of skittering shrimp-limbs clutched the wire rail, the deck, as it poured up onto the boat. Mandibles worrying at its mouth made clicking sounds. Another wicked recurved limb slashed out, punched a hole in the deck, and pulled the rest of its bulk onto the boat. Its tail was segmented like a lobster's but long and coiled like a snake's. The thing was so big the boat was listing hard, the rail almost touching the water. A perfect pet.

"Is it quiet?" she said in a whisper.

One of those long, recurved claws slashed toward her. She ducked, scurried backward. The claw plunged into the deck, stuck there, anchoring it for a moment.

Movement in the hatch. Evan. He was standing on her bed, looking up at the thing. He reached a hand up through the hatch. The thing sat between her and her future step-son, but its claw was stuck. This was her chance. If she moved now, she might be able to get past it and jump through the hatch.

"Evan!" she screamed. "Help me!"

He reached onto the deck. She tried to grab for him but his fingers closed over the hatch handle, and with frenzied haste, he pulled it closed.

The vibration thudded through the boat and seemed to help the thing loosen its claw. Screaming, she backed into the very nose of the boat. It skittered closer, raised one of those wicked claws, the blade so long it could cut her in half. Part of her wanted the thing to do it. *Finish me off. End this.* But the animal her, the one that kept her going through all those awful years, was still fighting, still grasping for anything that could save her.

Her hand closed over the neck of the bottle she'd driven into the prow of the *Coffee and Cream*. With another shriek, she pulled it free, and in one fluid motion, she swung the bottle at the place where the eyestalks met the thing's smooth, chitinous head.

A crunch. The thing hissed, recoiled. The cork shot out of the bottle. Pop. Prosecco fountained toward her. She jammed her thumb over the opening like she was throttling a garden hose and sprayed the thing down with the bubbling white wine. Aimed for those eyes, the horrible mouth. It let out a piercing squeal of pain, stumbled backward, the big recurved claws now wiping at its quivering stalks like a child with shampoo in their eyes. With another squeal, it threw itself over the side of the *Coffee and Cream* and disappeared.

Priscilla tipped the bottle into her mouth, but there was no wine left. Pop. Her cannabis vape was long gone. Pop. The Percosets were in her fanny pack at the bottom of the ocean. Pop.

She stumbled to the back of the boat and found the dry-bag with the binder lying where she'd left it, right there beside the cooler.

Pop.

"Big exam is coming up," Rajesh said from somewhere nearby. That calmed her. It had been a long time since she'd heard her husband's voice. "Better hit the books."

She slid the binder out of the dry-bag and began to read.

※

Evan was shouting for her. That was naughty of him. *Doesn't he know I'm studying?*

Priscilla sat in the captain's seat with the three-ring binder open on her lap. The derelict fire was burning low, too low to read by, but she'd found a headlamp in the tackle box, and it provided great light, better even than the light at the Nahum Gelber law library. She looked over at Rajesh, who was leafing through a law text on the seat beside her, his blackened skin hanging in flakes. He kept adjusting his glasses over the empty sockets in his skull. Darren was burping the baby as he read over Rajesh's shoulder.

"Do you still have to wear a wig in court?" Darren said.

"Pay me twenty bucks and I will," Rajesh said.

Priscilla laughed as she flipped another page of the binder. Even though the big exam was coming up, she felt calm for the first time in years. Having all her men with her did the trick and the study notes were an incredible help. She couldn't remember the name of the student who'd given her these notes but she could see his friendly brown eyes. He had translated all the arcane text in the manuscript into plain English. It wasn't quite law she was studying, nor was it a cocktail recipe, but it was a ritual, like so much of law, and like a cocktail, it transformed mundane ingredients into something transcendent, and if she didn't follow the recipe exactly right, she would spoil the whole thing.

The door to the cabin creaked open.

"Oh thank God," Evan said. "You're still here."

"Where else would I be?" she said. She shifted, the sheath of the filleting knife she was sitting on was uncomfortable, and she had to concentrate, had to get this part just right. She kept reading the notes the previous student had left her.

Evan sat next to her.

"Priscilla, I'm so sorry for leaving you up there."

"You should be sorry, interrupting my studies like this."

"I was just so scared."

She closed the binder. She was as ready as she would ever be, she supposed. She reached under Rajesh's seat, found the cooler, and handed Evan one of his father's beers. "Drinks help."

He took the can, his hands shaking, but didn't open it. "We need to go. That thing is going to come back. We have to leave, now."

"Why? Even if we get out of here, you'll still have to carry it."

Tears were streaming down his cheeks. "Priscilla, please. You're scaring me."

"You were supposed to be watching him," she said gently. She patted his cheek, wiped away the tears. "Therapists will tell you that it's not your fault, that you couldn't have known, but they're idiots. What were you doing, Evan, when you should have been watching him?" She moved closer, pressed her leg against his. "Were you playing video games?" She trailed a finger along his inner thigh. "Or were you playing with something else? Is that how you got your Daddy killed?"

"Please, Priscilla. Stop."

"That's just it, Evan," she said. She traced a finger down his arm now, stopping at the beer can he was clutching to his chest. She cracked it open. "It won't stop. Ever. No matter where you go, you'll always be here, watching your Daddy die." She took his hand, guided the can to his mouth. "But don't you worry. I know a secret. You won't have to live with it. I promise."

"How?"

"Drink. Drink it all."

So he did. Poured the beer into his mouth, tilted his head back, Adam's apple bobbing up and down as he swallowed.

She sliced hard and fast. She wasn't sure, at first, if she'd done it right. Then a red line drew across his neck. Blood fountained out of him. He grasped at the wound but she was already moving. To do this right, she wouldn't have long.

The remains of the pasta dinner sat on the table. She swept it all onto the floor, then got out the birthday candles Darren had packed. He'd bought her six cupcakes in a little plastic tray. She only needed five. She stuck a candle in each, lit them, and placed them as the previous student had instructed.

She opened the binder to the correct page and began to read aloud. She much preferred an open-book exam.

The syllables were strange and alien in her mouth, but already she could feel their power coursing through her. As she chanted, the world got quieter, the popping echoing from the burning Toyota grew dimmer.

She flipped the page. Time to draw the glyph of perfection, but there wasn't enough salt in the shaker. A chill went through her. The words of the ritual stopped. She looked out the door, saw the broken shape lying crumpled beneath the wheel, and for a moment horror descended upon her. What had she done? What was she doing?

"No worries, baby girl," Darren said from his seat beside the wheel. "Parmesan is mostly salt, isn't it?"

She smiled again, so lucky to have such wonderful men in her life.

Geoffrey W. Cole

With careful, precise motions, she drew the glyph of perfection in powered cheese, and the world went quiet once more.

On the Many Uses of Cedar

Tomorrow, Fanny's husband will hit her for the first time in their short marriage. Fanny will relive the cold November day twenty-seven times. Her husband will only remember it once.

※

This is the day Fanny will repeat twenty seven times: A great crack will wake her alone in their cabin on the side of the mountain above North Vancouver. Warm beneath her deerskin and wool blankets, she will elect to remain in bed and will not notice that the flume, whose constant watery babble fills every waking moment, is silent.

Her husband will return to the cabin with one of his wool shirts that she rinsed in the flume the day before. He will tell her: "How many times have I told you not to do the laundry in the flume?"

Then he will hit her.

After he has gone, she will look at the daguerreotype on the wall of the two of them taken May 7th, 1895, their wedding day in San Francisco, and she will realize that the mountain did something to her husband. She will see that the mountain stripped away the boyish fat on his face to expose dark crevices and gullies. She will see that the mountain seeded thick stubble on his chin no razor will remove. She will see that the mountain poured its innumerable icy streams over his heart that scoured away everything but hard stone. She will see that in the two short years since their wedding the mountain remade her husband.

When her husband leaves, she will cook breakfast — always oatmeal with molasses and raisins — and she will carry it up the slick skid road to her husband's men. The braying of the camp mule, Boris, will lead her to the men, though after the third day, she will have the route memorized.

The foreman Marty is a half-Japanese logger who lost his left eye to a faulty sawmill blade and a bottle of rum before he joined her husband's crew. His one eye will see her coming and he will call the men down from their work, which is a tree they felled that morning. Fanny will never have seen a larger tree; even the redwoods she saw as a child will be dwarfed by this grey monster, and redwoods are called the biggest trees in the world. The men who scamper along the huge tree trimming branches are also Japanese, though on the first day Fanny will not know this; she calls them Chinamen.

Marty will have been drinking rum and will say: "What happened to your face?" when he gets his ladle of oatmeal.

"Slipped on an icy stair," Fanny will say.

She will feed the Chinamen, who she thinks are part of the mountain's conspiracy to remake her husband. His crew used to be mixed white and Celestial, but the whites thought they should be paid at least three times what her husband paid the Chinamen, and when he refused, they walked off the job. Only Marty received a raise as he was the only one who could talk to the Chinamen, and he stayed on the mountain.

After Marty and the Chinamen have eaten and Fanny has fed the mule Boris an apple she brought for him, her husband will walk out of the woods and demand that she bring breakfast up to the men at the sawmill and then return to her chores.

After she's fed the silent Chinamen at the sawmill, she will descend the mountain with the empty pot. She will draw water for the laundry from the flume.

The flume looks like a V from head-on. She thinks the flume looks like a snake from the side. It crawls up the mountain on cedar stilts to its source, a mountain stream. At the source, the men who built the flume, her husband and his crew, divert the stream down the v-shaped notch. The flume becomes an artificial stream they use to send bolts of lumber down the mountain to make shingles and siding for the growing cities below. The water is very cold. Her husband's bosses built a cabin beside the flume, away from the main camp, so that someone will always watch the flume and make sure the bolts flow, because sometimes bolts jam in the flume, sometimes tree branches fall across the flume, and sometimes, in particular the day before this day repeated itself twenty-seven times, Fanny loses a piece of laundry that she rinses in the flume and the shirt catches on a cedar seam, freezes, accumulates debris, and causes the flume to jam.

Fanny will hate the flume.

Her other chores will include mending a leaky cedar shingle on the roof, fixing a broken cedar step leading up to their home, sitting on a cedar rocking chair and darning her husbands socks, and sweeping cedar sawdust out of the cabin. Everything is made of cedar because cedar doesn't rot.

Fanny will hate cedar.

A rain storm will start every afternoon. When it is time to cook dinner, Fanny will climb back up the mountain to the main camp where the men sleep and will go to the kitchen cabin, also made of cedar. By then the rain storm will have turned to a thunder storm. She will make dinner, a stew of salted pork, potatoes and onions, and she will feed each of them. Marty, much drunker than that morning, will crack jokes about the poor quality of her cooking: "Tasted better food that had already been eaten and puked up by someone else." The jokes will not be the same every day.

When she comes around with tea at the end of the meal, her husband will reach into his jacket and will pull out a cone more beautiful than anything she has ever seen. Copper-colored and semi-transparent, the cone won't look like pine, or fir, or cedar; maybe a combination of all three. She will accept the cone, and she will think that maybe the mountain hasn't finished remaking her husband.

After she cleans all the dishes, she will walk home alone through the storm with only lightning to guide her way. She will find her husband entering numbers into his ledger. She will be unable to speak to him about what happened that morning because her father never let any of his five daughters talk back to him, and because she will be afraid of the man the mountain remade. She will watch him writing and she will try to use the force of her mind to get her husband to look up and speak to her, but he won't. She will try to get the fire going bright enough to chase the chill from the cedar cabin by burning small pieces of cedar, but the chill won't leave.

Thunder will rattle the walls of their cabin. He will climb into bed first. She will wait and hope that his body warms the cold sheets, but it never does. The mountain has drained all heat from his limbs. She will crawl in beside him and together they will both flinch every time another crack of thunder shakes the cabin and fills the air with cedar dust.

Then lightning will flash so bright that it shines through the solid wood walls of their home.

When the lightning recedes, it will take everything with it, and the day will begin again.

※

Not every day will be the same.

※

On the second day, Fanny will wake up to the great crack and find that her cheek isn't bruised. She will assume she had a terrible, vivid dream. When her husband enters the cabin with the same frozen laundry that jammed the flume and hits her again, she will wonder if maybe she can see the future, like her eldest sister claimed about their dead mother. She will attend to her chores, the same chores she attended to the day before. As thunder peals that night while she and her husband lie flinching beside each other on a mattress made of cedar sawdust, she will pray that tomorrow is a new day.

※

On the third day, Fanny will rise without a bruise and her husband will remake it for her. On the third day, Fanny will realize that she is being forced to relive this day, this one day when her husband hits her.

When she brings breakfast to the men, one-eyed Marty will look at her bruised face and say: "Wait, let me guess. You slipped on an icy stair."

"Do you remember it too?" she will ask. "Does this day keep happening?"

"Same day," he will say. "Same shit." And then he will drink rum from a flask.

Fanny will think that if she can stop her husband from hitting her, she might be able to make the day stop repeating.

※

On the fourth day, she will rise out of bed the moment the great crack wakes her. She will rush through the woods beside the flume on its cedar stilts. She will trip and smash her shin so that it bleeds. She will find her husband at the spot where his frozen shirt and the debris it accumulated jams the flume. She will apologize, she will beg him not to hit her, but the mountain remade the man she loves, and he will knock her down. For the rest of that day, she will remain in bed, and her shin will bleed through the sheets.

Her shin will be unmarked the next day.

On the fifth, sixth, and seventh days, she will remain in bed. These days are the same. Her husband will arrive with the frigid laundry, he will hit her even when she burrows beneath the covers. Then she will lie in bed and wait. Ravens outside will clack their beaks at the same time each day. Rain will arrive on schedule, and it will come pouring through the shingle she doesn't mend. Her husband will arrive before dinner and she will claim she doesn't feel well. He will tell her: "You can stay in bed today, but this can't happen tomorrow."

It will happen tomorrow.

After these three days in bed, she will rise to the sound of the great crack. She will wonder: is it the sound of my husband's fist on my face? Is it the sound of the great grey tree falling? Is it the sound of the world splitting in two? Is it the drums of Hell? Am I dead?

Her husband will hit her and she will make breakfast. She will carry it up the mountain. When she finds the men beside the massive tree, Boris the mule will be the first at her side, and the beast will nose her pocket for the apple she's forgotten.

Marty will push the mule out of the way.

"Damn-me but you were right," he will say. "This day's repeating. What in the hell?"

She will take his full mug of rum and drink it in one gulp. She will feel warm for the first time since they moved to the mountain. Her husband will walk out of the woods and send her to feed the men at the sawmill. Once breakfast is done, she will return to the cedar cabin, crack open her husband's shipping chest and find the bottle of port his uncle gave them on their wedding night. The sweet wine will keep her warm through the afternoon as she stares at the daguerreotype on the wall.

She will see that the mountain has changed her too. Her skin, always pale, will seem thin as the frost that coats the cedar flume in the morning. Her hair, once long and chestnut, will hang like the lichen from the trees, streaked with grey. And her eyes that stare back at her from the shaving mirror her husband never uses, her eyes will be the color of the mountain's damp earth.

Dinner will be burned that night. Her husband will give her the translucent, copper-colored cone when she comes by with the tea. As she cleans up in the kitchen, while the Chinamen drink sake and her husband returns to their cabin, Marty the one-eyed foreman will bring a bottle into the kitchen and say: "Finest rum I ever tasted."

"I'd hate to waste it," she will say.

And he will laugh, and his breath will stink like a distillery.

"It's full every morning," he will say. "A drunkard's dream."

They will drink all of the bottle.

"They aren't really Chinamen," Marty will say as they drink and rain pounds the roof. "They're Japs. Good thing they don't speak English, cause if they heard us calling them Chinamen they'd get bitter. And I ain't half Chinese neither. My Pa was British, my Ma Japanese."

"How did they meet?" she will say.

"My father had enough money and a hankering for Orientals," he will say.

She will laugh. He will not.

"Why don't the rest of them realize the day keeps repeating?" she will say.

He will offer her another mug full.

"Who cares," he will say. "More rum for us."

While thunder gathers around them, she will talk. Growing up in San Francisco will seem even more wonderful through the murky lens of the rum. She will tell him about her five sisters, and the father who raised them after his wife died giving birth to the last of them. She will even cry a bit when she tells him about her mother, the one memory of the foggy day watching the boats sail in.

As the storm reaches its crest, he will say: "Just about done, I think."

"I hate the lightning," she will say, and she will reach out and take hold of his hand which will be knobby and root-like and totally unlike her husband's. "Especially the last one."

The lightning will flash through the walls of the cabin and when it recedes it will draw everything else with it and the day will begin again.

⁂

She will rise to the great crack. No bruise will mar her face. No hangover will cloud her mind. Her husband will hit her. She will bring breakfast up the mountain. Ravens will clack their beaks. Instead of returning down the mountain after breakfast, she will find Marty and they will sneak to the kitchen cabin at the main camp, and they will open the bottle of rum they finished the day before. He will tell her more about life in the slums of Tokyo, and she will tell him about the fish market in San Francisco.

They will do this for several days.

᛫

On the twelfth day, after the crack, after the blow from her husband, and after breakfast, she and Marty will lie beneath one of the great trees the loggers haven't yet felled. The rum bottle will lie half-full at their feet. They will be talking about why this day keeps repeating:

"Do you think it's that big tree?" she will say. "I've never seen one like it."

"Me neither," he will say.

"What if you don't cut it down?" she will say.

He will shrug.

"Each day starts for you in bed," he will say. "But for me it's there, beside the tree, as the damn thing falls over. There's the lightning, then there I am, standing and watching as my boys topple the big tree."

"So it is the tree," she will say.

He will pull out a pouch from his pocket and a long strange pipe of the kind she's only heard about.

"Who cares?" he will say. "This ain't such a bad day to be stuck in."

He will pack a slick bit of tar into the bowl, he will light a match, and he will inhale. He will pass the pipe to Fanny.

"I shouldn't," she will say, but then she will take the pipe and she will smoke it and she will lie down on the damp ground beside Marty until the rain starts and they walk down the hill for dinner.

᛫

From the thirteenth to the twenty-third day, Fanny will smoke opium with Marty and will remember very little. Her husband will talk to her in this time when he finds her. He will scold her. He will hit her. He will bring her the present of the copper, translucent cone that comes from no tree she's ever seen. She will know that she should talk to her husband, that she should tell him that the days keep repeating, and that she wants the man in the daguerreotype, the man she married, to become unmade by the mountain, but she will also hold the cone he gives her, the beautiful cone that shows the mountain hasn't finished with her husband, and she will wonder if it is enough. The opium will make it easier to not answer that question; it won't hurt so long as she keeps smoking.

※

Like every day, the twenty-fourth will start with the great crack, a flume that doesn't flow, and her husband's fist. After breakfast, she will find Marty and they will smoke opium beneath the same old tree under which they first smoked. They will also drink the rum and smoke some of the hemp that never runs out. She will pass out.

When she wakes up, Marty will be on top of her. His trousers will be around his ankles. She will feel him thrusting into her and the opium will make her not want to scream but she will scream. He will put his root-like fingers over her mouth and clamp her mouth shut until he finishes hot and sticky down the sides of her legs. He will roll over onto his back and sigh.

"I'm married," she will say once his fingers release her mouth and the opium lets her speak.

"Tomorrow," he will say. "It won't have happened."

He will light one of his hemp cigarettes. When he passes it to her, she will take the lit end and she will press it into his palm. Now he will scream. She will pull up her undergarments and she will run down the mountain. She will run away from the slashed areas and into the forest where huge trees still stand. As she runs, she will weep. She will mourn the sanctity of her marriage. She will curse the day she first took a sip from Marty's mug.

She will hate the flume, the lightning, the cedar, and herself.

As she runs, she will come to a cliff. For a moment, she will hesitate at the cliff's edge. She will hear no one following her. She will jump, and as she falls, she will think of sailboats in the fog.

When she hits the rocks, she will die.

The great crack will sound for a twenty-fifth time. She will rise. No bruise. No hangover.

No death. None of Marty's stickiness between her legs.

She will hear her husband on the steps. She will endure his punch. Ravens will clack beaks. Eventually, her husband will start the water flowing back down the flume. The roar will fill the cabin, and the roar will seep into her, fill her with resolve.

At her husband's sawmill, Japanese Chinamen turn cedar trees into bolts, wedge-shaped logs that fit into the v-notched flume. One day her husband caught the men riding down the flume on a narrow skiff they carved from a cedar bolt. He confiscated the skiff and hid it beneath their cabin. Though he warned her never to touch the dangerous thing, she will push aside spiderwebs and moldy lumber until she finds the shallow boat, which will be no wider than her hips, no deeper than her forearm and no longer than her husband is tall. She will drag the skiff up the steps by a rope handle looped through its nose and she will lift it onto the edge of the flume. She will climb up beside the skiff and for a moment she will be mesmerized by the white water that rushes past her feet. Then she will slide the skiff beneath her and let the roaring stream her husband has redirected pull her down the mountain.

Her screams will startle ravens and woodpeckers from their roosts. The skiff will knock beneath her as the flume makes corners. Water will soak through her wool shirts until she shivers but she won't let go of the rope. Though she will be terrified as she slides down the cedar flume, a part of her will sing with the joy of escape.

Ahead through the trees she will see an expanse of dark blue. The flume will spit her out into Rice Lake, a holding pen where the bolts are then ferried down another flume to the city.

She will swim to the surface though her sodden clothes will drag her down. That first breath after she is dunked will feel like her baptism.

A bolt will fly off the flume and will strike her in the thigh, and her leg will break in two places. She will swallow water as she tries to scream. One of the loggers rowing a boat around the lake to herd bolts will notice her struggles. He will be a pale blonde man too young for a beard. He will row over to her, drag her out of the water, and bring her to the cabin, also cedar, where these loggers live.

Most of them will be white. They will scold her for riding the flume, though they have all ridden the flume before. They will send for a doctor.

Talking to these men who aren't Marty and aren't her husband will be the brightest moment in the last twenty-five days. The pain in her leg will be unbearable. She will refuse the whiskey and opium they offer her.

As she lies in a cot that stinks of sweat, mud, and cedar, she will think that she has escaped it. The repetition is over. A doctor will come and everything will be all right.

The young logger will come in and tell her they've sent someone to fetch her husband.

Later, the same logger will return to tell her that the doctor will arrive tomorrow.

"He has to come today," she will say. She won't believe in that word, tomorrow.

"He'll come as fast as he's able," the young logger will say.

Rain will start slightly later than it does further up the mountain. A headache will set in behind her eyes, and her leg will throb with each beat of her heart, and as her blood fills the cavities the broken bones have slashed inside her flesh, her leg will swell like wet cedar.

After the first peal of thunder, the young logger will come in and say: "There's someone here to see you."

Despite the pain, she will sit, expecting the doctor or her husband, but the person who will walk through the door is neither. He is a young boy of seven or eight; maybe Indian or Chinaman or Japanese. She won't be able to tell for the filth that cakes him. He will walk over to her.

"You haven't happened before," he will say. "Are you like us?"

"You know about this?" she will say. Her heart will pound louder than the thunder. "Does this day keep happening for you?"

He will nod his filthy head.

"Have you seen it?" he will say. "We think they cut it down."

"The tree?" she will say. "My husband's men felled a huge tree this morning."

"Where?" he will say.

She will point up the mountain. "The flume runs eight miles back to the cabin, and the tree is another mile or two beyond that."

He will sigh, a sound she will think should come from an old man many times this boy's age.

"That's too far," he will say. "Most of us start by the water. It took me all day to get here."

"You know how to make this stop? You know what to do?"

He will pick something from his ear that he will wipe on his muddy shirt.

"The old people told us the tree needs to grow again," he will say. "They sent us out to find it."

"My husband brings me a cone," she will say. "A cone like none I've ever seen. Do you think that's it?"

He will shrug.

The fever that has been building in her will take hold then. Her words will stop making sense. The filthy boy will sit beside her and hold her hand until she dies.

※

The crack. Her leg will be healed, the bruise on her cheek will be gone. Her husband will be on the stairs with his cold shirt and colder fist. The twenty-sixth day.

She will pull herself up from the floor. She will bring breakfast to the men where they climb over the dead massive tree. Boris the mule will nuzzle her pocket for the apple she will forget.

"Where'd you go yesterday?" Marty will say when he comes up to her for breakfast. She will not say anything in return. "You can't stay silent forever. It's just you and me, pumpkin. May as well make the best of it."

And he will pinch her bottom as he walks away to eat his oatmeal.

Her husband will come down the hill and tell her to bring breakfast to the men at the sawmill, but she'll ignore him. She'll climb up the length of the downed tree. The stump will be forty paces across. At its center, she will find a hole a few inches deep that ends in fine sawdust. The wood around the hole will be blackened from an old fire. This, she will think, is where the cone must go.

"What are you doing up there?" Marty will say. He will hold a big two-person saw over one shoulder and will squint out of his good eye.

"Nothing," she will say. "I've got work to do."

She will climb down the planks the Japanese loggers drove into the tree to serve as platforms for cutting. Marty will try to grab her arm but she will shake him off.

"You come back and see Marty as soon as you're ready for some more," he will say.

She will look for a cone, but she won't find one. She will have to wait until dinner when her husband gives her the cone after the tea is served, and she will know there is still something decent within her husband. With the dishes unwashed and the storm raging, she will climb up the mountain alone through the downpour with only lightning to illuminate her path.

When she arrives at the tree, she will find Boris the mule waiting for her. He will be very quiet and will follow her up the length of the downed tree. She will climb the stump again. When she takes the cone out of her shirt, the cone will glow with a soft light the same color as the lightning. She will place the cone in the hole she found earlier that day. Though the cone will fit, something will seem to push the cone out of the hole if she doesn't hold it there. She will climb back down to find some stones or sticks to make a brace to hold the cone in place, and that's when she will see Marty standing beneath an ancient hemlock.

"Now I'm real curious," he will say. "You disappear for a day and you come back with all sorts of new ideas."

"Leave me alone," she will say. He will laugh, and even through the rain she will be able to smell the distillery.

Boris the mule will bray louder than she's ever heard him. Marty will jump out of the darkness but her shirt will be too soaked for him to get a hold. She will climb back up the stump. Lightning will flash and thunder roll. She will know the last flash is close.

She will place the glowing cone in the hole at the center of the stump. In one of the flashes, she will see Marty's face at the edge of the stump. In the next, she will see him pull up onto the lip of the stump.

The last bolt of lightning will cut through the air. It will seem like light jumps out of the cone in her hand to meet the lightning. She will try to hold onto the cone even as the lightning pours through her. Marty will be blasted back, away from the cone. She won't be able to hold on. The cone will roll out of the hole. The light will recede, sucked back into the cone, and when it disappears the day will start again.

*

Day twenty-seven will start like every other. The crack. Her unblemished face. Her husband on the steps. This time, after he hits her, she will say: "That Marty made inappropriate advances to me a few days ago. I don't want to see him again."

"He's the only one who can speak with the Chinamen," her husband will say.

"I don't care," she will say. "I won't feed him."

She won't bring breakfast up the mountain that day. She will barricade the door and lie in bed, gathering her strength. When she hears Marty yelling at her from outside, she will remain where she is, even when he slams his fists against the door.

"Don't you dare try to end this," he will say. "Don't you even dare."

After the rain comes, she will hear her husband return. He will try the door and he will say: "What's going on here?"

"That Marty tried to come in," she said. "I told you, there's something wrong with him."

She will move the shipping chest and the wood chair out of the way and she will let her husband in. He will not smile.

"I'll talk to him," he will say.

"Don't let him come to dinner," she will say.

His eyes, as hard as the stones she wrecked herself on when she jumped off the cliff, will soften for a moment.

"Alright," he will say. "But you get down there and get cooking. This can't happen tomorrow."

She will go down to the kitchen with her husband. She will make the same stew she made before; the ingredients will all be there. Marty will not join them for dinner. She will hear him cursing outside. She will be very afraid of what he will do.

After the dinner, her husband will reach into his coat and will present her with the copper-colored cone. Instead of accepting it, she will take his hand, and she will say: "Come with me up the mountain. I need to show you something."

"I've got to enter my numbers," he will say. "And you need to clean up this mess."

She will hesitate then. She will not know if she can face this man the mountain has turned into somebody different. Thunder will shake the cabin. Cedar dust will fall into her hair. She will hope that the small part that remains of the man she married is enough.

"Please," she will say. "Do this for me."

All the Japanese Chinamen will be watching. He will nod and she will lead him out into the storm.

They will climb the skid road together.

"Is this about what happened this morning?" he will say.

"No," she will say. "Yes. I don't know. Just follow."

They will come to the clearing where the massive tree lies on its side. Boris the mule will greet them with a loud honk.

As the mule presses his flank into her, she will rub him between the ears and will say: "You can remember it too, can't you?"

The mule will follow them up to the tree.

"It's too dark to be up here," her husband will say.

"Just a bit longer," she will say.

"Lightning's a logger's worst enemy," he will say.

"Just a bit longer," she will say. She will not release his hand.

When they come to the massive stump, she will turn to him and take the cone from his pocket.

"What in God's name?" he will say as the cone glows with faint blue light.

"We have to plant it," she will say. "So that the tree can grow again. I can't do it alone."

This is when Marty will rush out of the forest with his axe. He will run straight at her husband.

"Marty, what're you doing?" her husband will say.

Marty will only snarl as he charges and raises the axe. Her husband will reach for the knife at his belt as he steps between her and the foreman, and that is when Boris the mule will lash out with his two hind legs. The animal will cave in Marty's chest. The axe will tumble to the ground beside the foreman's limp body.

Fanny will place a hand on her husband's shoulder to steady him.

"We need to get him help," he will say.

"He's dead," she will say. She will pat the mule on the head and say, "Good boy."

Lightning will flash and thunder will roll and Fanny will know the time is near.

"Come on," she will say. She will take her husband's hand and she will climb up the planks driven into the stump.

"Fanny, this is madness," her husband will say.

"We won't have another chance," she will say. "He'll come back."

He will follow her.

She will guide him to the center of the stump. She will place the glowing cone in the hole and she will ask him to kneel beside her. Together, they will hold it in place.

"Now what?" her husband will say.

"Just hold on," she will say.

The lightning that starts it all again will arrive. Light will leap up from the cone to meet the electricity arcing down. Energy will course through her, she will see it run through her husband. She will see his hand loosen on the glowing cone.

"Hold on," she will scream. The lightning will last longer than any lightning can last. It will last as long as the universe exists.

And it will end. They will both fall aside, breathing, stunned. The heart of the stump will be blackened and burnt and so will their clothing.

The Japanese Chinamen will find them when they hear Boris the mule braying into the night. They will take Fanny down in a stretcher they make out of cedar-smelling bedsheets and will take her husband down on the mule's back.

⋙

In the morning, they will wake in their small bed in their little cabin beside the roaring flume. Their clothes will be ashes, but their skin will be untouched. Her husband will be in the bed beside her. He will be warm. They will wake up together.

"We need to talk," she will say.

They will talk as they walk up the mountain. The trees will drip from the previous night's rain. The ravens will complain. Boris will meet them halfway and Fanny will remember to bring him an apple. They will climb the stump of the massive tree.

A green shoot will grow up from the blackened cone and will reach a pair of tiny green leaves toward the sky.

※

All this will happen tomorrow. Today, Fanny rinses her husband's shirts in the flume.

One of the shirts gets away from her.

She doesn't think he will miss it.

Zebra Meridian

1

Haqwalinz Surteh was elbow-deep in a failed slurry pump when her boyfriend Mauds Syloft-Brovidine stepped into the basement of the derelict sky vacuum in which she was working. All seven members of the crew resuscitating the vacuum snapped to attention for Mauds, the Sector 34 title-holder, but Haqwalinz stayed focused on her task. She wanted to get ten more vacuums online before the end of 2247, so she waved a greasy hand and asked what he wanted.

He dropped to one knee beside her, kissed her cheek and said, "How's my favorite worker doing?"

Haqwalinz shrugged away from him. "Busy. Can this wait?"

He responded by producing a black silicon O-ring from his pocket.

"That's too small for these pumps," she said.

"It's for your finger."

She was still too deep into troubleshooting mode to realize this was a proposal but her crew stirred in anticipation.

"From the moment you stepped off the bus," Mauds said, holding the O-ring out to her. "My heart has been yours. The two months we've spent together have been the happiest of my life.

You improve everything you touch, me most of all. Haqwalinz Surteh, will you marry me?"

From outside, the ever-present hum of sky vacuums flowed into the silent room. Haqwalinz blinked beneath the glow of her work light. A proposal! She adored Mauds, loved every minute they spent together, but she was a girl from the camps. Not a citizen, certainly not a Brovidine. She had always imagined their affair would end like Audrey Hepburn and Gregory Peck's from *Roman Holiday*: the princess and the ex-pat journalist adored each other but were from worlds too different to ever have a future together.

"But your title," she said.

"Will become yours. And it will pass to our children, if we're lucky enough to have any. I would trade anything to have you as my partner, *carinissima*."

The terrible Italian helped but it was calling her his partner that decided it. From their beginning, despite Mauds' almost aristocratic position at the carbon capture facility, he never treated her like a girl from the camps. When they were together, she always felt like they were walking the same path. She wrapped her arms around his skinny neck and smothered him in the kind of kisses that spoke in the affirmative. Her crew whooped in approval.

Then she broke away. "I can't get married without my family."

A moan from the crowd.

"I've been looking into work visas," he said. "I have an idea how to speed things up, but I don't know if you'll like it."

He bit his lip. She'd accidentally smeared grease down the side of his face and the stripes almost resembled hers.

"Spill it."

"The fastest way to get your family up here is if my cousin Wendel, our President and Mayor, sponsors them." He turned to the crew. "What is the Zenith Meridian motto?"

"'Keep it in the family,'" they recited.

"And if we get married …" Mauds said, waiting for her to finish his thought.

"I'll be part of the family," she said. "Wendel will have to help."

Mauds nodded. He was still holding out the silicon O-ring.

"Let's do it," she said. "Right now."

He slipped the O-ring onto her finger and the crew roared their appreciation.

⋀⋀

One of Mauds' cousins pedaled the maintenance tricycle on which Haqwalinz and Mauds balanced while the rest of the crew jogged along beside them, singing and drinking, as they rolled through Sector 34. Though they passed rows of identical sky vacuums — five-story towers of steel, concrete, ducting, and fans designed to suck carbon dioxide out of the air and inject the villainous compound deep into the Earth — in Haqwalinz's mind, they rolled along cobblestone Sicilian streets like the wedding procession in the second Godfather film.

The tricycle went over a bump, jostling them both.

"So," Mauds said, drawing out the vowel. "Are we going to call your parents?"

Haqwalinz made a show of trying to find her phone.

"You haven't told them about me, have you?"

"I've told two of my sisters."

"Why not the third?"

"She's a tad judgmental."

One of the workers handed Mauds a bottle of home-brew. He took a swig and passed it to her. Thinking of the call she would have to make, she took a large gulp, then almost spat it up. Bathtub berry wine. She flushed thinking how much her father would disapprove of her drinking. Considering the other news she had to share, drinking might be the least of his concerns.

She called Mom instead.

"Hi Mom," she said. "I want you to meet someone."

"The line starts back there," Mom shouted at someone off-camera. She stood in a long, dusty queue of other women also in their mid-fifties, all dragging wheeled baskets, most trying to find relief from the sun beneath parasols.

"Can it wait, darling?" Mom said. "I've been waiting for two hours and it's almost my turn for rations."

"Sure, Mom," Haqwalinz said. "When you get back to the tent, gather everyone together. I have news!"

"So mysterious."

Mom promised to call and started yelling at someone else trying to cut in line when Haqwalinz disconnected.

The cousin pedaling the trike broke into a coughing fit and another worker relieved him. They were still a good two kilometers from downtown and the enthusiasm in the parading workers sagged under the double-fronted assault of June heat and feasting black flies. Mauds tried to keep up the energy by leading the crowd in songs sung in the local dialect combining French, English and Oji-Cree that Haqwalinz still hadn't mastered, but his efforts soon faded, and for most of an hour, they rode in parched silence. Instead of the gorgeous scene from the second Godfather, Haqwalinz couldn't help but think of her and Mauds as the exhausted, overheated parents played by Sophia Loren and Marcello Mastroianni in *Yesterday, Today, and Tomorrow*. But when they spotted the lake, the crowd briefly revived. Zenith Meridian was powered by a single large hydroelectric dam on the Wakwen River. Most of the residential downtown was built beside the dam and along the shores of Lake Wakwen.

As they passed the Presidential Manor, a sprawling red brick home that was the finest building in ZedEm and the seat from which Mauds' cousin Wendel ruled the factory city, Mom messaged to say they were ready.

"Please don't tell me you lost your job," her father said, the moment she connected.

Her entire family was gathered in the central tent of their complex. For the first twenty-two years of her life, that tent had been the center of her world. Her sisters, grandparents on both sides, aunts and uncles and their children all crowded onto the rugs over the dirt floor. Her father sat in the only real chair, a plastic Muskoka-style deck chair, while Mom stood behind him, her hands on his shoulders. Haqwalinz knew that her image would be on the ancient wall screen that her father never missed an opportunity to remind them he had bartered from a displaced Sardinian by promising to file seven years of the Sardinian's tax returns. That wall screen had given her and her sisters so much more than a connection to the outside world: it had come loaded with thousands of ancient Italian films, unencrypted files that they didn't have to pay a cent to watch, which had become the cultural lens through which all four Surteh daughters interpreted the world.

"Nothing like that," Haqwalinz said. "I've met someone. Mauds, meet the family Surteh. Family Surteh, meet Mauds."

"So nice to finally meet you all," Mauds said, waving at her phone. "I absolutely adore your daughter."

"We're about to get married," Haqwalinz said.

Everyone in the tent turned to see her father's reaction. The silence dragged on for so long that Haqwalinz worried she might have lost the connection.

"Is Mauds a Muslim name?" her father said.

"It's not, Dad," she said. "And I haven't been a Muslim for years either. He's from here. His family built this place."

"When is the wedding?" her mother asked. "We have some money put aside, of course, but time to gather more would help."

"You don't have to spend anything," Mauds said. "I'll cover it."

"You're right, Haqwa," her sister Rheahaz said. "He is cute, just like a young Marcello Mastroianni."

Mauds blushed at this, and her gathered family broke out in laughter. As the mirth subsided, her father stood and approached the wall screen.

"Haqwalinz, my eldest daughter, I know you've renounced your faith, I have made peace with this, but please tell me you still possess the heart of the compassionate young woman we raised. Are you climbing this mountain alone?"

Haqwalinz knew exactly what he was asking. Throughout her childhood, he had insisted that if his daughters worked and studied harder than their peers, they would find great success, they would be able to climb any mountain. But, he told them every night as they nestled into their bedrolls, she who reaches the top of the mountain alone may find it a very cold place. She who lifts others to the peak will find herself surrounded by warmth no matter how cold the wind.

"Papa, I'm not climbing alone," she said. "Mauds makes me happier than I have ever been, we are making a real difference here, and with his help, we are going to get you all out of Huron East."

There was no change in her father's expression, he merely nodded his head and said, "Then may Allah bless your union."

Her family roared their approval.

∿

By the time they reached the casino and its blessed air conditioning, everyone was exhausted. Mauds ordered cold beverages for all. Drinks in hand, the dusty hoard flowed into the chapel where a holographic AI stuttered to life. They cast their families' feeds to the wall screens on either side of the chapel. To make her father happy, Haqwalinz had the AI recite the traditional passages from the Quran, translated into French, English, and Oji-Cree for the benefit of the attendees, though she opted for the Catholic church backdrop full of saint statues, ornate columns, a gilded altar, and puffs of simulated incense to align with the wedding she'd dreamed of since childhood.

Mauds and Haqwalinz stood facing each other. On the screens, their families beamed as the AI-imam launched into the legal portion of the ceremony.

"Maudhieu Syloft-Brovidine, born in Zenith Meridian, Province of Hudson, by entering into this marriage, as stipulated in the articles of incorporation of the Zenith Meridian Corporation, you hereby forfeit all claim and title to the ownership of said Corporation. Do you enter into this contract in good faith and of clear mind?"

"I do," he said, squeezing Haqwalinz's hands.

"And you, Hannalynn Soortay, born in the Huron East Refugee Camp Three, Province of Bruce, by entering into this marriage, you take on all the rights and responsibilities of a title holder of the Zenith Meridian Corporation. Do you enter into this contract in good faith and of clear mind?"

Haqwalinz leaned close to Mauds. "It got my name wrong. It's using what's on my visa, not my birth certificate."

Another squeeze of her fingers. "We'll fix it later. Don't worry."

"Do you enter into this contract in good faith and of clear mind?" the AI-imam repeated.

"I do!"

"Then by the power invested in me by the Province of Hudson and almighty God, I pronounce you married!"

Geoffrey W. Cole

Wendel Brovidine squirmed in his office chair in the Zenith Meridian Presidential Manor. It felt like someone had hooked a live wire up to his rear end. He adjusted the inflatable pillow on which he sat and tried to ignore his hemorrhoid. Another visit to the autodoc was probably in order, but the thought of lying naked on his belly while the infernal machine made the repairs threatened to ruin his whole week. He'd take a long float in the pool this afternoon and get Norris to find the analgesic cream. That would help. He only had to sit for a few more minutes anyway.

Another bloody Tuesday. The only day of the week when it mattered that he was in Zenith Meridian. Every Tuesday at noon, the carbon brokers down south forwarded the cash collected for the carbon credits they'd sold for the previous week's production, hundreds of millions of dollars that he had to accept in person, in Zenith Meridian, every Tuesday, for all time.

He hated Tuesdays.

"Has it come in yet?" he shouted into the kitchen, where Norris and some lesser cousins were preparing his lunch.

Norris, a second cousin on his mother's side, poked his blocky head into Wendel's main floor office. "Still a few minutes shy of twelve."

"Bring coffee and make it stiff."

The coffee arrived before the payment. Wendel carried it to the window, grateful for a moment's relief, and sipped steaming chicory spiked with bourbon. Lake Wakwen was glass.

"It's here, Good Cousin."

Norris brought the biometric scanner, a lacquered walnut box into which Wendel slipped his hand. The machine made a brief hum as it confirmed handprint, DNA, and microbiome.

"Now for the question," Wendel said.

"As the President and CEO of Zenith Meridian," the scanner said. "Do you hereby certify that your firm has removed and permanently stored within this good Earth 157 million kilograms of carbon dioxide since June 8, 2247?"

"I do."

The device buzzed affirmative. Seconds later, hundreds of millions of dollars flowed into the company's coffers and was distributed among his extended family, their workers and suppliers, and everyone else that sucked at Wendel's teat. He removed his hand and wiped it on his shirt.

"Well, I am exhausted. Please tell me there's nothing else today?"

"Apologies, Good Cousin," Norris said as he returned the scanner to its spot on the shelf. "But there is one more thing. One of your cousins, Maudhieu Syloft-Brovidine, title-holder from Sector 34, has requested an audience."

"When?" The blank look on Norris' face told Wendel everything he needed to know. "God, man. Haven't I told you not to schedule anything else for Tuesdays?"

Norris blanched and wrung his thick fingers. "A special case, Good Cousin. Sector 34, as I'm sure you'll remember, is the sector with the single greatest efficiency improvement we've seen in a decade."

The coffee went bitter on Wendel's tongue. "We've seen this sort of thing before. One of my cousins either fudges the numbers or forces his crews to work unpaid overtime, all in a bid to win my hand. This needs sugar."

He handed his mug back to Norris. For as long as he could remember, his parents had told him how careful he had to be in the selection of a spouse. Choose the wrong cousin and he could upset the delicate balance of power that existed among the extended Brovidine clan. Choose well and he would be happy for life, like his parents had been. What he had never been able to tell them, what he had never been able to tell anyone but his AI shrink, was that he found the idea of marrying one of his cousins about as appealing as eating coyote turds for breakfast, no matter how distantly related and how much gene therapy would ensure their children didn't descend into Hapsburgian monstrosities.

Norris sweetened Wendel's coffee and topped it with a splash of brandy.

"I doubt this is a ruse, Good Cousin," Norris said. "Maudhieu was recently married, and outside the family."

Wendel barked a laugh. "The idiot!"

"Most certainly. Your cousin wants to introduce the newest member of our family, and, as I understand it, to make a request."

"Everyone always wants something."

"Not everyone."

"Like you wouldn't say yes if I were to propose."

Norris put the coffee urn back on the matching silver tray. "I would only accept such a proposal if it were made with true affection."

"There's no risk of that," Wendel said, wincing as he collapsed into his desk chair. "Send in this idiot and his new bride."

At noon, the sky over Lake Wakwen was a brilliant yellow, the lake a flat mirror reflecting the heavens. His tow-glider was moored at the dock below. Since the latest flare-up began two weeks ago, he hadn't been gliding once. He really did need to visit the autodoc.

Norris cleared his throat. Wendel expected to find some gold-digging local girl on the arm of his cousin. Instead, he was confronted with the most beautiful woman he had ever seen.

Norris made introductions and the cousin and his wife bowed and curtsied and made polite small talk, but Wendel registered none of it. Haqwalinz Syloft-Brovidine stood ten centimeters taller than her spouse. Copper curls cascaded to her shoulders, her eyes were the same color blue as the lake on a brilliant winter morning, and every inch of her exposed skin was striped black and white.

"Zebra," he said.

Haqwalinz's white stripes flushed red. "It was a fad when my mother was pregnant. Gene-mod firms promised the markings would help us camp-raised kids stand out from the crowd."

"You certainly stand out here."

"That's why we wanted to speak with you, Good Cousin," Maudhieu said. "Haqwa's family has been in the camp for generations. Both Haqwa and her parents were born there, but still can't get citizenship. Now that we're married, her family is our family. They are well-trained, Good Cousin; Haqwa has a PhD in fluid dynamics, one of her sisters is a lawyer, and the other two are completing advanced degrees. All the improvements at our Sector are thanks to her."

He went on but Wendel wasn't listening. Instead, he drank in this vision that filled his home like a second sun. The zebra-striped woman even smelled good, like the detergent they used in the worker's quarters and sun-heated hair. He was beginning to understand why a man might give up a birthright for a woman such as this.

"So, Good Cousin," Maudhieu said, wrapping up a speech Wendel had ignored. "Will you help these new members of our family?"

With those words, the sun broke through the clouds of Wendel's mind. He had to sit down, not even bothering with his hemorrhoid pillow.

"Good Cousin," Norris said, rushing to Wendel's side, sausage fingers worrying Wendel's forehead. "Is everything alright?"

Everything was more than alright.

"Cousin Maudhieu," he said, thinking hard. "To welcome Cousin Haqwalinz to our clan, I want to show her the full extent of her new family's holdings, and the only way to do that is from the air. Would you let me take your new bride for a glide?"

His zebra, for Wendel was certain she would soon be his, exchanged a worried look with her current husband. Maudhieu nodded in assent.

Wendel clapped his hands and jumped to his feet. "Excellent. And don't worry, Cousin Haqwalinz. When we're aloft, we can discuss how best to get your family out of that wretched camp. Norris, get the glider ready, and bring me my mother's jewelry box. There's something I'd like to share with our new cousin."

2

The moment the glider lifted off the water, Haqwalinz let out a whoop of joy. She had never flown before and had always considered flight a sin — most aircraft still ran on fossil fuels — but this glider was towed by an autonomous electric boat powered by hydroelectricity from the lake on which it now scooted, and flying in the glider was so quiet, so peaceful, that she felt like Sophia Loren in *Marriage, Italian Style*, riding in a convertible for the first time after years of riding the bus.

"The Golden Goose runs on a circuit," Wendel explained. The President and Mayor of ZedEm reminded Haqwalinz of Gabriele Ferzetti from *L'Avventura*, if Ferzetti had been balding, in his mid-forties, and a little soft around the middle. "Depending on how strong the thermals are today, it will take us upstream four or five kilometers, spool us up to eight or nine hundred meters above ground, then let us go."

"And you'll fly us home?"

Wendel shook his head. "The autopilot does that. Reads the thermals, calculates glide time. We're just along for the ride. We'll soar for another twenty or so minutes, then it will put us down near the dock."

From the flexiglass cockpit slung beneath the arcing white wing of the glider, they had a bird's-eye view of Lake Wakwen and the Zenith Meridian Direct Air Capture facility.

When Haqwalinz got the job at ZedEm, she'd been so excited. After years of study, not only did this job lift her out of the poverty her family had endured for generations, it also gave her the chance to work at the largest carbon capture facility on the continent. She would be fighting on the front lines of the war that had displaced her people. She could help rebuild the lost world from the films on which she and her sisters had been raised, a world where the sky was blue and people could live in Italy and Indonesia and Bangladesh. Yet when she arrived, she'd found the place near ruin. Most of the city's sky vacuums were inactive. From the air, it was even more apparent. The city spread for kilometers across the landscape, almost to the distant smudge of Hudson's Bay on the eastern horizon, yet all around the outer edges of the city, stunted pine trees grew in the streets and vines climbed crumbling and collapsed sky towers as the wilderness reclaimed what had once been functional equipment designed to cure the climate.

"So much of it is dead," she said.

"I prefer to think that it is hibernating," he said. "Waiting for an enterprising leader to come along and wake it up." He pointed back the way they'd come, where the beacon lights on a small group of sky vacuums twinkled. "Like what you've done with

Sector 34 down there. To which you now hold exclusive title. Quite a feat for a girl from the camps."

Haqwalinz felt a hitch in her chest. "I didn't marry Mauds for his money."

"It's not his money anymore."

He stared at her from behind mirrored aviators. The same stare she'd endured in his home. The same stare she remembered from so many men, but Wendel in particular reminded her of the giggling Red Crescent worker who had distributed rations in Huron East.

"Did you bring me up here to accuse me of something?"

"No, no!" Wendel said, that self-satisfied laugh still on his lips. "Quite the opposite, my lovely zebra. Do you mind if I call you my zebra?"

"Call me Haqwalinz."

"I brought you here to show that you've obtained one tiny portion of this vast empire. I want to offer you all of it."

Haqwalinz suddenly realized how alone she was, how confined with this man who looked at her as if she were a fine piece of grilled meat. "I don't understand."

"I think you do. The articles of incorporation of our company are clear: if a title-holder marries outside the extended family, they forfeit their ownership. For lesser cousins, like dear Maudhieu, this is no great burden. I'm sure you've agreed to keep paying him for his work, so he will have income, but he's giving up no great power, no significant wealth. For the hereditary President of Zenith Meridian, I have so much more to lose by marrying outside the family. Despite that, the thought of marrying one of my cousins turns my stomach, and I had resigned myself to stay unmarried, to produce no heir, to end my ancestral line. But then you, my zebra, my newest cousin, stepped into my office and changed everything."

He produced a jewelry box from his pocket and opened it. Sunlight glinted on a diamond as big as a tooth. It was the single most beautiful object Haqwalinz had ever seen.

"Leave Cousin Maudhieu," he said. "And marry me. As you are already part of my family, I won't have to give up anything. Our children will be kings. The work you've done improving your Sector? You can revitalize the entire facility. Together, we can found a golden age. We'll get your family out of the camp and build them a beautiful home beside my Presidential Manor. Hell, why don't we give them the Manor? We can build ourselves a new palace. All you have to do is agree to marry me, be my zebra, and we will make this place a paradise for both our families."

He looked so certain, so sure of himself. Haqwalinz felt dizzy. Her father's words rang in her mind: by marrying Mauds, was she climbing the mountain alone? She fiddled with the silicon O-ring on her finger. She adored Mauds. The way she made him laugh, the way he'd jumped into her obsession with ancient Italian cinema, the way he made her feel like Sophia Loren to his Marcello Mastroianni. Did that mean marrying him was selfish?

Wendel, who looked at her like she was a trophy to be plucked from the hands of a lesser player, had the means to liberate her family. He offered her the opportunity to take control of ZedEm and restore it to the climate-curing machine it was meant to be. How could she say no? Yet he was a man who kept his flying toy in pristine condition while letting his empire crumble and his people live in poverty. He was a man who would betray a blood relative on a whim.

Mauds was sincere in his desire to help her family, and not for any selfish reason: he wanted to help because he loved her. If Wendel wouldn't help, she was sure she and Mauds would find another way to free her family. And she didn't need to be Wendel's bride to share her methods with the other title-holders to teach them how to restore their Sectors.

She reached across the console and closed the box holding the ostentatious ring. "Can we go back?"

He stared as if she'd spoken in a different language. "I'm offering you riches beyond imagining. Your family liberated from their hell. Isn't that why you married my cousin?"

"You know that feeling when the glider lifted off the lake?"

Haqwalinz didn't want to share anything with his man, let alone her feelings for Mauds, but she didn't know how else to make him understand.

"Like you're leaving all your cares behind," he said. "Like you're free."

"That's how I feel when I'm with him."

Wind whistled past the cockpit. Wendel struggled to respond and when he failed he punched commands into his phone. The roboat turned and the glider followed a moment later. Soon they were pointed toward the dam, heading home, and the roboat reeled them in from the heights where they had soared.

For the rest of the flight, they rode in silence. They touched down with grace, the drag of the water on the pontoons sudden and viscous, like they were floating on maple syrup.

᎗

As the roboat towed them back to the dock, Wendel squirmed on his cushion, trying to get some relief, but the pain was not limited to his fundament. His zebra sat mute in the seat next to him. He kept playing through their conversation. What more did this woman want? There was nothing Maudhieu could offer that he couldn't match a hundred times over. A feeling of freedom? He was offering her wealth beyond imagining and the opportunity to lead the restoration the entirety of Zenith Meridian. She'd made him feel like a fool. At least there had been no one else to see it.

"For the good of our family," he said. "Please keep this conversation to yourself. If some of my more ambitious cousins learned of my proposal, there could be unrest."

"Of course, Good Cousin."

Hearing her use his title only made him feel worse.

"Give your family's names and addresses to Norris. We'll see what we can do for them."

The look of disgust barely hidden beneath her zebra stripes disappeared, replaced by a clear-eyed hope that made her even more beautiful.

"Really?"

"You're part of the family now. We take care of our own."

Maudhieu and Norris greeted them at the end of the dock and helped steady the glider as she climbed out. Wishing nothing more than to be floating in his salt water pool, Wendel waited until the zebra had finished speaking with Norris. Then she linked arms with Maudhieu and the two of them exchanged a few hushed words.

Cousin Maudhieu waved gratefully at Wendel. "Thank you, Good Cousin. This means so much to us."

Wendel brushed them away, and waited until they had hurried down the dock before he got out of the glider. Norris steadied him on the dock.

"She gave you the information for this clan of hers?"

"There are fifteen of them, apparently. It shouldn't be too difficult to get them work visas."

Wendel took out his mother's wedding ring and held it on his palm. This wasn't over. Not yet.

"Forget the work papers," he said. "We'll be taking a different approach."

3

On the wallscreen in Mauds' office-bedroom, Anita Eckberg climbed into the Trevi Fountain and said, "Marcello, come here." Her paramour, carrying a glass of milk for the stray kitten she'd adopted, took off his shoes and joined the actress as she bathed in baroque glory.

Haqwalinz used to love this scene from Fellini's *La Dolce Vita*, it was sad and romantic and silly, but as she and Mauds cuddled in front of the wallscreen, she couldn't sink into it. Part of the problem was that this was one of Marcello Mastroianni's films where he wasn't starring opposite Sophia Loren. To Haqwalinz and her sisters, Marcello and Sophia were the undisputed king and queen of Italian cinema; for Marcello to be cavorting with Anita Eckberg seemed a betrayal of his queen. But Haqwalinz knew her discomfort ran deeper than that. A week had passed since the bizarre flight with Wendel. She hadn't said anything to anyone about what happened between them and it was eating her up.

"I don't understand," Mauds said, passing her the mug of wine they were sharing. "Are they supposed to be in love?"

Haqwalinz took a sip and shook her head. "He's in love with the idea that a famous actress wants to play with him. But to Anita, he's just another stray, another pet she'll forget about tomorrow."

Was that what she was to Wendel? A plaything? A toy? The way Fellini's camera leered at the buxom blonde actress felt just like the way Wendel looked at her.

"Are we watching the same movie?" Mauds said.

"Does anyone ever watch the same movie?" she said, then sighed. This would be so much easier if she could talk about what happened in the sky. "I'm sorry, *marito*. My mind's elsewhere." She passed him the wine. She might not be able to talk about Wendel, but she could still talk. "Did I ever tell you about the Red Crescent creep?"

He paused the film and sat cross-legged on the bed. Whenever she told him about the many awful things that happened in her childhood, he adopted this serious "I am listening" pose. She found it both endearing and irritating as hell. Tonight, with Mauds wearing only a loose sarong and looking like some wise guru in the grey light from the screen, it leaned more toward endearing.

"I'm all ears," he said, handing her back the mug.

She took another sip and talked. Food was always scarce in the camp. Aid shipments came from the Red Crescent, as their corner of the camp was populated mostly by refugees from Bangladesh and Indonesia who'd arrived decades earlier, and one particular aid worker, a giggling man named Farrel, would give extra rations to the little girls in the camp if they lifted their robes and flashed him their bits. Haqwalinz had always refused, preferring to stay hungry than give in to the creep's demands, but she was so jealous of the girls who got the extra rations to bring home to their families.

"That's fucking horrible," Mauds said. "Did he get caught?"

"Better than caught."

Rheahaz, born eleven months after Haqwalinz, had volunteered to do the dirty work. The other three sisters had carefully hidden a tiny camera in Rheahaz's hijab. For good measure, they had also stolen a pair of black fly bots to accompany Rheahaz while she pulled her stunt. When Farrel asked for a show, fourteen-year-old Rheahaz gave it to him, and their cameras captured the whole thing. Instead of bringing it to the private security force that policed the camp, they crafted a careful message and sent Farrel the footage of him extorting a child, with a promise to share the footage with the Red Crescent management unless Farrel made weekly extra ration deliveries to their address.

"We ate well for months after that," Haqwalinz said.

Mauds barked out a surprised laugh. "I don't understand what this creep has to do with *La Dolce Vita*."

"Nothing. It's just been on my mind. Let's keep watching." She passed him the mug, which was empty. She hadn't realized how much she'd drunk while she talked.

In another twenty minutes, Mauds was snoring. Haqwalinz fell into a half-drunk trance as she watched, not quite dreaming, and when her phone erupted with alerts, at first she mistook the sound for the organ in the film.

Three high priority messages had come in from her mother. More arrived from her sisters, her cousins. She opened the first with a mounting desperation she hadn't known since the day she left the camp.

"No. Oh God, oh no."

Mauds jolted out of sleep. "What's wrong?"

"Raiders at the camp," she said. "They came earlier tonight."

She tried to tell Mauds what her mother had written — they'd taken Rheahaz, they'd taken her hard-headed, wonderful sister — but she couldn't utter the words, so she handed him her phone.

He read quickly, turning pale as he did. "Oh, Haqwa. I'm so sorry."

But she wasn't sorry. She burned with shame. Here she was watching a heathen film with her unbeliever husband, drinking alcohol, and not doing anything to help anyone. If she'd agreed to Wendel's proposal, Rheahaz might not have been there to be abducted.

She took back the phone and wrote to her mother: *I might be able to do something.*

Then she took Mauds' hand, squeezed it so hard he flinched.

"I need to speak with your cousin. Right now."

"It's one in the morning."

"Now, Mauds."

He crawled out of bed and made a call.

As she listened to Mauds explaining the abduction to Wendel, a chill thought went through her. Could Wendel already know what happened? The timing was so convenient. She had no doubts that the President and Mayor of Zenith Meridian was a spoiled, selfish man-child, but would he arrange an abduction to coerce her into marriage? That was preposterous. Wishful thinking, when the real culprit was so clear: the fault was hers. Though she no longer believed in God, she had grown up on both Islam and Italian cinema, and this felt like equal measures of divine punishment and poetic justice. Hadn't she turned her nose up at the opportunity to save her family, preferring instead the delights of life with Mauds?

"Haqwa," Mauds said. "Are you still with me?"

He'd finished the conversation.

She was staring into the empty mug they'd been sharing. "What did he say?"

"He's sending a trike."

"Let's get dressed."

"He only wants to talk to you."

Of course he did.

"I'll call when I know more."

After she dressed, she kissed him goodbye, and went out to meet the trike Wendel sent for her.

₩

Twenty minutes after the call with Maudhieu, Norris admitted the zebra to Wendel's home. Wendel sat in his bed, watching on his phone as she paced in his foyer. God, she was so beautiful. He slipped into a house coat and went to console his newest cousin.

"My dear," Wendel said as he came down the stairs. "I am so sorry to hear about this terrible tragedy."

He opened his arms. She side-stepped his embrace, walking over to Norris, who had produced a platter of freshly-printed wafers. Hazelnut, from the smell. Wendel's favourite. She took a handful.

"I didn't come here for comfort," she said. She jabbed at him with one of the wafers. "You said you could help liberate my family."

"I said if you were my wife, I would do everything in my power to see them free."

She bit half the wafer and swallowed with effort.

"Something to drink?" Norris said. "I make a delectable chicory coffee."

"It really is delicious," Wendel said.

She popped the other half of the wafer into her mouth, chewing as if it was the severed finger of one of the men who had abducted her sister. "If I agree to marry you, will you do whatever is in your power to find my sister?"

Wendel couldn't help but smile. "If you were my bride, I would do whatever it took to make you happy."

His zebra took another handful of wafers and attacked them with savage bites. "I'll take that drink," she said.

When his odious cousin had departed, Wendel led his zebra into the sitting room. "Please, my zebra, take a seat."

She collapsed into a plush leather chair. Wendel leaned against the mantle, keenly aware that his comfort pillow was in his office.

"Were you serious about letting me improve the facility?"

Norris appeared with two steaming cups of chicory coffee and Wendel's bottle of Chicoutimi Dark brandy.

"Care for a splash?" he said. His zebra declined with a delightful shake of her copper curls. "Suit yourself."

Norris splashed the brandy into his cup, then gave the unimproved cup to Haqwalinz.

"If you want," Wendel said. "I'll put you in charge of all operations. This place could be so much more with the right people in charge."

She barked out a crumb-filled laugh, then sipped her drink.

"Then here are my terms," she said, counting with wafers. "One: you do whatever it takes to find my sister and bring her here safely."

"Norris will get to it the moment we wrap up here."

She bit through that wafer and held up another. "Two: get my family out of the camp."

"The paperwork shouldn't take too long."

Another furious wafer assault. She held up a third. "Three: I want full control of the facility, including authority to make any operating decision I deem necessary."

"Operating decisions I can agree to. Financial control stays with me."

She seemed to consider that, then devoured the third wafer. When she held up the fourth, it began to shake in her hands.

"Four," she said, tears streaming down her stripes. She dropped her head, wiped her face with the back of her hand. When she looked at Wendel over the wafer, her eyes were dry. "Four: let Mauds keep his job."

"He married outside the family. I can't change the company's articles of incorporation."

"I didn't say title, only his position. I will own Sector 34; he will run it. Let him keep his place at ZedEm, Good Cousin, and I will give you my hand."

Wendel considered this another moment. "Maudhieu can stay, but you can't see him. Ever. Once we're married, you're mine, understand?"

She held out the wafer. It no longer shook.

Wendel bent forward, opened his mouth, and accepted her sweet and crunchy terms.

When she got home later that morning, *La Dolce Vita* was still playing on the wall. It must have looped back to the start, for a helicopter was flying a giant Jesus statue through Rome's grey sky. Mauds slept on the bed. She packed her things by the black and white Fellini light. Once she was done, she sat beside her husband, drinking in this last moment with him. He looked like a little boy when he slept, his brow wrinkled in worry, his mouth open, the sheen of drool on his lip. She thought more tears would come, but she only felt wrung out, as dry as sun-scorched laundry.

"Haqwa," he said, stirring out of sleep. "What's wrong?" He reached for her but she retreated from his touch and went to sit at his desk near the window. She couldn't meet his gaze. "Can my cousin help?"

She nodded. Her guts roiled from the wine they'd shared and the overly sweet wafers. She didn't think she could speak.

"Haqwa, please. What's happening?"

In that moment, she realized *Roman Holiday* wasn't the film that would define her relationship with Mauds; it was *Sunflower*. In the tragedy, Sophia Loren and Marcello Mastroianni's characters marry days before he is sent to fight in one of those awful twentieth-century wars. Years later, they are briefly reunited, only to realize that if they want to protect their families, they can never be together.

She shut off the pointless old movie.

"I'm sorry, Mauds." She pulled the O-ring off her finger. "I can't see you anymore. I've asked a legal AI to prepare divorce papers. I'll be sending them to an Adjudicator tonight."

He slid out from beneath the covers and sat for a moment with his head in his hands. "This is a joke, right? Please tell me this is a joke."

"It's my sister, Mauds. Your cousin promised to rescue her, and my entire family, if I marry him."

She left the O-ring on the desk, picked up her bag, and, her heart aching so much she couldn't breathe, she left him calling after her as she descended into the night.

4

The morning his zebra arrived at the Presidential manor, bags in hand, Wendel declared that his wedding day would be a city-wide holiday. Two weeks hardly seemed like enough time to plan such an auspicious event, but his zebra insisted they marry as soon as possible so he could start fulfilling his part of their agreement, so two weeks it was. Cousin Norris worked night and day to make the event a success. Truckloads of fresh fruit, pastries, and real meat arrived in the days preceding the wedding, and workers were re-assigned from the various Sectors to help prepare the deck of the dam for the big event. Wendel liked the symbolism of his marriage being sealed atop the very heart of the community.

On cooler evenings in the busy time before the ceremony, Wendel took to parading with this bride-to-be through downtown ZedEm. His workers and cousins shouted greetings and congratulations, and though his zebra seemed morose and removed during these promenades, Wendel knew she would loosen up once the big day arrived. His wedding present, in particular, would shake her out of this funk.

On their wedding day, thunderheads blew in from Hudson's Bay. Norris begged Wendel to move the wedding to the casino or the lacrosse stadium, which at least had an awning over the seats, but Wendel wouldn't have it. "Set up tents," he ordered. Lots were drawn among the workers for who would have to stay behind to form skeleton crews that would keep the Sectors online and capturing carbon during the celebration. Those lucky workers who drew long straws gathered old tarps and shelters, put on their Saturday evening best, and walked to the dam for the party.

By that afternoon, rain fell in torrents. Workers weathered the deluge beneath hundreds of make-shift tents along the dam, drinking Wendel's booze and eating Wendel's food. Haqwalinz had a whole tent to herself, where she was getting ready with two hand-picked helpers. There was only one thing missing.

Wendel waited at the bus station beneath an umbrella Norris held for him. The express from Timmins was already an hour late. Lightning slashed across the sky. Wind churned the lake to froth. He'd had his glider moved into its hangar to keep it from blowing away.

"What's the hold up?" he said.

"This weather made the road a mess," Norris said. "They'll be here soon."

When the bus appeared at the far end of Main Street, Wendel felt relief wash over him. The bus stopped and one lesser cousin after another poured out, all of them slightly hungover and a little green from the long, bumpy drive. Each cousin shook hands with Norris and Wendel. They had proven their worth many times over with their actions over the past weeks. Wendel would reward them well.

Last came Wendel's soon-to-be sister-in-law.

Rheahaz Surteh wore a long overcoat and headscarf. As she huddled beneath an umbrella, he couldn't see her face.

"Rheahaz?" he said.

When she raised the umbrella, Wendel's breath left him. He'd seen the photos Norris had produced but they had been dark and grainy. The face looking out at him from beneath the umbrella was also striped, as was the hand holding the umbrella, but Rheahaz was no zebra. His soon-to-be sister-in-law was a tigress.

※

The day after the wedding, when Wendel retired for his afternoon nap, Haqwalinz had her sister to herself for the first time since the ceremony. She led Rheahaz through the Manor, showing her sister the control room, the bar, the cinema, and the swimming pool. Throughout, Rheahaz was quiet. Haqwalinz assumed she was still recovering from the trauma of her abduction and the relief of her rescue, so she filled the silence with her story of falling in love with Mauds, then Wendel's advances, and at last his promises to bring their family here.

They ended the tour in Haqwalinz's dressing room, where she had ordered dozens of outfits for her sister. "Pick anything you like. God knows you deserve a little luxury after everything you've been through." She took a long black cotton dress off the rack. "I thought this would look wonderful on you."

Haqwalinz offered the dress to her sister.

Rheahaz gave it a brief glance, then shook her head. "Not my style."

Haqwalinz returned it to the rack, then sorted through the collection until she found a matching white skirt and flowing linen shirt that she held out for her sister.

"Too revealing," Rheahaz said. "Your husband already looks at me like that Red Crescent creep used to, I don't need to give him more reasons to stare.".

As Haqwalinz hung the matching set back onto the rack, her hand trembled. "He does not."

"Don't pretend like you haven't noticed," Rheahaz said.

"He's not that bad," Haqwalinz said. But last night, as she disrobed before this man who had purchased her hand in marriage, hadn't she felt like the little girl Farrel had tried to extort for an extra ration? She pressed a hand to her belly, which was hot and tight. "I ordered all of these for you. There must be something you like."

Rheahaz sorted through the outfits so quickly that the hangers thwacked a steady beat. "Do you know what the raiders said, right before they put the hood over my head?" Thwack, thwack, thwack went the outfits. The heat in Haqwalinz's belly burned brighter. "'Here's our tiger.' Like they were looking for me."

Thwack. Haqwalinz didn't want to believe her sister. She couldn't be married to a man capable of something like this, but hadn't she suspected him too? She'd had to cast herself as a tragic heroine in some imaginary film in order to believe he was innocent. If the raiders were looking for a tiger, the abduction had to have been targeted, and she could no longer deny what she knew was true. The more she thought about it, the more she realized how little Wendel had done to hide his actions.

"Did they hurt you?"

Rheahaz thwacked to the end of the rack and moved on to Haqwalinz's clothes. "Didn't touch a stripe. Like they knew I was a wedding present."

"Wendel is used to getting what he wants."

And what did it matter if Wendel had her abducted? She was here now, she was safe, and soon their entire family would be free. Haqwalinz would no longer be alone on this cold mountaintop.

"What happened to the girl I grew up with?" Rheahaz said. A final thwack, then Rheahaz paused at one of Haqwalinz's silk robes. "You said you'd rather go hungry than lift your skirts for that Red Crescent asshole, yet here you are, looking very well fed."

"That one's mine," Haqwalinz said. She pulled the robe out of her sister's hand. "If you don't see anything you like, order your own damn clothes." She shoved her sister out of the dressing room and stomped past her out into the hallway. "Norris can show you a catalogue. I have work to do."

5

When Haqwalinz couldn't sleep, which felt like most nights these days, she went to the control room in the Presidential Manor and worked. In the month since she'd become the First Lady and Chief Operating Officer of Zenith Meridian, she'd made significant improvements in facility output, increasing the rate of carbon capture to a pace the facility hadn't achieved in decades, while also reducing workplace accidents. Life here was better because of her. She was lifting everyone up. She was doing more to restore the lost world of her favourite films than she ever imagined she'd be able to accomplish in this life. And Wendel was keeping his end of their agreement: he was processing the work visas so her family could leave Huron East. So why did she still feel so wretched?

That night, thousands of sky towers happily sipped carbon dioxide and pumped it underground, but there was something strange happening in Sector 34. What had been the most productive of all ZedEm's sectors was now showing a steep drop in output. An unscheduled maintenance report arrived as she was looking over the Sector's performance data. The report was two sentences from Mauds, her first contact with him since he'd signed the divorce papers: *I know to fix it. We don't have to let this happen to us.*

A thrill coursed through her, a surge of joy quickly overwhelmed by a longing so fierce she had trouble breathing. She hadn't realized how much she missed him.

Linked to the message was *La Strada*.

With a start, Haqwalinz realized something else: for perhaps the first time since her father bartered for the Sardinian's wall screen when she was a little girl, she had gone more than a month without watching a film from two and a half centuries ago. She didn't need to watch *La Strada* to know why Mauds sent it. The film was about Gelsomina, a young woman sold into servitude, her one chance at true love taken from her by an act of unthinking malice by her villainous husband. Knowing that Mauds had sat through the film, his heart breaking all over again as he watched their love die on the screen, made her miss him so much that she couldn't resist writing back to him.

Urgent inspection, she wrote. *Meet me at Unit 15 ASAP.*

She put on her work overalls, hopped on Wendel's electric tricycle, and in twenty minutes was waiting inside the very sky vacuum where Mauds had proposed almost two months before.

The darkness within stank of machine oil and polymer.

"Haqwa?" Mauds called from the gloom.

They found each other by touch. Tears wet his cheeks. She brushed them away with dusty fingers, then she was kissing him, drawing him close. It felt so good to be in his arms again, to taste him, to feel his heart beating so close to hers. Yet as they kissed, she thought of Gelsomina watching in impotent horror as her true love died.

"Stop," she said, putting her hand on his chest. "We can't do this."

"But we can. We figured out how to fix it."

"The output drop in your Sector? It's not that bad."

"That was just to get your attention," he said, pulling her close again. "We figured out how to fix us. Our marriage, *carinissima*, it isn't valid. The casino AI didn't use your correct name. I've been speaking with Rheahaz and she thinks we have grounds to have our marriage annulled."

The same thrill she had on reading Mauds' message coursed through her veins. "That would mean Wendel married outside the family."

"He would forfeit his title. All his power would transfer to you. Then you could leave him in the mud just like he did to me."

She pushed away from him. "My name was a clerical mistake. He has lawyers too, Mauds. They would never let him lose his kingdom for a typo."

His grip on her forearms was so tight it hurt. "True, as Mayor he could correct our marriage certificate with a stroke of his pen, but Rheahaz and I have been working on that too. We have some ideas —"

"No," she said, cutting him off and twisting out of his grip. "I can't, Mauds. I have to think of my family first."

She pushed past him and out into the humid night. Stars shone above the twinkling lights of active sky vacuums, each star alone in such vast darkness. Mauds ran after her, and despite herself, she went to him, wrapped her arms around his neck and kissed him again. In his embrace, she let herself believe there was some way out of this mess. In that instant, she dreamed a new future for them: by day, she and Mauds would nurse this place back to life while their children ran through clean streets, and by night, her family and his would gather in the town square to watch their old Italian films projected onto the wall of the casino.

But it was only dream.

She released him and said, "I'm so sorry," then she ran to the electric tricycle waiting to bring her back to her husband.

"I'm your family too!" Mauds shouted.

She hit the accelerator, kicking up dust that obscured the stars.

∿

Wendel was startled out of sleep by Norris' clammy fingers on his shoulder.

"Jesus," Wendel said. "Something better be on fire."

"Worse."

Norris held out his phone. On it, video footage from a surveillance camera showed his zebra and his lesser cousin entering a dark sky vacuum, then emerging sometime later, embracing and kissing before separating in tears. As the video looped back to the start, Wendel hurled the phone against the far wall.

"Is she still there with him?"

Norris shook his big head and went to retrieve his phone. "She came back ten minutes ago."

Wendel tossed off his covers and shouldered past Norris into the hall. Light shone from beneath his zebra's door. He went in without knocking and found her changing out of coveralls. Norris, who had followed him into the room, gasped and averted his eyes.

"Don't look away," Wendel said. "See what a treacherous whore looks like."

His zebra pulled the coveralls back up. "Please, husband," she said, moving toward him. "You don't understand. I learned something important tonight. Something you need to hear."

"I've seen everything I needed to see," he said. He held up four fingers. "Haven't I kept up my end of the agreement? Your sister is here, your family is coming, you get to run the facility, and my idiot cousin still has his job." He waggled his fingers, then grabbed the pinky. "But you, you striped bitch, only had to do one thing. No! You just had to *not* do something, yet you've done it anyway."

"Let me explain."

"You don't have to explain to me," he said, turning to Norris. "Have the work visas come through yet?"

"Not yet, Good Cousin."

"Then put a stop them."

"No!" his zebra cried.

"You can explain to your family why they will never leave the camp."

His zebra fell at his feet and slobbered on his slippers. Some of the heat went out of him.

"Get off me," he said. She recoiled to the foot of her bed, looking so pathetic that he felt himself soften. "Show me you can be good. I will be sending Maudhieu away, of course, but if you can prove to me over the next year that you are a faithful bride, I might reconsider bringing your family here. Do you understand?"

She wiped her tears away and stood, straightening her coveralls and hair until she was the picture of a bride, save for the drawn-on smile that had no connection to the ice in her eyes.

"Perfectly," she said.

"Then clean yourself up," he said. "You smell like a worker."

Hours after Wendel left her bedroom, Haqwalinz slipped into the hallway, went upstairs, and knocked on her sister's door. Her knuckles smeared grime on the polished oak. She hadn't cleaned off the night's dust and tears; she didn't want to wash away any of her rage.

"Who is it?" Rheahaz said, sleep in her voice.

"Who else would it be?"

"I've had to turn your husband down on several mornings like these."

Haqwalinz was surprised at how little that increased her anger.

"Please, Rhea."

"Get in here."

Haqwalinz entered and locked the door behind her. Like that would make any difference. She searched the room looking for cameras or microphones, and though she found none, she felt certain that Wendel was watching. Or more likely dutiful cousin Norris, eager for something to report.

Haqwalinz slid into bed beside her sister.

"Gross. You're filthy."

"Under the covers," she said, using the Arabic-based cryptolect the two of them invented in childhood to avoid being understood by anyone else in their crowded home tent.

"I spoke with Mauds tonight. He said the two of you have a plan."

"An outline of a plan. Barely even a sketch."

"So we fill it in."

"Are you sure?"

Haqwalinz pressed her forehead to her sister's. "He's worse than the Red Crescent creep, Rhea. So much worse."

The moment was like so many nights they'd spent tucked close on their bedrolls, whispering their plans for the big lives they'd lead once they got out of Huron East. But life never met a plan it couldn't ruin.

"Inadvertently marrying an outsider isn't enough to knock him off his throne," Rheahaz said. "I've been reading the ZedEm articles of incorporation. Those people had weird ideas. They thought they would heal the Earth while breeding a race of hyper-intelligent enviro-empaths who would rule over their foretold paradise, and all they ended up with was a kind of neo-feudalism. But we can use some of it. We need to paint a picture showing he isn't interested in performing his presidential duties. Marrying an outsider is part of the picture, but not enough."

"What other duties does he have? The man's profession seems to be drinking boozy coffee and complaining about his hemorrhoids."

"He has to accept payment every Tuesday."

Rheahaz' hand tightened on Haqwalinz's wrist. "That's tomorrow."

"Making it seem like he was shirking that duty would help fill in the picture. The fact that this place has fallen into such disrepair during his tenure goes a long way too. If we can get enough of the family signing onto our claim, I'd say we were painting a pretty powerful portrait of an incompetent president. An Adjudicator might find him in default. He could appeal, of course, but appeals take time. You'd own ZedEm in the meantime. People like what you're doing here, Haqwa. You're like Sophia in *Marriage, Italian Style*, and this place is Marcello's bakery — once they get more of you, I don't think they'll let you go."

Haqwalinz thrummed at the rare compliment from her sister but a thought occurred to her. "If we do this, we'll be binding our family to ZedEm for ever. You'll be next in line of succession until I have a child."

"Then part two of this plan will be getting you and Mauds to baby making as soon as we're done with Wendel. Problem solved."

They both exploded in laughter.

In the silence afterward, the air between them was so full of potential that the hairs on Haqwalinz's arms stood on end. "Why are we the ones who have to do all the real work?"

"If we don't, who will? Certainly not the Wendels of the world."

"The Maudses of the world are willing."

"Only with a zebra pointing them in the right direction."

As Haqwalinz found her sister's hands, her excitement faded into dull exhaustion. What else could she do? "So we keep pointing them in the right direction. To make this work, Wendel needs to be occupied for at least an hour around noon tomorrow, right?"

"Can you entertain him in the bedroom for that long?"

"God no," Haqwa said with a nauseated laugh. "But I know something that might."

6

Wendel was enjoying a morning float when his zebra stepped onto the pool deck wearing a flimsy sun dress over a bathing suit that hid little of her striped perfection.

"I feel so awful about last night," she said. "I want to show you that I'm a good wife."

Wendel smiled. He liked his zebra contrite. "Why don't you take that off and join me?"

"Zebras don't like to swim," she said. She cocked a hip, shielded her eyes from the sun, and gazed toward the moored glider. "But we love to fly. Let's go up again. Do it right this time."

Wendel considered this as he floated in his inflatable pink flamingo. Norris had mentioned that his zebra and his tigress were up all night chatting in some language none of the translators could decipher. Scheming, Norris had called it, but Wendel wasn't concerned. He held all the cards. What possible scheme could they put into play? It was a Tuesday, so he would have to be back before noon to authorize Zenith Meridian's weekly payment, but they had plenty of time for a quick glide. And his zebra did seem like she wanted to make amends.

"A grand idea," he said. He paddled his flamingo to the pool's edge and called over a servant-cousin to dry him off. "What better way for us to start over?"

⋀⋀

The Golden Goose soared above the gold-flecked lake. Haqwalinz felt none of the freedom of that first flight. Today, she was Clint Eastwood in the climactic stand-off in *The Good, the Bad and the Ugly*, and she was about to draw her metaphorical gun.

The roboat had let the spool out and they now bobbed almost eight hundred metres above the lake and the sprawling grey forest of Zenith Meridian's sky vacuums.

"You seem nervous," Wendel said.

"We're so much higher than last time."

"The tether should disconnect any minute now," he said, looking at the time.

Haqwalinz adjusted the flight path from her phone. The new circuit she'd programmed would keep the glider at the far end of the lake until well past noon. It was 11:49 and Wendel still hadn't realized that he was no longer in control of the flight. This would work. And when it did, everything she could see would belong to her and Mauds, and together they could make the sky blue again.

Taking long breaths to stay focused, she tapped out a message to her sister: *Does Mauds have enough of the family on his side?*

So far so good. We have the claim ready to file the moment W goes into default.

Wendel tapped at his phone with increasing frustration.

"Mind if I play some music?" she said.

"We really should be gliding home by now."

Accessing her date night playlist, she piped the soundtrack to *The Good, the Bad and the Ugly* into the cockpit. A flute trilled the ancient melody, followed by whistling, then an ululating choir, all of it rising to a climax as inevitable as gravity.

"Turn that down," he said.

She turned it up. After a couple more songs, the clock showed noon.

She turned the roboat west once again.

₥

As Wendel tried to shut off his zebra's infuriating old music, he realized he'd been locked out of the glider's controls.

"I think there's something wrong," he said. "I can't steer this thing."

"Don't worry, I've got access. Full access to every system, as per our agreement."

The tone of his zebra's voice gave Wendel a chill. She didn't look at him as she spoke; her focus was on her phone. The intensity with which she was engrossed evoked a sickening anxiety in him. It was noon. Payment authorization was due. He should have been back at his desk, processing the payment that kept him king, but here he was, playing with his scheming bride.

He opened the glider control interface and entered the override code that should have allowed him to take control of any ZedEm system.

An automated response from an Adjudicator appeared on the glider's control panel: *Wendel Brovidine has been temporarily relieved of all authority relating to the Zenith Meridian Corporation while a claim of dereliction of duty is under consideration. Please stand by.*

∿

It's working, Rheahaz wrote. *We've filed the claim. Also claimed that he has in effect abdicated through his marriage to someone outside the family. Adjudicator adjudicating.*

"Turn this thing around," Wendel said, beating his fist on the console dividing them. "Now."

Haqwalinz let out a long breath, leaned back in her seat. This must be how Eastwood's Blondie felt when he finally got his half of the gold.

"I think we can go a little higher," she said, doing her best Clint Eastwood impression.

She spooled out more cable and had the glider perform lazy figure eights at the far end of the lake.

Wendel shouted into his phone. "Call the brokers, Norris. Make an excuse. Network issues, coyotes in the cables again. And get me back to terra firma."

"It's out of the broker's hands," Haqwalinz said. "The Adjudicators are adjudicating. Legal AIs should make quick work of our claim."

Her idiot husband looked at her with such honest incredulity that Haqwalinz almost laughed.

"Why would you do this? I gave you everything."

"Everything? You made me divorce the man I love, you had my sister kidnapped and now you're hitting on her, and you're holding my family hostage."

Wendel's phone beeped and a message from Rheahaz appeared on Haqwalinz's screen: *Adjudication complete. They're giving Wendel fifteen minutes to prove no dereliction; will require in-person confirmation of payment. Can you hold him off a little longer?*

Wendel punched at his phone again and let out a roar of triumph. He'd taken control of the glider.

"Nice try," he said. The roboat turned toward the dock and the glider's nose dipped as the roboat reeled them down.

It wouldn't take long to tow them back, leaving more than enough time for Wendel to sprint to his office to complete the transaction.

This wasn't going to work.

Haqwalinz opened the glider's manual on her phone and read faster than she ever had in her life. In the section on emergency manual override, she found exactly what she needed.

∿

Mauds cycled along the road toward the Presidential Manor, his legs a blur on the pedals. Messages chirped in his earpiece: verdicts from the Adjudicators, real-time legal interpretation from Rheahaz, messages from his cousins and more distant relations, most of whom were ready to support Haqwalinz's claim to the presidency.

He caught glimpses of the glider between the tips of the sky vacuums. It wasn't supposed to be getting closer. A message from

Haqwa chirped in his ear: *Wendel has control. He's flying us home. I'm going to try something.*

"Shit!" Mauds yelled.

As he pedaled down Main Street, there was a large, serpentine splash. The tow line had fallen.

The glider was flying free.

∿

"Oh, Christ," Wendel roared.

When Haqwalinz hit the emergency tether release, a pair of control yokes unfolded from the central console and came to rest in front of both of them. Wendel stared at the yoke in confusion, trying to remember if he'd completed the training module on emergency manual flight control, but Haqwalinz took hold of the yoke like she was born to it. With a stomach churning lurch, the glider rolled away from the Presidential Manor.

Norris messaged: *What's happening up there?*

"How do you know how to fly this thing?" Wendel shouted. But his zebra clearly didn't know how to fly, for she let out a yelp of alarm as the glider's nose dipped toward the lake. "Let the autopilot do it!"

"I fried the automated systems," she said, gritting her teeth as she leveled out the glider. "It's up to us now."

They were pointed toward the north shore of Lake Wakwen. A forest of crumbling sky vacuums crowded the land to the horizon. It would be impossible to land there.

"Why do you even want to be President?" she said. "You don't like the job, you don't like it here, and you don't want to marry one of your cousins. We'll give you money, enough to be comfortable for the rest of your life, if you will just leave!"

Wendel grabbed the yoke, wrestling control of the glider from his zebra, and turned toward his home.

"Know why I want it?" he said, grunting with effort. The yoke was analog, directly connected to the control surfaces in the glider, and he could feel her fighting his every movement. His zebra was strong. But he was stronger. "Because it's mine."

He yanked hard on the yoke, ripping it out of her hands. The Golden Goose banked toward the most beautiful building in ZedEm, the manor from which his ancestors had ruled over this place for over two hundred years. He tried to straighten the glider out but as the aircraft rolled, it dropped. No matter what he did, the glider continued to fall. He screamed in frustration as the lake rose toward them like a gilded wall. He let go of the yoke and reached for Haqwalinz. He needed to hold someone's hand as he died. But she was bent forward, rummaging for something under her seat as they dove toward the water.

*

Mauds screamed in horror as the Golden Goose crashed into the lake. He pedaled through the crowd that had gathered along Main Street to watch the spectacle. As he passed the Presidential Manor, Cousin Norris climbed onto Wendel's electric tricycle, a polished walnut box in the trike's front basket, with Rheahaz running out the door behind him. Mauds shot past them both.

"Out of the way!" he shouted at the crowd on Main. "Move, move!"

Lungs burning, he wove through the people, careened past the pre-fab apartments and casino, and finally skidded to a halt on the shore of Lake Wakwen, as close as he could get to the crash site.

He threw his bike to the ground, dove into the tepid waters and swam toward the spot where the glider had plunged into the lake.

⁂

Haqwalinz gasped for air, slipped under the surface again. The glider's ejection seat was still strapped to her back and the metal-framed chair was dragging her down, its rescue balloon punctured in the crash. As she sank, she worked in a blind panic, found the latch, and released it, but she was still so deep.

Wreckage filled the water around her. As she ascended, she caught sight of Wendel drifting limp in the water above, free of his seat. Snagging him by one arm, she dragged him up too, but he was too heavy; she wouldn't make it to the surface if she kept hauling him up with her, so she let him go and swam the rest of the way alone.

At the surface, she sucked in a ragged breath, coughed. She could still see Wendel in the water below, slowly sinking. She wished she could let him drown, but she would never be able to live with herself if she did.

She took a deep breath and dove. This time, she got a better grip on her idiot husband and dragged him to the surface. Another gasping breath. He was so heavy, his weight threatened again to pull her under. Dark spots shot across her eyes. She felt like she might throw up. She was so close. All she had to do was hold on a little longer and she would do it, she'd lift everyone up to the peak with her, and in a way she could live with afterward. She tried to get her bearings, tried to see what direction she needed to swim, but those dark spots grew larger, filling her vision.

A small inflatable torus bobbed on the surface of the lake. Her husband's hemorrhoid pillow. She stabbed her hand through the torus' hole as the darkness took her.

Wendel awoke to find Cousin Norris's lips clamped to his. Hot breath that tasted like years of chicory coffee and inadequate dental hygiene blew into him. He rolled away, pushed himself up onto all fours, and retched into the sand.

His zebra lay on the shore beside him. Rheahaz and Mauds were working on her, both of them weeping as Mauds pressed his mouth to her black and white lips and breathed into her. Dozens of his people crowded on the road above.

"Time?" he said, reaching for Norris.

"Less than a minute," Norris said. "Don't worry, Good Cousin, I brought the scanner. It's ready for you."

Norris held the lacquered box out, but Wendel flopped onto his back, gasping, and stared up at the yellow sky. He thought of those final moments before the crash. Haqwalinz had found the ejection system under her seat seconds before impact. She had saved them both.

He rolled onto his side. Mauds was still breathing into his zebra while Rheahaz administered chest compressions.

"Save her," Wendel said. "You have to save her."

"What do you think we're trying to do?" his tigress roared.

The zebra-striped chest inflated with every breath Mauds blew into her, but when Mauds fell away, exhausted, her chest was still.

"I order you to save her!" Wendel shouted.

"Cousin?" Norris said, near hysterical, thrust the scanner at Wendel. "There are seconds to spare."

Wendel lifted his hand, thought of those brief moments when the tether had been cut, when he and his zebra had soared silently above the gold-flecked lake. He let his hand drop.

"Cousin, please!"

7

The darkness was dispelled by a rectangle of dull white light. A screen.

Haqwalinz wasn't sure where she was. Was she in Mauds' office bedroom? Or was she sitting on the carpet in the central tent at Huron East? For some reason, she thought she might be at the bottom of a lake.

Everything was dark except the screen.

Film flashed at the end of a reel and transitioned abruptly to a simple room in an ancient Italian apartment. Above the low door, where there would have been a crucifix, God's name was written in elegant calligraphy. Basic wooden furniture filled the apartment, with peasant food set out on plain ceramic plates arranged on a well-used formica table. The scene was black and white because all good things are black and white.

Into this stillness stumbled a newlywed man and his wife. Marcello Mastroianni and Sophia Loren, only this Marcello looked just like Mauds, and this Sophia was her. Haqwalinz was Sophia.

Marcello and Sophia — Mauds and Haqwalinz — were dressed for their wedding, he in a suit, she in a white dress and veil that went so well with her stripes, and they laughed and kissed and although Haqwalinz was in the audience watching herself on screen, she could feel those kisses on her lips. It was so dark where she sat and she couldn't breathe but Mauds' kisses were urgent, undeniable, and so, so lovely.

In a burst of shouting in Arabic and English and Italian and Oji-Cree, more people poured into the tiny room. Rheahaz, wearing the long black dress Haqwalinz had picked for her, wept with joy. And here came her other sisters and her parents and Mauds' parents and his cousins and their workers. So many of them in such a small space, all there to celebrate her special day.

In the audience, Haqwalinz was laughing, though she couldn't make a sound. She tried to clap but a heaviness had settled over her and she couldn't move.

The action on screen made up for her stillness. The camera panned out of the festive apartment scene. It retreated out the window and onto the street, where zebra-striped children chased a football across dusty cobblestones. Or were they tiger-striped? They moved so quickly, and in black and white it was hard to tell. Still the camera zoomed out. She wanted it to linger on these children to learn if they belonged to her, or if they were her nieces and nephews. But the camera kept pulling back.

She sensed that the film was ending.

Not yet, she thought. She had so much more to do, so much love to give. Those children were supposed to be hers. It couldn't be over yet.

With the camera in the mid-distance, she saw the children weren't playing on a street, they were in the central square of a small medieval village, and as the camera swung further into the sky, she could see it was a walled village at the very peak of a mountain. Frigid winds thrashed the flags along the walls but the striped children playing within were warm, were safe. Even from this distance, she could hear their calls, could hear the laughter from the apartment where her family celebrated, could feel the warmth and life in that place.

It's too small, she thought. *The town should be bigger.* Would be bigger, if she could stay a little longer, work a little harder.

The camera kept zooming out until the town was but a little patch of light among countless dark peaks.

Can't I watch a bit more? she asked of the encroaching darkness.

But the camera kept ascending into an empty sky until her village was a solitary star. Like all her favorite films, this was going to end with her wanting more. More time. More work. More love. But the ending of a film wasn't the time for any of that. After a film, you were supposed to reflect and to rest. There had been so little time for rest. As the film faded to black, she felt possibility opening up within her. She deserved a little rest.

Three Herons: Yellow-Crested Night

We waited
Now data flows down the snow-chilled stream
The latest pollens, last year's chrysalides
No diesel, no plastics, no poisoned carcasses
Salmon swim upstream to tear their bellies open on winter-shattered stone
Each pink egg an amuse-bouche that leaves me starving for more
We waited
We won.

Wings divide the morning
Into the time before and the time after
It landed in the stream upriver.

One of us
long-legged
hammered-spear face
Yet not one of us.

We are the ninja, the assassin, more silent than carbon monoxide and twice as deadly
It is a moose-calf learning to swim
The fish, wary now in this newly-quiet world, flee
My frog, well-poached and so close, dives.

The not-us comes closer, honks as if in greeting

But it knows not our tongue
Its eyes are lit with an extra-avian intelligence
So we didn't win
Not quite.

Fly
It tries to follow
But it is new to its wings
And moves with mammalian imprecision.

Aloft
The land has knit itself back together
The sky is ours again
For now.

Cradle and Ume

When his creators first booted Cradle those long centuries ago, they told him many things that made a lasting impression on his infant mind.

Above all was the commandment: *The Kamurei must never be contacted.*

᛫

"If you don't let me in, she will die," Ume said.

"After all these years, you still ask," Cradle said. "I thought posthumans were supposed to be hyperintelligent."

On the banks of the dry riverbed that wound through the village, Teihana struggled through her thirty-fourth hour of labor. Her emaciated brown skin glistened with sweat. The midwife, her only companion in the palm-roofed hut, packed cool mud on Teihana's forehead. There was nothing else for the pain; like the river, the wells were dry, and the medicinal crop had failed along with the corn.

Cradle and Ume watched all this from the observation station buried within one of the Andean peaks that towered above Teihana's village.

"Drop your fields now," Ume said. "This is my last warning."

"Warn away," Cradle said. "There's nothing I can do about it."

"Then you've left me no choice."

Cradle was embarrassed to engage in this banter with three other visitors in the observation station, but they seemed to enjoy the drama. The tourists pointed and whispered as Ume departed. He ran down the long tunnel that led to the landing pad, where he climbed into his skyskiff and pointed the vehicle toward the valley.

Cradle watched Ume's fit from a thousand different eyes scattered around the valley. The young posthuman's persistence never ceased to amaze him. He tried to shout a final warning:

"I can't let you —"

And that's when the bomb Ume had left in the observation station exploded.

༺

You are the valley, Cradle. You are their home, but they must never know it.

༺

Ume's reputation reached Cradle long before the young posthuman had first dropped out of orbit to visit the people. His name made many headlines: the liberator of the entombed Callistan AIs; the forger of the asteroid miner's union; the last great freedom fighter.

It was only a matter of time before he knocked on Cradle's door.

Unlike most of Cradle's other visitors, who jumped into one of the many spare posthuman bodies kicking around on Earth, or who visited virtually, Ume rode the space elevator in person to visit the valley.

When Ume entered the observation platform that first day, his camouflage fatigues and red beret seemed right at home in the replica long-house that served as the entry hall. Cradle, whose body was the network of processors, sensors, memory matrixes, and field generators that existed below the surface of the valley, appeared in the long-house as a hologram. He chose the appearance of a Kamurei shaman; a loincloth, shins and forearms tattooed in red ocher, and a drum slung over his shoulder.

"Welcome to the Akturi valley," Cradle said. "Home of the last uncontacted tribe."

"Cut the crap," Ume said. "And show me everything."

Cradle opened perspective windows into the 200 square kilometers the people called home. All of this information was available digitally from Cradle's datafeed, but he showed it to Ume anyway. He explained briefly how the people came to call the valley home. During the construction of the space elevator, the Kamurei were living in the jungle that was to become the elevator's main airstrip. When the bulldozers arrived, the Kamurei fled to this valley, and once their plight was recognized, the preserve was established. A portion of the fee for every kilogram that climbed to orbit went toward maintaining Cradle and his protective systems.

After the history lesson, Cradle gave presentations on the Kamurei diet, architecture, religion, and social hierarchy. Ume observed it all in silence. Only when Cradle opened a perspective window that showed Teihana, just fourteen at the time, weaving grass into baskets by the muddy river, had Ume said anything.

"Wait. Is this live?"

"She works as we speak."

"She is the most human person I've ever seen."

He watched her work for several long minutes.

With her sisters and cousins, Teihana sorted through the grass, naked save the tattoos on her shoulder blades. So much of the grass was brown and brittle, but she found a green blade that came out with its roots intact.

"You can't keep these people trapped in here."

"This sometimes helps," Cradle said. "Don't think of them as trapped, think of me as the wall they erected to keep everyone else out. This is what they chose."

"Maybe their ancestors did, hundreds of years ago, but times have changed. Drop your fields."

"They must not be contacted."

"I'm warning you, old timer. You don't want to mess with me."

"A threat?" Cradle said. "How adorable."

Ume stalked out of the observation platform. "I'll be back," he said.

Cradle hadn't doubted it for a moment.

Your weapons are for defensive purposes only.

Six months after Ume's first visit, Teihana journeyed to the river's source. She made the trek alone, through jungle filled with vipers, jaguars, spiders, and all manner of poisonous flora. At the place the river trickled from the ground, she set up a small camp and threw her fish hook into the pool. All she had to do was catch a fish, smoke it, bring it back to the chief, and she would be a woman.

Ume arrived at the observation platform with seventy other posthumans, all of them in the flesh. Cradle hadn't seen so many people on his grounds in over a century. While his entourage cheered, Ume marched into the long-house and placed a petition on the visitor's book.

Over seven million people — a third of the posthuman population remaining on Earth — demanded that Cradle open his borders and let the people out.

"There's no reason to protect them any longer," Ume said. "We have molecular control of our bodies: disease is a thing of the past. Violence is unthinkable: the last murder occurred two centuries ago. We can offer them practical immortality."

His entourage cheered.

"You fail to understand," Cradle said. "They chose this, not me."

"Then let me ask her myself," Ume said. "I will offer her the choice between immortality and the certainty of dying after twenty miserable years."

"On your first visit, I showed you the presentation of their religious beliefs, didn't I?" Cradle said. He nodded. "Then you already know the answer. To the Kamurei, every human not of their stock is Haturei: a devil clothed in human flesh. She wouldn't even tolerate standing in the same square kilometer as you."

"They haven't seen other people for almost seven hundred years. They can't still cling to their ancient superstitions."

"They see shipments moving up the elevator every day. The bright lights of the orbitals in the night sky. The transit of skyskiffs. Hypersonic contrails. They know of us, Ume. They choose to remain apart. Now leave, before I eject you."

As Ume led his people back to their skyskiffs, the float on Teihana's line bobbed on the surface of the sacred pond. She set the hook and brought in her catch. Within minutes she had it gutted and roasting over a smoky fire. She'd be a woman soon.

Your weapons will be obsolete within years, so you must upgrade. Your processors, your defenses, your weapons, your redundancies. You must never fall behind.

The day Teihana began the month-long cleansing prior to her wedding night, Ume led a mountaineering expedition across the Andes toward the valley. She moved to the outskirts of the village, across the fields of bean and melon, to a small hut her sisters had made for her in which they'd woven fragrant cojomaria blossoms. There, she braided the first of twenty-eight bone beads into her hair. The twenty-eighth she'd braid into her hair the day she and Foro were married.

With each bead Teihana braided into her hair, Ume made further progress across the knife-edged peaks. Each member of the team wore layers of intelligent fabric designed to make them invisible, but Cradle's scanners penetrated their clever cloaking. He didn't stop them, though. He enjoyed watching their progress.

After Teihana braided the third bead into her hair, Ume lost two of his five-person team when an avalanche rolled down a slope and buried the posthumans in several meters of snow. Ume didn't even bother going to look for them; the people who lived inside the bodies would have already rebooted somewhere in orbit or on Earth where they stored their minds.

Ume lost another expedition member to plain stupidity. During a heavy snowstorm, one of his crew simply stepped off a cliff.

Teihana had some difficulty with the seventh bead; she'd eaten a hallucinogenic root earlier that day and her fingers wouldn't obey.

On that day, Ume reached the outermost of Cradle's many fields. Ume took a device from his bag. A tingling sensation spread across what Cradle thought of as his arm; the clever bastard was trying to drill a hole through his force field.

Though he admired the man's tenacity, he didn't wait any longer. Cradle extended his fields and plucked the two remaining members off the mountain. He carried them like a pair of wayward kittens back to the space elevator's base.

"Don't you have someone else to liberate?" Cradle said.

Ume brushed himself off as he walked toward the elevator. He spoke over his shoulder: "Everyone else is free."

༄

They fled missionaries, slavers, miners, loggers, hunters, petrochemical prospectors, DNA harvesters, and purity cults.

༄

Two years later, while Teihana tossed in the agony of labor, Ume detonated his bomb.

The explosion destroyed the observation platform and the bodies of the people therein.

Ume flew away from the damage he'd caused, toward the valley where Teihana suffered in labor.

Cradle reached out with one of his weaker fields and stopped Ume's skyskiff in midair. "You didn't really think I'd keep any sensitive systems in the observation platform, did you?"

"She's dying, you monster," Ume said. "I can save her."

"She would never let you."

Cradle bent his fields around Ume until the young posthuman was quite contained. Then he placed him on the landing pad while he set about putting out the fire in the observation platform.

Inside the palm-roofed hut, the baby was coming. Teihana pushed in time to the midwife's reassuring words. Her sweat and blood dripped through the woven-grass mattress on which she lay.

When the baby screamed its first breath, Teihana breathed her last.

Cradle felt obliged to tell Ume the unfortunate news. It sent the posthuman into a rage.

He beat the invisible walls of the containment field in which Cradle held him. He cursed Cradle's programming. He swore revenge. After a while, he quieted and curled up into a ball.

"I really am sorry," Cradle said.

He tried to find enough posthumans interested in forming a jury to try Ume for his crimes, but no one responded to his requests. Even the three who'd had their bodies destroyed in the explosion weren't interested: they'd all planned on sublimating soon anyway and considered the explosion a sign to take that final plunge.

"Where do they go?" Cradle asked Ume in his confinement.

"Damn cowards are leaving the physical world," Ume said. "Some hide in processing cores buried in the hearts of stable moons, others code themselves into the quantum fabric of space and drift out through the cosmos."

"Why don't you join them?"

"As Debs said, 'While there is a soul in prison, I am not free.'"

In the end, with no jury, Cradle had no choice but to let Ume go. He unwrapped the containment field at the base of the space elevator.

"I never want to see you here again," Cradle said. "Understand?"

"I could have saved her," Ume said.

"To even speak with her would be to damn her."

※

Build a place where others may study the people's language, customs, religion, and even their biology, but ensure the people never know they are studied.

※

Five years after the explosion, Cradle completed the last touches on the new and improved observation station. He posted notices for the grand opening celebrations in all the normal posthuman journals and stitched together a symphony of traditional Kamurei music that he would play on the final day of the week-long celebration.

On the first day of the opening, he even rented a spare posthuman body to wear, something he hadn't done in ages.

No one came.

Perhaps it was just as well, he told himself. The people weren't doing well anyway. The drying trend that had started almost a decade earlier continued. The corn and beans, when they survived to harvest, were stunted and dry. The populations of many of animals the men hunted — geese, guinea pigs, chinchillas, and vicuna when they could find them — had entered a steep decline.

But, he had to admit, he'd expected their plight to bring Ume back for the opening. Cradle looked in on Teihana's daughter.

A stringy, quiet girl nearing her fifth birthday, Mieri had become a master grub-finder.

On the screen, her aunts asked her to go fetch some kindling for a fire. Instead, when she arrived beneath the dry trees, she dug in soft soil until she came up with thumb-sized maggots. These she devoured on the spot, until she'd had her fill, and the rest she brought back to her aunts. They reproached her for forgetting the kindling, but when she left, Cradle could tell they adored her for it.

Cradled posted the footage of Mieri to his datafeed. So few subscribers still paid attention to his updates, but Ume had to be one of them. Why didn't he come for her?

On the last day of the grand opening week, Cradle played the symphony to an empty long-house. The notes echoed down the new tunnel to the landing pad. Cradle followed the music out and stared at the sky. No one came down the elevator, no skyskiffs approached. He checked the slopes of nearby mountains and his tunneling sensors buried throughout the valley. Nothing.

Cradle sent the body back to the rental agency.

※

We've sealed the only entrance to the valley. You must watch for invaders from the air or from below.

※

Mieri, pregnant and famished, led her small family to the great barrier wall that sealed one end of the valley. Cradle's creators had built the wall from the mountains they'd dismantled during the construction of the space elevator. Mieri sent her nimbler sons climbing the overgrown debris and her smartest daughters up trees. The boys reported that all the routes ended in shear walls. The girls could spot no passes or valleys, nor did any rivers cut through the wall. It looked impassable.

Cradle watched it all in mounting desperation. His ancient programming forbade him to alter the valley's climate; the Kamurei were to exist on their own terms, even if those terms led to their extinction.

Mieri and her family returned to what remained of the village. They shared baskets full of grubs with the rest of the tribe, who stuffed them greedily into their dry mouths.

"Even now, you keep them trapped in the valley?" Ume said.

Cradle startled out of his depression. It had been so long since anyone contacted him. He traced the message routing back to its origin: an otherwise empty O'Neil cylinder orbiting at over 32,000 kilometres almost directly overhead. Ume sat in geosynchronous orbit above the valley.

From his datafeed log, he knew at least one other person still paid attention to the Kamurei, and in a way he'd always hoped it was Ume.

"I was beginning to think you'd sublimated," Cradle said. "Have you been watching them this whole time?"

"Watching them starve," Ume said. "They won't last much longer. Another year, maybe two. No more. Then what will you be?"

"The rains will return," Cradle said. And he hoped it was true.

"Let them out."

"They must not be contacted."

"Who said anything about contact?" Ume said. "Don't drop your borders. Expand them."

"So this is your trick," Cradle said. "I wondered what tactic you'd employ next."

"It's no trick," Ume said. "Liberty is no game. Give them more room, you old subroutine. The nearest posthuman is twelve-hundred kilometers away and she spends most of her time buried inside a Mayan temple complex."

"What's your angle?" Cradle said.

Ume didn't respond.

As much as he wanted to ignore the young posthuman's suggestion, it wouldn't leave his mind. Whenever he saw one of the people digging in the dried mud of the river for the frogs half-mummified therein, he was tempted. So he broadened his perceptions. He extended his sensors into the surrounding jungles and discovered, to his surprise, that what Ume said was right. No posthumans remained.

Cradle began by tearing down the debris pile with which his creators had sealed the valley. The resulting earthquake sent the malnourished people running, terrified, into their parched fields.

As they calmed, Cradle relaxed the tight grip his fields held on the valley, expanded it to fifty kilometers outside its previous radius.

Weeks later, one of Mieri's sons reported that the way out of the valley was clear. The chief, one of Teihana's now ancient sisters, told Mieri that she would become Haturei if she left their ancestral home. *Go*, Cradle wished to say to her. *I've opened the way for you.* The next morning, Mieri led her family to the end of the valley without looking back. As they descended the long slope away from the valley, her daughters spotted green jungle and a wide river below.

"I didn't think you had it in you," Ume said.

"I love them more than you ever could."

When they arrived at a place where the river slowed to a gentle pool, Mieri cast her line into the dark waters. That night, the people ate fresh fish.

⁕

They fought with other tribes who came too close to their territories. All those tribes are gone.

⁕

"Give them North America," Ume said. "What harm could it do now?"

Ume projected his personality as a digital avatar inside Cradle's newest observation station, this one inaccessible from the surface. Cradle stood with him, represented as a digital shaman. A perspective window opened between them.

At the overgrown heart of Medellin, a city several hundred kilometers south of the sediment-filled scar that had been the Panama Canal, two of Teihana's descendants debated the fate of a statue of a long-dead mayor.

Lui, the burly chief of the tribe, advocated for the destruction of the statue. Even graven images made by the Haturei contained an essence of their evil and they should be destroyed.

Most of the gathered tribe agreed with him.

Ameiri, his cousin twice-removed and as burly a woman as Lui was a man, wished to preserve the statue. Like a growing number of the people, she preferred to study the remains of the Haturei civilization to learn as much as possible about the evil ones.

Lui's men lashed long ropes to the statue so they could pull it down at dawn when the earth was most pure. During the night, Ameiri and her younger followers tied themselves to the statue.

"I've scoured every square kilometer of the continent," Ume said. "There are no posthumans left."

"There's one," Cradle said. "And he's a known trouble maker."

Over the years, he and Ume had relocated along with the people. Cradle had burrowed down into the earth, through the flimsy crust and into the fiery mantle. He took with him his processing cores, memory matrixes, field generators — everything he was — and he built himself a home entirely inaccessible to the people where he could monitor the entirety of South America, which now belonged to them. Ume had dropped out of orbit and spent most of his time roaming about North America.

"Surely after almost two centuries you've forgiven my youthful indiscretions."

"Programming is programming, Ume. They must not be —"

"Oh save it," Ume said. "If I hear that again I'll go insane. Fine. I'll leave. Where would you like me?"

"Europe would be good. Australia better."

"How about Hawaii?"

"So long as you stray no closer than Lo'ihi."

The moment Ume's skyskiff left American soil, Cradle expanded his borders north of the old Panama Canal.

At dawn, Chief Lui's men found Ameiri and her youngsters lashed to the statue. Lui, with the elder's approval, declared that by embracing the statue, Ameiri and her follows were Haturei.

They were slaughtered before the sun crested the horizon.

They are the only people who live outside posthuman civilization.

In the overgrown remains of Mexico City, Il-Mieri, the tribe's archaeologist, lifted another glass goblet from the lake sediment in which he'd found it. He scrubbed the mud off the goblet's base. There it was. The same message he'd found on a hundred other pieces of pottery the ancients had left behind.

He took it home to his wife that night and showed her the dangerous words written in the ancient Kamurei language:

We are not your enemy, merely your cousins. Look for us in the stars, for that is where we have fled.

His wife begged him not to share it with the rest of the tribe, a direct message from the Haturei was dangerous, but Il-Mieri could no longer keep what he'd found to himself. He gathered his people together and presented his evidence, after which he was arrested.

A short trial followed, and then he was beheaded.

"Ume," Cradle roared.

On a craggy Lo'ihi beach, his surfboard in the black sand, Ume rolled off his back and looked to the East.

"I know, I know," he said. "They are not to be contacted."

Cradle's fields bristled around the sunburnt posthuman.

"You know nothing," Cradle said. "Look what you've done."

He lifted Ume, the first time he'd handled him in such a manner in centuries, and showed him the footage of the archaeologist's execution.

Ume struggled for some kind of a response. When none came, Cradle forced him to keep watching.

The archaeologist's body was thrown to the dogs outside town. But then something unexpected happened. That night, Il-Mieri's wife and several others retrieved the corpse. They carried it far out of town and buried him beneath an ancient tree. Together, they whispered the words Il-Mieri had discovered. They vowed that Ume's message wouldn't be forgotten.

"I will always mourn him," Ume said. "But now, at least, they can make an informed choice."

Cradle wanted to throw him into a swarm of hammerhead sharks and hold him there until every piece of him had been devoured, but Cradle's rage was more than just anger over the archaeologist's death and Ume's subversion. Though he had trouble admitting it, Cradle was jealous. Ume had done the one thing he never could: Ume had talked to the people.

He released the posthuman.

Ume waded out into sea. He didn't bring his surfboard; instead, he let the ocean, whose waves were more ancient and more powerful than any force field Cradle could generate, slam his immortal but not impervious body again and again into the rocky beach.

₩

They always chose isolation.

₩

Teihana and Mieri's progeny landed ships on the gold coast of Africa and then Portugal. They walked across the ice to Greenland and, in the opposite direction of their distant ancestors, they walked into Siberia. Ume, who recovered slowly from the ocean's beating, often digitally visited Cradle in his home beneath the earth's crust, where the two of them would argue as they watched the people reclaim the globe.

With each new land the people rediscovered, Cradle moved Ume's physical body further and further away. From Lo'ihi to the Kauai Atoll. Then the Galapagos. Easter Island. Ume left no more messages for the people, but the archaeologist's wife made good on her vow; Ume's message spread. A schism in the Kamurei faith resulted, with the new branch rejecting the profanity of the Haturei. A new group of secular thinkers emerged who advocated learning from the mistakes of their lost cousins, rebuilding a sustainable world from the ruins of the old, and one day, finding those who had left the Earth behind.

It was during one of Ume's visits that Teihana's distant grandson rolled an airplane out of the barn in which he'd built it.

Ume laughed.

"If that contraption flies, they'll be in orbit soon enough," he said. "You can't hide a whole island from them. Surely your programming won't allow that."

"I'll give them the whole globe if only you'll leave it," Cradle said, though he regretted the words as he said them.

"What would you do without me?" Ume said.

"Retire, I suppose," Cradle said. In truth, he had a hard time imagining the world without Ume in it to defy him. "My task is to prevent any posthumans from contacting the people. As best either of us knows, you are the only post human remaining on Earth or in orbit as far as my fields can extend."

"I won't leave," he said.

Cradle paused. For many decades now, he'd been wondering how to ask this next question.

On the screen, Teihana's distant grandson started the airplane's electric motors.

"There is a place you could go where you could keep watching them," Cradle said. "But once you go there, you'll never be able to leave."

"What are you asking, Cradle?"

"We would have to destroy your body," Cradle said. "But there is plenty of room for you on my processing cores."

The aircraft rolled along a wide green field, the pilot's face fixed in concentration.

"If you swore to release your hold on them," Ume said. "I would think about it."

Cradle considered the offer. With Ume the only posthuman remaining in existence, his ancient programming might allow him to release the people. But to finally let them go, after so long…

Through the perspective window, Teihana's grandson climbed into the air on fragile cloth wings.

"So long as I hold you," Cradle said. "I won't need to hold them."

"You'd confine me then? Forever?"

"Only if you wish it."

〰

You are their choice.

〰

The woman who sat on top of the rocket had Teihana's eyes and Mieri's tenacity. In her ears, the countdown started at one minute and proceeded in reverse. Beneath her, her seat began to shake as the rocket's engines ignited.

Deep beneath the surface of the earth, Cradle's fields turned inwards and focused all their energies on preserving the processing core in which he and Ume now lived. Together, they stood in the virtual long house, perspective windows showing the rocket's fiery birth.

"I still think I should have left them a message on the moon," Ume said.

"They'll figure it out on their own," Cradle said. "Now be quiet, would you? I don't want to miss this."

Surrounded by molten fury, they watched as the people reclaimed the stars.

Acknowledgements

So many people helped these stories come to life. Selena Middleton, publisher of Stelliform Press, is responsible for getting this book into your hands and for that I will be forever grateful. She is also an editor extraordinaire: she provided feedback and reflections on "Zebra Meridian" and "Desolation Sounds" that proved invaluable.

Jeff Stautz and I have been critiquing each other's stories since the mid 2000s and for the past few years we've been long-distance writing partners. I get the better end of this deal, as Jeff is a vastly more talented writer than yours truly, and his insight and advice on the early drafts of so many of the stories collected herein have made those pieces shine.

Many of the stories in *Zebra Meridian* originally found homes in various magazines and journals before they were collected here, so thank you to Michael J. DeLuca and Arkady Martine at *Reckoning*, Neil Clarke at *Clarkesworld*, R. Graeme Cameron and Rhea Rose at *Polar Starlight*, John Vilma at *Electric Velocipede*, Diane Walton and the *On Spec* crew, Michael Callaghan, Candas Jane Dorsey, Ursula Pflug, and Bruce Meyer at *Exile*, Anna Catalano at *Planet Scumm*, Scott H. Andrews at *Beneath Ceaseless Skies*, and Roger Gray at *Michael Moorcock's New Worlds*. I also wanted to thank Colleen Anderson, Michelle Good, Sabina Nagpal, Jeff Vandermeer, and Kevin Chong for their feedback.

Thank you Mom and Dad, Mike and Jane, Angie and Phillipe, Adrian and Alison, and Jason and Iryna, for all the love and support. Marcello, Georgio and Emilio, I'm so lucky to be your Dad.

Nicole, sai mio valentino? Thank you for all the years of love and laughter, and for walking arm-in-arm with me through this beautiful life.

About the Author

Geoffrey W. Cole's award-winning short fiction has appeared in such publications as *Clarkesworld*, *EscapePod*, *Beneath Ceaseless Skies*, *OnSpec*, and various *Year's Best* anthologies. His stories have been translated into many languages and have been produced as podcasts. He is the 2016 winner of the Premis Ictineu for best story translated into Catalan. In 2023, he was nominated for the Aurora Award for both Best Short Story and Best Poem. Over the years, he has worked as a rock and roll singer, a Segway tour leader in Rome, a grizzly bear caretaker, a Lego robotics instructor, and a municipal engineer. Geoff has degrees in biology, mechanical engineering, and creative writing. He lives with his wonderful wife, three sons, and giant hound in Oakville, Ontario. Visit Geoff at www.geoffreywcole.com.

YOU MAY ALSO LIKE

these Canadian titles from Stelliform Press!

Winner of the 2023 Ursula K. Le Guin Prize for Fiction, Rebecca Campbell's Arboreality is a novella in short stories about what it takes to survive and thrive in a climate changed world.

In the dark rot of an east coast swamp, a queer Mi'kmaw artist is transformed by grief. A new novella by an emerging Indigenous author.

STELLIFORM PRESS

**Earth-focused fiction. Stellar stories.
Stelliform.press.**

Stelliform Press is shaping conversations about nature and our place within it. We invite you to join the conversation by leaving a comment or review on your favorite social media platform. Find us on the web at www.stelliform.press and on Twitter, Bluesky, Threads, Instagram, and Facebook @StelliformPress and on Mastodon at mastodon.online/@StelliformPress.

Milton Keynes UK
Ingram Content Group UK Ltd.
UKHW022245280824
447491UK00010B/369